MY KIND OF TROUBLE

MY KIND OF TROUBLE

A Novel

L. A. SCHWARTZ

This is a work of fiction. All of the names, characters, organizations, places and events portrayed in this novel are either products of the author's imagination or are used fictitiously. Any resemblance to real or actual events, locales, or persons, living or dead, is entirely coincidental.

Published in the United States by Alcove Press, an imprint of The Quick Brown Fox & Company LLC.

Alcove Press and its logo are trademarks of The Quick Brown Fox & Company LLC.

Library of Congress Catalog-in-Publication data available upon request.

ISBN (hardcover): 978-1-63910-890-9
ISBN (ebook): 978-1-63910-891-6

Cover design by Stephanie Singleton

Printed in the United States.

www.alcovepress.com

Alcove Press
34 West 27th St., 10th Floor
New York, NY 10001

First Edition: October 2024

10 9 8 7 6 5 4 3 2 1

For my sister Melissa,
my partner in musical theater crimes

AUTHOR'S NOTE

My Kind of Trouble is a romantic comedy celebrating its fat and autistic characters, but it also touches upon possibly sensitive topics. It includes backstory mentions of a fatal car accident, parental loss and abandonment, and alcoholism. There is also discussion of bullying of autistic characters (by schoolmates, community members, and parents), brief discussion of ABA therapy, discussion of parental and societal homophobia, moralistic food talk and mention of fatphobia, and mention of church abuse of minors. Finally, the book contains some off-page minor violence, on-page minor blood and shoving (not between hero and heroine), and on-page sex. For anyone who may be sensitive to these topics, please read with care.

CHAPTER ONE
HARMONY

Sitting in the gazebo in the center of Brookville's grassy town square, Harmony Hale took a long sip of her iced coffee and thought it didn't look like the kind of town run by the most corrupt man you'd ever meet.

Then again, in her straw fedora, teal surplice jumpsuit fitted over her generous curves, and strappy kitten heels, Harmony probably didn't look like the kind of person who could shatter the life of the most corrupt man you'd ever meet, but that was exactly what she was here to do. That was what she had done to dozens of others—who'd all deserved it for one reason or another. But none as much as the mayor of Brookville.

"You ready to charm him?" Alice, sitting on the bench beside her, asked with a grin, before slurping up some of her own blended coffee through a bright pink straw.

Alice Burrows. Harmony's reconnaissance woman, assistant, and best friend. She'd arrived in town a few weeks ahead of Harmony, getting the lay of the land.

Harmony raised the coffee Alice had brought from the café where she'd gotten a job (perfect for meeting people and hearing gossip). She made a little toast and smirked. "Like I always do." But she wasn't talking about charming the mayor—not yet. Today she had her sights set on a different man. The last cog in the trap that the mayor would greedily walk into and spring himself, like the rat he was.

Her fingers tightened around her plastic cup, pressing into the cold condensation. "When is this guy supposed to show?" That morning she and Furiosa—her convertible—had driven up from a small town outside Santa Barbara, where she'd taken the life savings off the football coach of a private university who'd covered up the sexual misconduct of his star athletes for years. Unsurprisingly, it had been easy to tempt him with the opportunity to invest most of his ungodly salary in a soon-to-be-announced college sports streaming platform that didn't actually exist. And without any of that cash left to pay off witnesses and campus police, she figured he wouldn't have his job much longer either. The latest victim would be able to get a fair trial against his star cornerback—especially with the chunk of the coach's money Harmony had anonymously donated to her legal fund. But the high of that recent victory had already worn off, and Harmony was buzzing with the need to get this job rolling.

The job. The one she'd had her sights on since she started grifting. At first, she'd worked for others, learning the tricks of the trade, but soon she'd set up her own operation and brought Alice on board, the two of them going after her favored targets. And now the time was finally here. Not that she wanted to rush the con—she intended to enjoy this.

She swished another sip of sweet, creamy coffee over her tongue. It had taken a few years to amass the resources she'd need to pull it off. Those leftover football coach funds were going to such a good cause. Now she only had to line up one last piece of her plan. So where was the guy?

"Every day at three on the dot." Alice scrunched her long, thin nose. "Man's like a machine with the routine. He's been too easy to follow. Barely goes anywhere. He leaves the library for the school every weekday, same time."

Harmony stared at the wooden doors of the library, willing him to appear. The building's white plaster walls made up one side of the town square, along with a senior center and a parking lot. Across the lawn, where a small group was practicing yoga and a few children toddled around scattered blankets, crouched the red brick town hall. On this early spring afternoon, several people occupied benches along the paths, drinking coffee or scrolling on their phones, and others strolled before the storefronts that made up the rest of the square, their doors open invitingly, sandwich boards blazoned with daily specials or sales.

Every small town was essentially the same. Contrary to popular belief, not everyone in town knew absolutely everyone else, but the people *were* nosy and judgmental, yet far too trusting at the same time. So easy for Harmony to play like violins to get closer to her targets who hid among them. She savored the bitter aftertaste of her coffee, imagining a few months from now when all these people would know Mayor Travis Weaver for what he truly was. They'd be ready to tar and feather him—metaphorically, at least, spreading the news of his downfall to social media. He'd be done in Brookville—and the tech world, where he'd made his millions—forever.

You know who didn't usually have millions, or acres of real estate holdings? Full-time civil servants. "And you're *sure* this is the guy who owns the land?" she asked Alice. "A librarian?" He was a last-second addition to their plan; Alice had originally found a hobby farmer for Harmony to target, some middle-aged divorcé looking to move away from Brookville, the type she could always have eating out of her hand in minutes. But then Travis goddamn Weaver happened to put in an offer on the very land she needed for her scheme, and they'd had to scramble.

"Don't you trust me?" Alice dropped her jaw and batted her lashes, hand spread over her chest.

Harmony rolled her eyes. She didn't trust anyone.

They broke into laughter at the same time, Alice's staccato cackle against Harmony's throaty chuckle.

"You've gotten mixed up before," Harmony reminded Alice. "One cute clerk at the records office in San Diego meant I spent three days seducing the wrong Paul Thompson." One who hadn't even owned a car, let alone a franchise of restaurants where he'd been fighting unionization efforts by reporting his own employees to immigration.

"That clerk *was* cute," Alice admitted with a sigh. "He had *dimples.*" Harmony snorted, still grateful for Alice's help. She was easily distracted but good with details about their marks and tracking down targets who were practically begging for someone to come along and charm them out of their ill-gotten gains. It was a public service, really, providing benefits for everyone. Justice for society and cash for Harmony's untraceable bank accounts.

"I double-checked," Alice reassured her, dragging her straw through the lid until it made little squeaks. "The land's not zoned for development, so the family's just passed it along through the generations."

Which meant it would be a piece of cake to convince the librarian to lease the land to Harmony for her plan. She tried to douse her impatience with another sip of sugary coffee, letting her attention follow the long roll and clatter of skaters attempting kickflips on the pavement around a fountain at one corner of the green. For some reason, someone had given the statue above the trickling water a wide-brimmed and well-feathered hat like he was off to the derby. Just beyond, older kids ran through the entrance of an arcade—the VRcade, its neon sign declared, beckoning Brookville's youth to the metaverse.

"There he is."

Harmony's gaze shot back to the library. A man who had to be over seventy shuffled down the path that led to the street, library book tucked in the crook of his age-spotted arm.

"Alice, what the hell?" Harmony laughed. "You told me this was gonna be a charm-and-disarm. I think I may need a different approach." She could get anyone wrapped around her little finger, but strategy was everything. Setting down her coffee, she grabbed her Staud purse from the bench. She had time to wipe off this red lipstick; the mark was still barely to the curb.

"Not *him*." Alice shook her head, brown hair fluttering around her narrow face, which was breaking into a grin as she pointed past Harmony. "*Him*. Preston Jones. Full charm ahead."

Harmony turned back to see a very tall, very lanky man—white, just about her age, maybe mid- to late twenties—emerging from behind the senior citizen. He hurried down the steps, dark hair ruffling and herringbone jacket flapping. Nervous energy practically crackled up and down the long length of him as he fumbled his leather messenger bag open to stuff a book inside and furrowed his brow above glasses glinting in the afternoon sun.

"Oh, god," Harmony said thinly, setting down her purse. "I think if I turn the full strength of my charm on that flagpole wrapped in tweed it might actually kill him." A bubble of laughter broke from her chest.

Alice snickered.

Harmony stood. She shook her hair back over her shoulders and cocked her hat at what she knew from plenty of practice in front of the mirror was a rakish angle. Then she strode down the gazebo steps and across the lawn toward the next lucky victim to fall under her spell.

She and her charm met Preston halfway up the path to the library. "Can I trouble you a moment?"

Though his thick eyebrows shot up at her words, the librarian didn't slow, just mumbled, "Oh, god." He barreled past her. "No."

Not the usual reaction. Harmony fell into step beside him, matching each of his long strides with two of hers. "It'll only take a moment." She let her smile spread wide and released a gentle half laugh. She'd pinned politicians and millionaires in place with that soft huff of breath. Men hated the idea of being laughed at, but they loved being in on a joke—even a nonexistent one—with a beautiful woman.

"Sorry." Her current mark kept his gaze aimed straight ahead, missing out entirely on her bewitching smile, as he sped up and turned from the main path, where a branch split off toward the parking lot. His fisted hands twisted the strap of his bag across his chest like he was wringing the neck of his mortal enemy. And did he actually mutter "*Not today, Satan*" under his breath?

Even with her heels clip-clopping over the pavement like a show pony on Adderall, Harmony couldn't keep up with his ridiculously long legs. But when he stopped beside the bike rack at the front of the parking lot, she caught up with him.

"It's an important matter," she said, as he unlocked a green bike and slid a white helmet from its handlebars. He obviously had somewhere to be—the school, Alice had said, though what could be so important at a school of all places Harmony couldn't guess. Some kind of book emergency? Pressing an open palm to her ample chest—such a crude technique, but when in doubt, draw attention there—she reassured him, "Though I have an appointment soon, so just a word and then I myself must be going—"

He slammed his helmet over his brown curls, snapped its buckle shut, and swung one long leg over the bike. "Great," he pronounced sternly.

And with that, he launched himself and the bike out of the parking lot and down the street, leaving Harmony gaping after him.

She clamped her mouth shut. Nope. She didn't gape. And she never panicked. Harmony always rolled with whatever her grifts threw her way, taking everything in stride. Except she'd just been out-strode.

What had just happened?

Maybe he was gay. Or ace. Harmony could work with that. Switch to another approach. She was lovable in so many ways. Maybe he was fatphobic. Then she could teach him a lesson along with his mayor. There was no limit to the number of assholes she could take down in one town. But she needed this asshole to get to the one that mattered.

Harmony traced her finger along the empty bike rack, thoughtful. Maybe he simply needed her to show even more charm. This wasn't schmoozey L.A. or social-climbing San Francisco, where she could dangle the promise of an opportunity like a handkerchief and everyone would jump for it. People could be stubborn in small towns.

Either way, this was going to be a challenge. She recalled the librarian's tensed full mouth, the flash of blazing blue eyes behind his thick glasses. Harmony rolled her shoulders back, her gaze chasing down the tree-lined street where he sped away. She loved a challenge.

This was going to be fun.

CHAPTER TWO

PRESTON

Preston Jones did nothing halfway.

As he cycled down Main Street, shoulders hunched over his handlebars, he considered how this had likely gotten him into trouble over the years.

Like when he'd go on too long about books or music until people made that uncomfortable face they always eventually made. The face that meant they'd stop inviting him to coffee or their club or anywhere at all.

Or the way he'd follow rules exactly until it annoyed even his teachers or bosses—or completely ignore the rules when they made no sense, which somehow also annoyed the same teachers and bosses.

And worrying. Preston was a full-time worrier. If worries were bought at the store, Preston would come home with a Costco-sized pallet of them.

Worries that he wouldn't be allowed to do his job properly. That it would be taken away from him entirely.

About climate change. And police brutality. Fucking *gerrymandering.*

That he was fucking everything up.

And, always, always, about Lacey.

He shot out an arm to signal his turn down to the school, his stomach churning faster than his pedals spun.

His therapist had called it black-and-white thinking. Given him exercises to improve his mental flexibility. To better function in neurotypical society. Avoid getting into trouble.

Like speaking rudely to a patron at work.

But he hadn't been at work. He'd been *outside* work, on his way to pick up Lacey like he did every day.

Except today. Today, he'd received a call from the school—accompanied by a sharp spike of anxiety until the office lady explained why. Lacey had hit a classmate. Preston had been summoned to the principal's office.

So, no, he didn't have time for another of the "concerned citizens" who wanted to purge his shelves and cancel his storytimes, who'd been in to complain more and more frequently, interrupting his work, and were now taking to lying in wait to accost him outside. Not even for an incredibly hot one. With curves poured into that vibrant outfit and a smile like a sunrise.

Wait, no. Preston let the rush of air as he rode cool his flushed cheeks. No. Bad. Book banners were evil. The enemy.

Why did the enemy have to be *so hot*? Why did evil get all the hottest people on its side? All the poor beleaguered library had was him.

Just like Lacey.

When he arrived at the elementary school she wasn't waiting in her usual spot by the front gate. The place had emptied out. There was none of the usual childish shouting and shrieking like in the mornings when he dropped Lacey off. Just the flap of the

U.S. and California flags on the pole before the administration office and the forlorn clink of tetherball chains out on the playground. He locked up his bike near Lacey's, not thinking about the woman who had stood beside him when he'd unlocked it, or her waves of golden hair playing over her shoulders. She likely had a problem with Saturday storytime including a book about a trans boy, or the Black History Month display he'd created last month somehow making her two-point-five white children feel bad, or the teen Genders and Sexualities Alliance now meeting weekly in Conference Room B. He could worry about all that later. He *would* worry about it later.

His boss had asked him to represent the library at the next town hall meeting, where one of these concerned citizens had gotten an item on the agenda about the library's collection and events serving the community, and clubs like the GSA. Probably Cheryl Weaver, the mayor's wife, who'd been in to politely yell at him more than once. Give Preston a book to read aloud to four-year-olds while their parents scrolled through social media in the back of the room and he was in his element, but public speaking in front of a hundred attentive adults? Streamed live online? He'd been in the middle of trying—if he was honest, failing—to write up some notes for the meeting when he'd gotten the call from school.

Inside, Preston met the polite greetings of the secretaries with what he hoped was a pleasant smile but knew was probably more of a pained grimace. There, sitting cross-legged on one of the blue plastic chairs along the wall outside Principal Swann's office, backpack dumped on the worn carpet, waited Lacey.

The admin secretary, from behind her computer monitor, told him, "Hi, Preston. You can go on in, he's ready for you."

Preston dropped his bag on an empty chair and crouched down in front of his sister. He balanced on the balls of his feet, forearms resting on his thighs. "Hey." She was stimming with the velcro on one purple shoe, peeling the strap open and pressing it shut, over and over. "You okay?"

Lacey, dark hair falling in front of her face, didn't say anything. Not that he'd expected her to, with the secretary just there.

"You want to tell me about it? Why you hit Asher?"

The velcro ripped open and crunched closed faster. "We're supposed to go home. It's time to go home."

"Yeah. I have to talk to Mr. Swann first."

"It's not okay to hit," Lacey said quickly. "We're pacifists."

"Well, yes." At home Lacey could talk his ear off like any ten-year-old, asking questions about every aspect of the world and discussing philosophical or political beliefs. Especially at bedtime. "We are. I'd still like to know what happened with Asher before I talk to your principal about it."

Lacey's voice was small, like it always was with other people around, if she spoke at all. "He took my sandwiches."

Sandwiches? Preston had thought it strange when Lacey asked for two this morning. They were both creatures of habit, and she had the same thing for lunch every weekday: veggie straws, a fruit puree pack, and a sunbutter sandwich on potato bread. But he'd figured it was a growth spurt, she'd been so hungry at dinner lately—

Shit. "Just today? Or before that too?"

She nodded.

Preston drew in a long, thin breath. It did nothing to help the tightness in his chest. He had fucked up, but he had to stay calm right now for Lacey. "I'm going to take care of this, okay? And then we'll go home." He stuck out a pinkie. "Promise."

Lacey wrapped her own around his before returning to her stimming. He stood and went into the principal's office and shut the door behind him.

The little office's walls were plastered with artwork and certificates. Rubber duckies lined the windowsill and the tops of bookcases, a joke gift begun when Swann started here as assistant principal, back when Preston attended this same school, and carried to ridiculous lengths by parents over the years. Now ducks of every color with football helmets and devil horns and pirate hats watched over Preston's return to the room where he'd been disciplined so many times, back when he still had meltdowns every week or so.

Mr. Swann stood and gestured at the wooden chair before his massive cherry desk half covered with framed photographs. "Preston, good to see you."

That made no sense, considering the circumstances. "Is it?" Preston asked, sitting. "Because it seems unfortunate, kids shoving. And stealing."

Mr. Swann's mouth hung open a moment before shutting in an indulgent smile. "Yes, well—" He settled back into his chair, adjusting his suit jacket, weathered face creasing with confusion. "Um, stealing? I asked to speak with you because Lacey hit another student." He spread his hands flat over his desk. "You know our zero-tolerance policy on violence. Lacey's been doing well overall with push-in support, but perhaps she needs more reinforcement outside the classroom. How are the private therapies going?"

They were going well, the various appointments Preston took Lacey to a few afternoons a week. Music therapy, social skills group. Things he'd have no way to pay for if he got fired and lost their insurance and *goddamn* those book challengers making his life a misery ever since he took over Youth Services.

And now he was hyperfocusing, staring at a rubber ducky wearing black sunglasses and missing what Principal Swann had been saying. "—there are therapies that can reduce unacceptable behaviors—"

Preston snapped his gaze back to the principal. "ABA is off the table." If there was one thing Preston was not going to fuck up, it was that. His mother's wishes had been perfectly clear. Hell, ABA therapy was banned in several countries now, for good reason. Some of his own earliest memories were a blur of too many hours spent in Applied Behavior Analysis—rewards and punishments, acceptance always conditional, the things he wanted about to be snatched away. He pushed up his glasses. "But what is the school's policy on theft?"

Mr. Swann's easy smile grew more tense. He ran a hand over his salt-and-pepper hair. "We're against it, obviously."

"Lacey pushed Asher because he's been taking her lunch every day."

Mr. Swann nodded. "The playground supervisor asked him about that. Asher says he asked Lacey—"

"Asher knows she won't say no. She can't." Her selective non-speaking was most present at places like crowded lunch tables. "Which is why her classmates need to be taught to understand her accommodations and not take her food from her."

The principal's fingertips pressed into his desk, his hand making a little tent. "I'd really like to see Lacey, as a fourth grader, advocating for herself, with words and positive actions." Like she had when she asked for two sandwiches. Only after Asher took them both had she lashed out. "We have free lunch available every day, which Lacey could have made use of."

"She can't eat that." Preston scrubbed a hand over his face. God, he was tired. Of explaining, of having to explain. It had to be the same food. The same brand. The exact same texture and taste.

"Look, we understand Lacey is particular—"

Preston's voice went flat. "Yes, because of her autism." This wasn't mere pickiness.

"But we have to handle *all* the children with understanding. I know you see this as very black-and-white—"

Preston dropped his hand to his armrest with a sigh. "Yes, because of *my* autism." He refused to believe that was the only reason it was very clear to him this had been poorly handled. "Why isn't Asher's guardian also in here right now?"

"Because Lacey is the one who hit another student. Brookville Elementary must foster a safe environment."

Fine. Call it black-and-white thinking if they liked. A failure of perspective-taking. A lack of empathy—that one always bothered him the most, setting a spark of anger up his spine. To Preston, anything else was simply trying to blur the line between right and wrong. "We are not doing this," he told the principal, hands gripping both armrests. "Unless this school is okay with teaching a boy that as long as a girl doesn't say no in just the right way he can take whatever he likes?" Swann's eyebrows shot up. "No?"

The principal shook his head. "Physical violence still—"

"No one noticed or helped." Preston's slow, certain words were almost strangled by the emotion tightening his throat. He swallowed down his own remorse. "Lacey wasn't given the support her disability requires. She was bullied. If the school wants to promote a safe environment for *everyone*, I hope it intervenes sooner next time." He stood. "I'm taking Lacey home."

"All right." Swann's voice followed him out of the office.

Preston was already grabbing his bag and the backpack and jerking his head at Lacey. "Let's go, Lace Face."

Outside, they climbed onto their bikes and buckled their helmets, Lacey's with iridescent stars stuck all over it. "Strawberry yogurt smoothies when we get home?" he asked. Her toothy smile at this almost soothed the unease stirring through his chest. If only he could fix everything else as easily as with a snack.

He dug his foot back to lift his kickstand. Bullies. That was the problem. And nobody doing anything about it. It started with stealing sandwiches without consequences, and then they grew up to try to tell everyone in town what they weren't allowed to read.

He'd work on those notes for the town hall meeting tonight, after giving his piano lessons and ineffectively enforcing Lacey's bedtime. He'd be ready the next time he faced one of those book banners. No matter how pretty. At least he could *try* to save the books and the clubs and his job. Even if he wasn't confident it would turn out well.

Nothing halfway. Knowing himself, it would be a complete disaster.

CHAPTER THREE
HARMONY

"C'mon, I know there must be someone." Harmony, lying on her crappy hotel bed, elbowed Alice where she perched on its edge.

Alice squealed in protest and shoved her away. Pretending to focus on the laptop balanced across her knees, she said primly, "I don't know what you mean."

Harmony snorted as she lifted her phone above her head to scroll through more of Brookville businesses' and residents' social media. "You'll have to do better than that if you want to run your own grifts someday. I can hear you blushing over all that hunting and pecking." Harmony clicked through to a local moms' group. "And if there wasn't someone, you'd have done a better job tracking down information on our librarian."

Instead of leaving Harmony out to dry with him this afternoon. Preston Jones had been her first online research target, after she and Alice had gotten her checked in here and grabbed an early dinner at an Indian place out by the freeway, near the olive processing plant and the big Brookville welcome sign with the motto *Olive What's*

Brotherly and Beautiful! But the man had like zero social media presence. And he was only a small part of all the work a con this complicated involved. No wonder Alice had given up so easily. That, and the *someone*, who obviously existed.

Harmony rolled onto her stomach and kicked her feet back and forth, pretending to scribble on her phone. "Dear Diary," she said in her breathy sex-kitten voice, "today I came to the most boring town in California and met a guy!" She rolled back. "So what's his name?"

Alice's fingers stilled. "Evan Sargent. He works at the shelter and food pantry at the Unitarian church."

"Oh, hon." Harmony peered at her friend from over her phone. "A church boy?"

"Not a boy. Not with those biceps." Alice scrunched her mouth to one side, like she was savoring some delicious flavor.

"Even worse." Alice fell for someone on every job. Sometimes harder than others. And it did affect her work. Not like Harmony—she stuck to one-night stands. No strings. No distractions. No looking back.

She wriggled her shoulders into the lumpy mattress. She hadn't even had one of those nights in a good while. Not since Zach. And Zach—well, he wasn't available anymore, was he?

Her phone fumbled in her hands, nearly smacking her in the face. *No looking back.* Harmony sat up and swept over to the stiff little upholstered chair squeezed next to the window offering a charming view of a parking lot. "You'll just have to leave him," she reminded Alice. "Sooner rather than later."

The sooner the better, if these were the best accommodations to be had in this town. This barely passed as an extended stay suite as advertised. Bed, chair, TV she'd never turn on. Desk that doubled as a coffee station. Sink, minifridge with microwave, and a single burner stove she definitely would never turn on. Shitty art on the ugly walls. On the bedside table, a lamp shaped like—was that supposed to be a cowboy? Were there cowboys in Brookville? If there were, maybe Harmony could find one to help pass one night she was stuck here.

"I know," Alice grumbled. "And it's such a waste, because I think Evan actually likes me. He's started coming in for a second coffee most days."

Harmony clicked through another Facebook profile with a variation of the perfect Brookville family: mom and dad, their arms around each other and hands resting on the shoulders of smiling or disaffected children. "Maybe he just needs the caffeine because he's so tired—of living in Brookville."

Alice threw one of the bed's thin pillows at her. "Never mind. There's no one. I haven't spoken to a single person in Brookville since I arrived." Still a horrible liar. She wasn't even trying.

Harmony hugged the pillow to her chest and rested one cheek atop it, smiling innocently. "Oh, you know I don't mean half of what I say."

Alice shot her side-eye. "We can't all be knockouts with every man falling at our feet."

Not every man. Annoyance buzzed at the back of Harmony's neck at the thought of Preston Jones sailing right past her today. Her scrolling finger paused as she tilted her head and imagined him falling. Someone would have to shout "timber" or half of Brookville could be taken out in one blow.

Harmony smirked, then told Alice, "That's not fair." Her partner in crime could fade into the background, yes—essential in their line of work, especially as Harmony was physically incapable of not causing a scene wherever she went. But with a smokey eye and the right dress for her angular frame, Alice was a knockout herself. Being able to play different roles like that was a huge asset. "You're so pretty," she cooed.

"You suck."

"I do suck," Harmony agreed, "and also I don't suck; in fact, I'm wonderful. You love me." She kicked out her foot to nudge the edge of the bed. "Tell me you love me, Alice. Tell me I'm pretty." Her toe prodded the mattress, until the laptop jostled in Alice's lap.

"Ugh! Do you want me to make these other social media accounts for you or not?"

"Yes, please." Alice had already set up a few, mimicking Brookville residents, for Harmony to start manipulating local public opinion to be more receptive to her grift. This plan relied on more than just tricking Travis Weaver. "You know I need you on this, one hundred percent." And Harmony needed to get back to work too. Focus on the grave trouble Brookville was dealing with—or would be, once she did her thing.

Conning was all about emotions. The trick was to stir people's up and make them feel like they had a problem, so when you arrived on the scene everyone saw you as a solution. In their panic, they'd grab on to you as their savior, gladly letting go of logic—and their wallets—for the privilege. All Harmony had to do was craft enough worry over Brookville's kids rotting away on the internet—people loved worrying about kids being online—and suddenly they'd be *begging* to host the outdoor music festival Harmony would claim to be bringing to town. The fake festival would ultimately be the trap for Travis.

The fact that he happened to own the VRcade, which she'd use to crystalize all those anxieties into a useful moral panic, was a delicious bonus.

She propped her elbows on the pillow and jabbed a finger at her phone, switching between fake profiles and planting seeds of discontent that would come to fruition at the town hall meeting next week. An article about the dangers of screentime shared here. A comment about the importance of diverse extracurriculars for college applications made there. A fake screenshot of a report on human traffickers using the metaverse to find young victims posted everywhere—this one in particular blended in perfectly among the many paranoid warnings between well-off suburban parents, without any of the real problems others faced, who were convinced entire flocks of kidnappers roamed the aisles of their incredibly safe grocery stores.

Alice prodded Harmony's thigh with her own toe, her brow wrinkled into neat little lines. "But you're sure about going with the festival grift? Is that the best way to come at Weaver? What about a multilevel marketing scheme? His wife is already deep into one, something with jewelry." Alice had done some good current research on the Weavers, at least. "There might be an in there."

"Mmm." Harmony dropped a comment about drug deals going down in the metaverse into a conversation among Brookville parents discussing the dangers of vaping. "I did have fun with those for a while. And made serious bank. Women will really go bananas for their unicorn prints." But then someone took their own MLM pyramid scheme too far, ugly yoga pants became the latest Nigerian prince, and now the whole game was greeted with too much suspicion.

Nope, selling fake festivals was her old standby. If she trusted anything anymore, she'd trust that. Especially when local politicians or other community leaders were the target, and she needed to do more than disappear with a suitcase or offshore account full of cash. This con was her go-to when she needed to destroy a man completely, ruin his reputation, turn everyone against him. Leave him, after all the sparkle and shine of her lies, with nothing but dust. She'd used it on a megachurch with a promised Christian music lineup. (Why let its leader steal from his parishioners to buy cars and planes and new wives, each with taller hair than the last, when Harmony could do it for him and expose to his flock what he was really doing on all those youth group trips at the same time?) She'd used it with an imaginary stable of country stars on an agriculture magnate whose daughter wanted to be the next Kacey Musgraves (and whose factory farm was illegally dumping pollution into the local watershed).

The swindle was as simple as one, two, three. First, get as many businesses in town as she could to invest in the festival as vendors, suppliers, and support. Second, declare the headliner act was pulling out, threatening the festival and everyone's livelihoods. Finally, get the target to save the day paying through the nose for a new, last-minute headliner.

Of course, Travis would say no at first to such a large risk of his own money—these guys *always* balked at helping others out. They'd never have gotten as rich as they were if they weren't in the strict habit of putting their bottom line above everyone else. That was all part of the plan. Only when Harmony pointed out that refusing would ruin their reputations and rob them of their power—all their suddenly struggling friends knowing they could have prevented the disaster and chose not to—did they crumble. They'd suddenly be just as eager to hand over their money as any mark, to hold on to their image as great men by playing the hero.

And of course, the payment wouldn't actually go to any headliner, because there was no festival; Harmony would use some of Travis's money to make things square with the local businesses before blowing him her final kiss goodbye: she'd have secretly recorded his inevitable initial refusal to help and blast it into everyone's inboxes before skipping town with the rest of his cash.

She shook her head. She was sure about this. She'd planned it all out perfectly, and now she had the funds to pull it off with mainstream acts. The biggest names, to take down the biggest crook.

She said with certainty, "The festival is the way to bring Weaver down."

Alice worried her thumbnail against her front teeth. "This grift means you stay in town all the way until the headliner switch-up. Months."

"What?" Harmony asked. "You're afraid I'll start seeing things in the pattern of this wallpaper by then?"

"You'll get bored. And using your real name? That's risky."

"Just my first name." Harmony wanted Weaver to realize, once she pulled the plug and his life went down the drain, who it was who had stolen it all back from him.

"It's risky," Alice repeated.

"It's worth it." Heat rushed up through her, warming her cheeks and tightening her throat. "For my dad."

Alice's gray eyes softened. "Yeah."

Travis Weaver had made his first millions selling an algorithm to a major music streaming app, as the tech world rebuilt from its burst bubble and tried to tamp down the popularity of file-sharing sites. The algorithm was a brilliant, elegant piece of code that served up just what listeners wanted and kept them hooked in for more.

Except he hadn't written it. His business partner—Harmony's father—had. And Travis Weaver stole it. Iggie Greene had trusted Weaver, and he lost everything.

He and Harmony had never had much. Her mom had taken a hike before Harmony had even formed permanent memories. They'd moved constantly, always just ahead of eviction. Slept in the car more than one night. But they'd had each other. And her dad had promised once the algorithm sold, everything would change.

And everything had.

Travis said it was her father's own fault for not reading their contract more carefully. Travis came from a real nice family. His own father was a lawyer. Harmony's dad had taught himself to code while working multiple jobs through high school. After Travis's betrayal, he was never the same—drinking, health problems, depression. No insurance to help with any of it. His heart gave out before Harmony turned eighteen. Her dad trusted the wrong man, and eventually it killed him.

After that, Harmony had no one and nothing. Not until she learned to take it.

She jumped over to the VRcade's Yelp page and began typing a one-star rant about her fake son spending $300 on in-game purchases. Travis Weaver had, like so many tech bros, eventually left the Bay Area for wider pastures. He'd bought a McMansion, run for mayor, and now he'd opened this little arcade that Harmony would, with a wave of her hand, turn into a threat to Brookville's youth and the key to his undoing. Especially once she started planting stories of people using it for cybersex.

"You know I've got your back," Alice said. "But you will get bored. And then you'll get in trouble."

"Well, I'm plenty busy for now," she reassured Alice before digging through the VRcade's Instagram feed, swiping through pictures of elaborate gaming equipment and following links in the likes and comments into profiles of other Brookville residents. Launching this big a con was like getting a dozen plates spinning. While singing opera. And juggling. "Town hall soon, to really kick things off."

Plus, she recalled with a pang of annoyance, she still needed to nail down the festival site. Even if the festival was fake and would never happen, she needed that documentation to convince Travis to get on board—and Preston Jones's land was now the only available around the town that the millionaire mayor hadn't snapped up himself over the past few years. Harmony couldn't have Travis getting *that* close a look at her dealings and possibly catching wind of anything suspect. She'd take another crack at the librarian once she had everything else in place.

A post from last August caught her eye, and she stopped scrolling. A red-haired boy held up a summer-reading certificate and a prize bag. No one was tagged, but behind a long counter, at the edge of the frame, like he was trying to escape right out of the image, stood Preston Jones. Harmony's fingers dragged the picture wide, so the librarian filled her screen between the crosshairs of her manicured nails. "And then I bet I can find something to keep myself entertained."

CHAPTER FOUR
PRESTON

"Good night," Preston called to his last student. He watched from the piano bench as Mason climbed into his mother's car. The headlights swept across the little fenced yard and the darkened windows at the front of the house.

Finally everything was quiet and still. Just Preston and the piano, the walls covered in bookshelves, the glow of the lamp. It wasn't as if more work wasn't waiting for him—the dishes, and figuring out what the hell he was going to say at Tuesday's town hall meeting—or that the couch and his book resting open on one armrest didn't beckon temptingly. But he couldn't seem to move from this spot.

Now that it was peaceful, the stress from the day came rushing back to him. He'd thought he'd been holding everything together, but he hadn't noticed Lacey wasn't getting to eat her lunch, and god knew how long it had really been going on. He was fucking things up again, and Lacey was suffering for it. Again.

He began playing to drown it all out. Rachmaninoff. Variation 18. If Lacey was actually in bed like she was supposed to be, maybe it would help her fall asleep. Then he started noodling around with a new melody, something that felt like moonlight.

He hadn't had time lately to compose much, but he didn't really mind. He loved his sister, and he loved his job. He didn't mind going into work on Saturdays for concerts in the community room swarmed by seniors and families, or heading back over with Lacey some afternoons to supervise whatever clubs the teens who had nowhere else to go after school wanted to try out. He wanted the library to be a haven for everyone, like it had been for him when he'd been a weird kid looking for someplace to hide. Before he had sorted out all the ways being autistic made certain things hard for him and honed the skills and tricks to cope, the library had been his retreat. And he'd been able to bring that peace home, even. Escape inside the stories he'd found, when his parents were arguing again about him.

And these "concerned citizens" were trying to take the books away. The books that kids needed most, books where they could find characters like themselves, where they could see their lives and what they could be. Preston's hands danced over the piano keys faster, fiercer. Imagine thinking kids needed to be protected from books, of all things. Not parents who weren't safe to be around, or prejudice, or mental health issues, or anything like that. It must be nice, to live the kind of life where you could believe kids only faced problems that could be solved by Mom and Dad with milk and cookies or a hug.

Preston's fingers stilled on the keys, white and black. He'd really fucking like a hug.

But his own mother was gone, nearly five years now, and Lacey's sensory issues meant she preferred pinkie promises and high fives to any other contact. And no one else was offering. So he did the next best thing, and called Dani.

"Preston, hey." He could picture his mom's oldest friend in her studio at her place outside town, short curly hair bound back by a silk scarf, phone on speaker while she shaped clay or painted. "How's it going?"

He set his own phone on speaker and rested it on the piano. "Fine."

"Uh-huh. Fine fine or you're spiraling but won't admit it fine?"

Preston spun the silver ring on his thumb. "Can you take Lacey next Tuesday?" Dani had helped his mom out a lot when Lacey was tiny, after their dad left and Preston was off at college. They'd kept up the routine after Preston moved home. Routine was important for Lacey.

"Sure. You got a hot date?"

Annoyingly, the image of the woman from that afternoon, outside the library, flashed through his mind. "Er—with my civic duty?"

"What?" Dani sounded distracted. Definitely working on something.

"With the town council and probably several angry parents?" What if they got an entire group together to mob the meeting? These people had too much time on their hands. And money and energy and more than rudimentary social skills cobbled together from years of therapy.

"Oh, god, Preston. You have got to get out there. Do something for yourself for once."

"I don't have to listen to you; you probably have clay in your hair."

"I do." Dani laughed. "But you should still go on an actual date sometime."

"Yeah." A familiar longing stirred through his chest. He did want that. And more. The whole romance thing. Someone to be with in the quiet at the end of the day, instead of just his own worries. Hugs. But he knew from experience how unlikely that was, how hard he was to love. Besides, he had no time. "I'll do that, during the forty-five minutes while Lacey's at group, maybe."

"When was the last time *you* saw *your* therapist?"

Besides the grief counseling sessions he'd gone to with Lacey? His last therapist had worked for his grad school's health services. So. About five years.

He pushed up his glasses and deflected. "What are you working on?"

"Oh, a vase. Supposedly. A thing of beauty is not what this is. Gonna smush it down and try again tomorrow."

"You still good with supervising the GSA on Friday?"

He wasn't sure if Dani's grunt was of acknowledgement or from her working the clay. But she said, "I'll be there."

"Even with all the extra attention we've been getting?" He spun his ring again. "Can't promise an angry parent won't show."

"Preston, I have been an out lesbian in a small town for decades. Nothing can hurt me. And I really like working with the kids. And helping you out. If you wanted to go out more," she added meaningfully.

Dani made it sound so easy. Go out. With—someone. But this was a small town and people weren't exactly lining up to date a twenty-seven-year-old bookworm with a budget-frozen civil servant's salary and a fourth grader. Who wasn't selectively nonspeaking like his sister but who was still much better talking to family or within the set scripts of work.

"I want to be there for Lacey *and* for you," Dani went on. "It's okay to lean on me, babe."

His mouth quirked. "But you're so short."

Her snort crackled over their connection. "Respect your elders."

"Right. I forgot you're very old and wise." His fingers began plinking out the minuet he'd worked on with Mason that evening. Beethoven.

"Forty-six is not old. *You're* just an actual, literal baby still."

His fingers traveled lightly over the keys. "And babies should be dating?"

He could hear the smack of her palm against clay. "Yes. That is my wisdom. Go on a date, you infant."

"You first."

"Oh, Preston, I had my chance." The resigned sadness in her voice was chased by the next smack of the clay. "Sometimes it just doesn't work out. But I don't want to see you miss yours entirely because you're making it harder than it has to be."

A door slammed somewhere upstairs, bringing Preston's playing to a halt. That meant a window was open. "I should check on Lacey."

"Ha, good luck. Night, babe."

"Night."

He made his way upstairs, thinking about scripts. He needed to plan out exactly what he wanted to say at that meeting. He was not going to pull the books Cheryl Weaver had complained about—supposedly because of sexual content, but funny how they were all only books with queer or POC main characters. And one was a picture book, for god's sake. Pronouns were not sexual content.

But he also didn't want to get fired. There were plenty of libraries in California, but that would mean moving away from Dani's support, and disrupting everything he and his mother had worked hard to establish for Lacey—her therapists who understood her, the home she'd always lived in. Routine and consistency. He couldn't uproot her like that.

Just like he couldn't pry her away from her telescope, where he found her crouching in her pajamas at her bedroom's open window.

He leaned a shoulder against her doorframe. "Bedtime, Space Lace."

She kept her face glued to the eyepiece. "It's not my fault this crab is nocturnal."

"Cancer? That's the—" He knew this, she'd been telling him.

"Beehive cluster." She turned to her desk and began jotting something down in a notebook. "I'm already at a hundred and ten observed member stars. Galileo found forty."

"Um, wow. Should we alert the university?"

She looked at him sternly. "There are over a thousand." She returned to her notes. "I've logged a thirty-two-point-five percent rate of red dwarfs so far, which is under half of what the Smithsonian says is the total—why do you think that is?"

Preston blew air through his cheeks. "Is this one of those questions where you ask but then just tell me?" Lacey didn't answer and didn't stop scribbling in her observation record. She couldn't manage bothering with shoelaces or pouring her own milk for her cereal, but for her beloved stars she tracked and predicted paths of constellations and measured magnitudes, doing calculations he already couldn't quite follow. Shit, should he be getting her a tutor? An astronomy tutor? Did those exist? Books and the Chromebook he'd gotten her for Christmas— which was open on her desk—would have to do for now. He walked over and shut its screen. "No computers after dinner," he reminded her.

Lacey peered back through the telescope. "I needed to check if I was right about 42 Cancri's magnitude."

"Yeah." He folded himself into Lacey's desk chair. He was used to the intensity in her voice that so many took as defiance or rudeness, when she did speak around them. Getting Lacey proper accommodations had been like a third job for a few years there. He ran his finger along the spiral binding of her notebook. "And you need to tell me right away if someone's picking on you again, okay? Asher or anyone else."

"I thought he was my friend. Because we were sharing. The recess supervisor said maybe he picks on me because he likes me." Her nose wrinkled. "She said boys used to pull on her pigtails."

"No." Preston leaned forward and tugged Lacey's hand, gently facing her toward him. "That's not right. When the right someone comes along, they'll be kind to you and just tell you they like you. They won't pull your hair or steal from you." Again he felt that ache, keen as the stars up there against the black, for something like that for himself.

Lacey wound a strand of her hair around one finger, like she often did when she was calculating. "Good. Because I like my sandwiches, but I do want a boyfriend."

That was officially one thing too many for Preston to deal with today. "Did you brush your teeth?"

"I forgot."

Like pretty much every night. He waited while she finished getting ready, shut the window, and flicked out the lights, leaving her star projector dimly casting blurry constellations over the walls and ceiling. "Night, Lace Face."

He headed back downstairs to where only work waited for him and, if he was lucky, a little reading time. Despite Dani's cajoling and offers of babysitting, that was how his nights mostly ended. Looking for a relationship was way down his to-do list, as much as he might have wanted to find someone. Someone who might want to curl up and discuss what they were reading. Someone kind, like he'd said. Though he wasn't against a little hair-pulling among consenting adults.

And yeah, maybe he spent too many of his slivers of free time retreating into books. But autistic burnout was no joke. He couldn't afford to fall back into more sensitivity and meltdowns and trouble communicating, less able to take care of himself, let alone Lacey. He had to work to be accepted, to be masked, to be useful—sometimes he wished he could just *be.* Or be someone else, who didn't have to work so hard at it all. Books gave him that. So, he'd have to settle for reading love stories for the time being. He knew their solace was mostly fantasy, but it was enough to blot out for a while the truth he'd learned, indelible as the ink on their pages, that he and his life were too difficult, too much, for anyone to love. Not love enough to want to stay, anyway.

It was enough to let himself imagine that there could be someone.

CHAPTER FIVE
HARMONY

Harmony marched into the Brookville town council chambers and surveyed the scene.

Seven high-backed leather seats ranged before a large mural of the local farmland and countryside at the front of the assembly room, raised above a few wooden tables with office placards for regular non-council meeting attendants: secretary, sheriff's deputy, school board rep, associated student body president from the town's one high school. These all faced the rows of stackable padded chairs already filling with Brookville residents.

She noted the main contingents present in the overwhelmingly white crowd. Business owners. Chatty retirees. The helicopter parents with already-bored-looking kids and teens beside them, most of them doing homework in their laps or on phones. Granola parents with babies in wraps, amber necklaces, and fancy water bottles. Here for the agenda item about pesticide use at the local parks, no doubt. These were her vanguard, to be called up in service to her plan first.

Making her way toward the back, Harmony's attention snagged on someone in a rich brown corduroy sports coat, long legs escaping into the aisle next to where he sat. "Nerd alert," she sang under her breath. She couldn't believe her luck. Well, she could, because she prided herself on cultivating a charmed existence. Still, she was delighted she'd caught him here. Two birds, one Harmony.

"Just who I needed to talk to!" she exclaimed. She was wearing a coral flared blazer over a black jumpsuit with a thin patent-leather belt and her highest aqua heels. So when she leaned in nearer, clutching the leather folio case she carried tightly with both arms, even with the man's height her plunging surplice neckline was right at his eye level.

At her words, Preston Jones stopped shuffling the stack of notecards propped against one bouncing knee and looked directly into her cleavage.

Let's see him ignore me now.

She kept an innocent look plastered on her face as his mouth fell open a gratifying amount—probably not gay—before he lurched back, almost into the lap of his neighbor. He looked up at her, and, behind the fluorescent gleams cutting across his glasses, she swore he rolled his eyes. Through a clenched jaw, he told her, "If you want to yell at me, you'll have to wait until your scheduled turn."

Huh. She was getting distinct weirdo vibes off of this guy. He looked stressed. His thick hair was parted with wicked precision but tousled as if he'd just run one of his fidgety hands through it. She stayed near, pitching her voice low. "But I really just need to inform you—"

"Yes, yes," he hissed back. "I peddle pornography, I'm the devil, books are more dangerous than gun violence or climate change, please won't someone think of the children?" He snatched up his notecards and squeezed past the next few seats, toward the middle of the chambers.

Yikes. So he was *deeply* chaotic. Almost as outrageous as she could be. She straightened and made for a seat in the center back. She really might need to reassess her charm-and-disarm strategy. But now it was time to put the rest of Brookville under her spell.

The town council, some of whom had been chatting with constituents or the people at the front tables, filed into their seats behind a large shared desk. They unbuttoned suit jackets or adjusted the little mics set before each of them. Mayor Weaver, taking his place in the center chair, called the meeting to order.

Harmony had kept tabs on him online, but it was the first time she'd seen the man in person for—damn, *well* over a decade. His hair was still light brown—dyed, clearly—but his hairline was drawing higher, especially on the sides, like holiday bunting festooned above his tanned, punchable face. He had that well-moisturized, easy look of someone absolutely comfortable in his skin and in the world.

God, she was going to enjoy crushing him.

She took a seat and texted Alice, already planted on the far side of the audience. *Everything set?*

Yup. Accessed display controls. That would allow them to take charge of this meeting—literally, altering the agenda projected on a flatscreen mounted to one side above the mural—whenever Harmony found the most promising moment to jump in with her festival pitch. *Something's hinky with the sound system, don't know that I can lower mic volume if they try to cut you off.*

There were always a few bumps on the road to glory. *Then I'll just have to be louder than them.*

Alice replied with three megaphone emojis. Harmony smirked and sat patiently through the council's opening procedures and discussions of old business, addressing items down that displayed agenda. To pass time during a discussion of the local fraternal brotherhood's donation to the senior center, she squinted hard at the back of Preston's head, easily visible above the people behind him, wondering if she could psychically implant the impulse to not say strange things and then run away the next time she tried talking to him. *Be nice to Harmony and agree to give her everything she wants.* She sat up a little straighter when Cheryl Weaver stood to address the council, including her husband and his smug little smile.

Cheryl minced up to the podium in her black suede booties and smoothed down her Ann Taylor belted tunic before speaking, pink lipsticked mouth pursed. She was entirely what Harmony had expected from her Facebook and Instagram and occasional appearances in regional media—a woman pleased with herself and with holding the audience's attention hostage to her self-satisfaction. "As you know," she said, turning her blonde head to address one side of the chambers and then the other slowly, "the Brookville Ladies' Association has been working to bring enriching, enlivening experiences to the children of our town for many years, and we're proud to announce our sponsorship of Brookville's fifth annual Earth Day celebration. This event will allow Brookville youth to participate in crafts, learn about the environment, and enjoy outdoor fun."

She paused, inviting a smattering of polite applause. Harmony noted the group of well-dressed women who clapped the loudest. Power players in the town hierarchy. She'd need to spend some up-close-and-personal time soon with the Real Housewives of Brookville.

Like a bad beauty pageant contestant, Cheryl gestured to a portion of the mural along the back wall, where the town motto flowed across a golden ribbon twining between olive tree branches. "Thanks to the association, our children can enjoy all that's brotherly and beautiful in Brookville."

The mayor's wife continued her stilted recitation patting herself on the back, but another noise began rising through the chambers. Barely perceptible at first, a song played through the speakers mounted on the walls, gradually overtaking Cheryl's projected voice. Harmony glanced over at Alice—had she somehow messed up with the sound system?—but she was looking around just as confused, brows drawn together sharply; this wasn't them. Kids giggled as the lyrics of Nicholas Fraser's "Why You Always Lying?" blasted. Parents gave up hushing them as the music grew in volume. Cheryl, eyes and nostrils flaring, tried to carry on with her speech until she was practically shouting and finally threw up her hands, waving her bright pink nails in the air and letting out a little huff.

The music blared louder. Preston's head ducked between hunched shoulders as he crashed a palm to one ear. Travis banged his gavel, adding to the cacophony. "What is that? Where is that coming from?"

Harmony, bemused, could only sit back and drink in the chaos as a text popped up from Alice: *I KNEW someone else was in the system!!!!* Apparently, they were not the only ones with nefarious designs on this meeting. Respect where it was due. The music had completely disrupted things—sending the sheriff's deputy jolting up from his seat and looking around bewildered, half the audience shouting pointlessly, and most of the teens sitting to one side near their ASB prez laughing. Harmony was enjoying the increasingly dark shades of red Travis's face was turning. She bopped her head in time with the song.

Then, from the fringe of the group of teens, a dark-haired Latina girl in a black tee and jeans shot up from her seat. She punched a button on a remote, and the music cut off.

Travis's frown carved deeper. "Jordan DaCosta, what the hell—excuse me—what do you think you're doing? This is not the place for your juvenile delinquent behavior! This isn't funny."

The girl opened and closed her mouth, arms crossing and then falling to her sides stiffly. At last she blurted, "No, this is a *protest*. The women's association is participating in the destruction of the environment with their hypocritical event."

"Excuse me," Cheryl said, breath puffing harshly off the mic she adjusted nearer. "We are fostering a love of the outdoors and personal responsibility. Teaching how to reduce your carbon footstep."

"Foot*print.*"

Cheryl ignored her. "And if you don't think that's a worthwhile and nice thing for our kids, maybe *you're* the problem."

The deputy marched up to Jordan and confiscated her remote, but she came back at Cheryl. "Running bounce houses off gas generators and handing out coloring sheets sponsored by a multinational oil corporation is *not* helping the environment or the kids of Brookville." A cloud of anger and discomfort shadowed the teen's face. "It's going to take more than a few of us choosing paper straws and reusable bags to save the planet. My generation needs real action now if we want anything beautiful left for when we're adults. Everyone knows you're gonna cut down a bunch of our trees to build houses. Since climate change disproportionately affects minorities, it's like no one *cares*—"

Cheryl's fingers clawed against the side of the podium. "Are you calling me *racist*? We're just trying to create a nice day for *the children.*" She circled one hand in front of herself, with an air of being unfairly put upon yet generously obliging. "We'll do a carbon offset."

"You own half the town, why don't you actually protect the local environment instead of just talking out of your—"

Travis roared into his mic. "That's enough!"

Harmony fought back a grin. That Jordan had given her quite a present, letting her see the Weavers so upset before she'd even begun her own campaign. The kid reminded Harmony of herself when she was a teen, after her father died. Clearly a natural at brewing up trouble, but angry and lacking the skills to effectively direct it so it didn't rebound on herself. And none of her classmates were standing with Jordan; only the ASB president shot her a small pained smile, while the others tilted their blonde heads together to giggle and whisper or leaned away like they couldn't even see Jordan.

Harmony knew the type. When she'd stolen an address to send herself to a top public arts high school across the city, those rich kids had ignored her an entire semester. But all Harmony had wanted then was to escape being the girl at her old school whose dad had died. She hadn't yet taken on their costume, learned how to wear the right labels—their passwords were tragically easy to guess, their bank accounts too flush to notice light skimming—and drop the right names of vacation spots and semi-famous friends. It really was a good education she'd gotten there—nothing like already being rich to get people to give you things for free, to let you charge things to random rooms in hotels, to let every eccentricity from a chaotic upbringing and outsize personality slide.

But Harmony had been doing this a long time now, so she was also reading the heightened energy in the room, like static dancing through the air just waiting to be harnessed. She'd planned to take control of the meeting later, when people were worn out and more malleable, but when opportunity presented itself, you had to be ready to swoop in.

And Jordan clearly needed some help. Travis was studying the confiscated remote and saying something about cybercrime, and when one of the council members laughed like she thought he was joking, he actually called the deputy to *arrest* Jordan so they could move on to discussing the library.

Cheryl plopped back into her seat, nodding to the friend at her side wrapping one well-toned and braceleted arm around her in support. "That's the kind of kid who goes to those new library programs. Wasn't I saying that?"

Harmony caught sight of Preston's shoulders tensing before she texted Alice: *Now.* She couldn't let all these volatile feelings stay focused on Jordan or fall next on the library of all things. Not when she could use them, nudged toward the right target—Travis's new business—to make her festival proposal even more attractive. As she leaned down to where she'd tucked her purse at her feet, she muttered, just loud enough for the people sitting near her to hear, "That's rich, coming from the owners of a cybersex arcade." Slipping a pair of thin black frames from her bag, she straightened, blinked innocently at her neighbor, and listened as if rapt.

But her work on social media must have paid off because a woman sitting in front of her with a baby in her lap called out, "Why are we discussing the library when the mayor's opened a cybersex shop in our town?"

Travis turned positively crimson, peering into the crowd. "My business is *not*—" He looked from the rest of the crowd to Jordan and back, like a particularly foolish tennis fan. "First, we have to deal with her—"

"It was just a prank," his colleague beside him said. "Let's get back to the agenda so we're not here till midnight."

Jordan scowled. "It wasn't, I told you, I'm protesting—"

The councilor who'd laughed about the mention of cybercrime shrugged. "Free speech. I think removal from the meeting should suffice for speaking out of turn."

One nudge more should do it. Harmony pitched her voice just beyond the general murmur of the audience reacting to the drama unfolding. "More than enough. Get on with business." Soon there was a swell of agreement urging the council to move on.

Travis let out a sigh. "Give someone an inch and they'll take the shirt off your back." But he gestured at the deputy. "Escort her out. We'll be calling your mother, young lady."

Jordan asked sullenly, "Can I have my remote back?"

Harmony savored the way Travis looked like he nearly choked before declaring, "No, you may not have your remote back!"

Jordan raised her chin defiantly as she left with the deputy in her wake, to some admonishing looks—Cheryl was shooting her daggers—but also laughter from the teens and some adults too.

Travis banged his gavel again, for absolutely no reason, and said, "Now, we're meant to hear from Mrs. Weaver about the library next—"

Several people in the audience murmured in protest and pointed up at the digitally displayed agenda, which—thanks to Alice—now showed an open comment period after the Ladies' Association announcement. Travis frowned down at his desk, shuffling through papers, while the woman in front of Harmony declared, "Looks like we have plenty of time to get back to this arcade where people plug themselves into computers all day doing god knows what."

Another parent joined in, echoing one of Harmony's social media posts. "Yeah, I heard kids have been hooked in for hours after school!" *Hooked* was good—it would make parents think of drugs.

Harmony perched her frames on the bridge of her nose. Anticipation crackled under her skin. She loved this part. She'd always done theater at the schools she'd moved around to and for a little while afterward in L.A., but grifting was even more of an immediate performance. Visceral. Electric.

The orchestra was warming up, the curtain rising—if the work she'd done the last few days had truly taken root, and her own disruption of this meeting didn't fizzle out.

One of the crunchy-granola parents cast a disgusted look at their neighbor. "I'd *never* let my children have that much screentime."

"Letting perverts raise your kids," another said with a sage nod. "Picking up ten kinds of gender."

Yeesh, this was getting out of hand. One thing you *could* always trust was that people could always be uglier than you expected.

The first parent leaned over, a hard look in her eyes. "We all know your kid is probably in some anti-feminist chat room right now, Patricia."

People assumed all Californians were open-minded hippies, but there were plenty of haters here, especially in its smaller towns. Could make for some powerful fireworks between them, but Harmony needed all that aimed in the direction she chose right now.

Fortunately, an Asian woman in a pantsuit with a teen sitting next to her turned to the council and demanded, “What’s going to happen this summer? We don’t have enough city rec programs; kids are going to end up doing nothing but video games.”

“Sucking money out of *my* bank account,” added another parent closer to Harmony. He leaned toward the people next to him. “Did you hear about that kid that spent three hundred dollars in one day on that stuff?”

“Forget that, did you hear about the child who was *human trafficked* after being on there?”

The meeting erupted again in a racket of concerned comments and demands that the council address them. Amid it all, Harmony rose from her seat.

Showtime.

CHAPTER SIX
HARMONY

"I don't know if you always conduct business like this here—" Harmony let the full force of her powerful voice carry across the room to an exasperated-looking Travis, and several people stopped their side conversations to give her their attention. "But I would be really glad if we did get to the open comments part of the agenda? I actually think what I came here to talk about will be of interest to all these obviously good and clearly concerned parents."

By the time she finished this opening, most of the crowd had quieted and turned her way. The air in the room became a held breath. Harmony, right at the center of attention, where she loved to be, felt like a conductor raising her baton. Time to steer this meeting just where she wanted it.

"Excuse me, Miss, uh—" Travis furrowed his brow at her. No way he'd recognize her—she'd been a tiny thing when he'd last seen her, a child with secondhand clothes and unbrushed hair, and he'd always been too far up his own ass to notice people unimportant to him anyway. Maybe he needed glasses but was too vain to wear them. Funny, because her own lenses were prescriptionless. But the frames made her look older, serious, more trustworthy.

Ha.

"Harmony Hale, Rhythmic Events." Mentally, she snapped a hand shut at Travis. *Silence from you right now.* She called upon her first chairs—the anxious parents. "And I hear what these people are saying. Nothing is more important than the well-being of a community's children."

Nods and murmurs of agreement buoyed her hold over the room, forestalling interruption by the council, even without Alice cutting their mics. A few people chimed in more loudly, with "That's right!" and "What is the town doing to address the needs of parents in the community?"

They hadn't been asking Harmony, but she answered anyway. "Kids need a village. Values. Somewhere to direct their wonderful energy. And that's just what we do at Rhythmic—strengthen communities, through world-class cultural events. I'm in town to scout potential sites for the launch of a new music festival."

This earned raised brows, mouths formed into little *O*s, whispers of excitement. Along with the majority of the room, the possibly mentally unstable librarian's attention was locked on her. He'd twisted his long body around to look her way, arm bent along the back of his chair.

Travis tried to regain control once more, holding up whatever paper he'd finally found in his pile. "Actually, the agenda—"

Preston glanced back and forth between the mayor and Harmony—and once at his notecards—as if he wasn't sure which way he wanted the power balanced between them to tip.

Harmony barreled forward with oblivious purpose. "Yes, my agenda is to introduce the concert proposal and gauge interest on the part of potential stakeholders." She tapped her finger against her folio, signaling Alice.

Faithful Alice was right on cue with her counterpoint. "A *rock* concert?"

"No, all kinds of music!" Harmony carried on, knowing this would reassure the seniors and plenty of others. "My firm's interested in being the first in California to host a multigenre, multicultural musical festival focused on the whole family." And *that* would catch the attention of everyone who'd just witnessed Jordan's protest, goad them to prove how worldly and accepting they were, along with providing an alternative to Cheryl's tarnished community events. "We anticipate it being a clear success. Within just a few years this festival will rival every midsized fest out there, like Pilgrimage or Firefly back east, while establishing its own unique brand. Family-friendly. A chance for togetherness. We're currently in talks to secure a major name headliner. Picture it—" She raised one hand, fingers splayed. "*Coachella North*!"

Now a buzz of excitement carried from the teens on one side of the room and sparked across the rows of people.

But not everyone was on board, not even close. Harmony dropped her gaze to a pursed-lipped businessman a few seats over, her eye contact subconsciously granting him just the permission he needed to feel like speaking up. "How do a bunch of concertgoers descending on our town help strengthen the community?"

Harmony bathed him in her brightest smile. "I'm so glad you asked." She slipped off her glasses and folded them. "I've managed several previous projects like this, and the heart of our operation is ensuring the local municipality and businesses have both a voice and interest in the execution and success of the festival." She pointed with her glasses at the different elements in the crowd. Seniors. "Of course, the community-held values of coming together and culture." Parents. "And we integrate with local schools to offer teen internships, where they can learn vital leadership skills working in a dynamic industry and in the fresh outdoors." Business owners.

"Importantly, we strive to use local merchants for as much of the festival's needs as possible—restaurants and food trucks for catering and beverage services, merchandise, even printing and signage." The deputy. "Security is hired from local off-duty peace officers, offering extra income." That they would never actually see, of course, since the festival would never happen. Harmony only paid cops when she was bribing them.

Each group's energy was palpable, adding to the swell of excitement building.

And then, right as she should have thrown all that momentum into a crescendo sealing the deal, leaving this meeting with an appointment with the mayor and the goodwill of the people, one of the council members jumped in. "This kind of event sounds expensive and risky." The man to the right of Travis leaned back in his seat. "It would be a significant undertaking with unknown impacts."

His sour note broke her spell. Other councilors began shuffling paperwork. Parents leaned over squirming children.

She was losing them.

Harmony didn't panic. Like she always said: when they're running you out of town on a rail, grab your baton and pretend you're leading a parade. They'd end up following wherever you led.

"Of course," she said with an easy smile, like it was her idea to pull back on her pitch. "It's a major opportunity that deserves careful consideration." She rocked back gently on her heels. "I'm still in the exploratory stages. I've focused the search on Brookville specifically, because other towns in the area have established centers of tourism—the spa in Heraldale, the winery scene in Cranton." Both were nearby towns that Brookville existed in the shadow of, with no specific draw of its own. And the Heraldale Herons were the Brookville Bobcats' biggest rivals. "Brookville has the closest access to SFO, but what's more important is finding a location *fully* invested in being the home of this festival." She made a little shrug, as if it didn't matter to her much. As if her retribution on her father's behalf wasn't riding on these next few moments. "But maybe this offer would be more attractive to the council of Heraldale."

The councilor who'd had Jordan's back folded her hands under her chin. V. Newell, her placard read. "No—I'd like to hear more."

Bless you, you're a treasure, I love your hair. "Well," Harmony dove back in with a patter too fast to interrupt again, "we use a cost-sharing model that ensures the community benefits from the success of the event." And ensured, once she pulled the headliner switch-up, that Travis would be on the hook or see his town and reputation crushed. (Not that she wouldn't still crush his reputation on her way out anyway.) "But businesses that participate directly with the festival aren't the only winners; tourists will make a vacation of it before and after the actual concert, and for local retail, our previous festivals have produced an average sales increase that outpaces holiday shopping." She delivered an assured look at the businessman who had questioned her before and threw him a bone. "One week of hosting concertgoers keeps the lights on the rest of the year." He pulled the corners of his mouth down appraisingly, and she knew she had him. She was hitting that high of working her magic, that freewheeling place she loved to soar without a net, trusting herself to bring all her riffing and promises home eventually. "And the town's newfound name recognition typically results in a healthy bump in year-round tourism, boosting hospitality and recreational sectors"—she paused finally, before hitting them with the keynote—"to say nothing of the town's tax base."

The councilors were almost all nodding now. V. Newell offered, "Perhaps when we next convene—"

Travis held up a hand. "We'd need to see documentation."

Harmony let her widest smile unfurl at him. "I have all the figures and would be glad to go over them in more detail at your earliest convenience, tomorrow if you like—"

"I'd want to see all the details," Travis emphasized. "The site, traffic impacts—"

Which meant she needed that land use lease signed yesterday. "I can get those for you." Once she had the site locked down, she and Alice could get to work on the rest of the paperwork—some real, some not worth the expensive fees when she knew a good forger.

With a sharp nod, the man who'd stolen her father's work invited her into his life. "Bring them along to my office whenever you do."

Along with a world of pain, buddy. Harmony had to stop herself from jumping and clicking her Valentino heels. She could laugh maniacally in her hotel room later.

Travis glanced at the councilors to either side. "After tonight's confusion, I think it's best if we table the rest of the agenda items until we next convene." He was probably worried what new chaos might break out if his wife tried addressing the council again.

No one objected. Even as people began gathering bags and children and chatted with each other, they were all still held in the echo of her spell, completely won over and ready to spread the good word of Harmony Hale and the festival through their town. But as Travis banged his goddamn gavel again, she felt a sharper gaze on her.

Preston was still turned in his seat, peering her way. Suspicious? That wouldn't do. There were much more fun, less spoil-her-plan emotions he could be feeling about her. So Harmony waited a beat; then, with a demure glance away and back, she tucked a lock of hair behind her ear and bit her lip. *Oh, you're staring at little old me?* Her smile escaped, turning wolfish. *I'm flattered.*

In the municipal fluorescent lighting, the ruddy blush that swept over Preston's long, handsome face was marked. Now, that was more like it. Maybe some of the color was from frustration, as his brows zipped together, and he gave a little shake of his head before spinning back in his seat, flustered. But not all of it.

She definitely wanted to take advantage of that. Preston was certainly good-looking, in a straitlaced sort of way, so she'd assume he had a girlfriend—except surely he'd have popped up in the girlfriend's social media if he did, and Harmony had been searching nonstop through anything tagged locally in preparation for tonight. Anyway, she wasn't trying to marry the guy, just charm him long enough to get what she needed. See if now that she'd made her pitch he'd be open to discussing the use of his land.

But Alice had held up Travis and his wife at the double doors leading out of the chambers, as they'd arranged. Harmony couldn't help taking the chance to look the mayor in the eye before knocking his lights out. Metaphorically. And Preston would have to get past her before he could run off again.

When Harmony neared the bottleneck at the door, Alice was rambling some nonsense about a pothole outside the coffee shop while Travis and Cheryl barely concealed their impatience. When Alice saw Harmony, she babbled, "Anyway, thanks, g'night!" and abruptly took off. Harmony was about to sweep in for a quick word, when Jordan DaCosta tried slipping back into the room.

"Ah, ah, ah!" Travis twirled a finger in the air. "Turn around, young lady."

Jordan gestured at the kids still chatting around the table where their ABS president was sliding her notebook into her purse. "But we all drove together from school—"

"And you're leaving alone," Cheryl told her, shooing her back along with all the people streaming from the room. "I don't want our kid spending any more time with you." Harmony wondered which of the discount Regina Georges over there who'd snickered at Jordan's protest was the Weavers' pride and joy.

Travis shrugged. "Guess you're walking."

Jordan stood open-mouthed, looking suddenly young and vulnerable even in her choppy bangs and Green Day tee.

"That's consequences." Cheryl glanced around looking for agreement, falling on Harmony. "If people would only discipline their children, maybe they wouldn't grow up so out of control."

Travis noticed her there too and shook his head ruefully. "As exciting as your proposal is, with all the hands-on opportunities for young people," he said, "I'm afraid nothing is going to change a troublemaker like that. Can't teach an old dog not to holler."

Harmony didn't want to get on their wrong side, especially when they might be touchy about the VRcade fuss, but it was dark, and she didn't know how far Jordan lived from downtown. "Still, as your lovely wife says, anything for the children." She pulled a twenty from her purse and held it out to Jordan. "That should cover a lift home. Maybe spend the ride thinking about your actions." Specifically, how awesome they were.

Jordan's brows darted together uncertainly, before she grabbed the cash and left, muttering, "Thanks."

Travis looked at Harmony with grudging thoughtfulness. At least throwing money around might pique his interest some more. "That's awfully nice of you, Miss Hale."

"Like I said, I'm hoping to make a real impact on the community." She matched his gaze. "Never too soon to start."

She didn't get long to enjoy looking at Travis face to face, though, because behind him, just down the hallway where people were chatting in clumps or making their way out into the evening, Alice was half subtly, half frantically waving one hand and pointing with the other back inside the chambers. Harmony broke her gaze from Travis to glance over her shoulder, and almost swore. Along with a few others who must not have wanted to fight the crush at the main entrance, Preston was escaping out a back door she hadn't known led outside.

Her librarian—and her path to revenge for her father—was getting away.

CHAPTER SEVEN
PRESTON

What was *that?*

The question cycled through Preston's mind as he biked along one side of the town square. He'd been going to speak about the library collection and events. He had definitely been next on the schedule. And then.

Harmony Hale.

Interrupting the agenda. Talking not about books or the library at all but a festival. Causing them to push things back until next month. He'd have this hanging over him *another month*. And yet the immediate reprieve had unlocked all the tension in his shoulders and stomach. His mind went around and around again, unable to decide how it felt. Good, bad, good, bad.

Headlights spilled across the road from behind. The purr of an engine crowded nearer. "Go around," Preston gritted out under his breath. However he did feel about the delayed agenda, things not going to plan always unsettled and irritated him in the moment. The car didn't pass him, though, even when he rode as close to the curb as he could. He reached the stop sign at the square's corner and waved the driver by.

A red convertible rolled through the stop sign until the driver was even with him.

"Well, hello to you too!" Harmony Hale called, waving back with a wiggle of her fingers. "We've gotta stop running into each other like this."

He rounded the corner and pedaled on. "Please don't run into me."

She laughed. "Now, if I did that, I'd never get you to agree to lease your land to the festival."

Preston's wheels wobbled. "My—?" He gripped the handlebars and steadied his bike. The convertible still rolled along beside him.

"For the festival site. I've been trying to talk to you about it for a week."

"So, you're *not* a concerned parent hoping to censor books from the library's collection." When she'd started speaking to the assembly, it had taken only a minute for him to realize his mistake. He'd had the rest of the abbreviated meeting to ponder why that revelation had brought him such a swell of relief. But his land? The old walnut orchard?

"Oh, *that's* what the devil talk was about earlier." She tossed her head back, comprehending, then shook it. "Nope." Her hair sort of shimmered over her bare shoulders when she did that—her blazer was thrown over the passenger seat. "Don't have kids." She cocked a brow. "But I might be interested in some of that other stuff you mentioned sometime."

What he'd—?

Porn. The word lit up through his mind like the neon sign outside the Moonlight Bar across the street. He'd said he'd peddled porn. *Don't say porn again.* That seemed like a low bar for a conversation, even for him. "Gun violence?" he asked weakly.

She laughed again. He dared another glance her way as he stopped at the next intersection, wondering if she was laughing at him. Sometimes he couldn't tell. Didn't get the joke—which was sometimes him. But as Harmony laughed now, something softened in her face. Like her smile shifted: false to true.

Then, still smiling at him, she rolled right through the intersection.

"That"—he kept his eyes forward even as he wanted to direct a glare her way—"was a stop sign!"

"Preston, we're going like three miles an hour."

"Because you're driving practically on top of me!"

"I think that stop sign might actually be going faster than we are."

"Your eyes should be on the road," he said.

"How do you know they aren't if yours are?"

Because he'd looked over at her again and caught her smile beaming at him still. It was like a fucking *magnet.* Like when she'd swept into that meeting and confidently spoken before that crowd, somehow getting everyone to listen and agree. Connecting so easily with people she hadn't met until that moment. How had she done that? It was like a magic trick. One he couldn't figure out no matter how many times he watched others do it.

Instead here he was arguing about traffic laws with her. Annoyance heated his neck. "Ms. Hale, I don't like reckless drivers." Reckless *people.* Thoughtless of others, breaking rules without considering the impact upon anyone else. Messing up town meeting agendas—even while taking the heat off Jordan and the library—was the least of it.

Preston suddenly pedaled up a cutout in the curb to a path leading across the green, leaving Harmony Hale behind. Enough of the unexpected for one night. He had to get home. Lacey should be getting ready for bed soon, and Dani would be waiting to drive back to her place.

A few people were walking home or sitting on benches eating ice cream from the shop Lacey always asked him to take her to when she'd hung out at the library all afternoon. He navigated carefully past them and came out on the other side of the square.

Where Harmony Hale waited in her car.

"Again," she said, elbow propped on the steering wheel, "you're going, like, five miles an hour at best."

The foam of his handlebars compressed under his grip. He blew out a long breath. Preston knew he could go a little overboard sticking to a schedule. Plus, it wasn't lost on him how she'd jumped in when Travis Weaver was going full school-to-prison-pipeline with a teen trying to improve the community.

He shot her a challenging look. "Then it should be easy to keep up." And if she wasn't a book-banner, then that wouldn't be bad.

Satisfaction flared though his chest when she followed, stopping precisely at every stop sign, signaling every turn. Keeping pace even when he sped up. The two of them were like the tiniest, most ridiculous parade ever. As they reached wider residential streets, she pulled alongside him again. "Look, can we go grab a coffee? It'd be easier to talk."

"Have to get home. You have until then to talk." He still felt prickly at the idea of breaking from a plan—which included gorgeous women bringing giant festivals to town.

"Can we set a meeting for your convenience? You heard the mayor—I need to secure a potential site before I can get all that paperwork for him and make this thing happen and finally hear my bosses at Rhythmic sing praises to my name as they should."

She was joking around, he knew that, but some deeper emotion chafed against her glibness. When he braked at another stop sign, at the turn onto his street, he dropped his foot to the pavement and stole another look, wondering if the desperation he heard in her voice would show on her face.

They'd stopped under a streetlight. It washed over her, lighting up her hair all caramel and gold, making the freckles sprinkled over her cheeks almost seem to sparkle. Revealing more freckles on those bare shoulders, spilling over her collarbones. It was like a spotlight, pulled to her like all that attention she'd drawn back at town hall.

Like the attention he was giving her right now. Because she wasn't one of Cheryl Weaver's clique and that, apparently, meant his mind felt free to explore the possibility of this woman being the most attractive person he'd ever met. His eyes were getting in on the exploring too, roving over her plush, undeniably sexy curves and the admittedly adorable quirk her full lips made—probably because he was still staring. Shit. He blurted, "It's not my land."

She raised a brow. "County records say it is."

County records hadn't promised their dead mother her family's old farm would be for Lacey if she ever needed it. In his mind, it belonged to his sister. It was her last safety net, if something happened to him. "I'm sorry I can't help you." It was true, not mere politeness—because he knew if he agreed, she was sure to blast him with that smile again. And he wanted that.

"You wouldn't just be helping me, you'd be helping the entire town." The glow of the streetlight limned her hair like a halo. "You heard me back there; this is an amazing opportunity for everyone." There it was again, as her mask of confidence slipped just a little with a tightening of her mouth: that false smile.

Preston might have wanted to talk more—to try to explain—but the words for all that, his family's infamous past and uncertain future, were buried deep under his own careful mask he always wore. His usual scripts were failing him with this woman, and when he got like this his rule was to shut up. He lifted his foot back to his pedal. "Good night, Ms. Hale." He headed down his street, into the shadows under reaching oaks.

"Harmony," she corrected. Her ridiculous car rolled behind him, and she kept talking, making her pitch again for the festival, complimenting what she'd seen of Brookville so far, extolling the not-too-chilly spring evening. "It'll be perfect in early fall; people will flock here from places back east already freezing their tits off." Preston coasted to a stop at his driveway and Harmony took in the house. "Huh, nice place."

He locked his bike to the porch railing, and still she was talking. He was honestly beginning to think she might follow him inside and keep commenting on his decor as he said good night to Dani and checked in with Lacey and got ready for bed. What would she think of his choice of wall art or the color of his weighted blanket? Picturing Harmony Hale in his bedroom shut down his imagination. Impossible. He didn't bring women home around Lacey unless they were serious. And that had happened exactly never since he'd become her guardian. Not that Harmony was making him *that* kind of offer. He didn't think she was, anyway. Not that he'd accept. He really didn't like bad drivers.

He'd better get inside.

"Man, this is why I gotta move. L.A. rents are killing me." Harmony ruffled a hand through her hair, car idling behind Dani's Jeep. "You *must* have roommates?" Keys, where were his keys? "Good night!" she called with an easy wave.

Without meaning to, as he fought the door open, Preston broke the rule he'd made and answered with his own call of "Good night."

And at this, before she at last drove off, Harmony Hale granted him a final flash of her wide, wolfish grin, brighter than the car's headlights.

CHAPTER EIGHT
HARMONY

After her success at town hall and strike two with Tweed on Wheels, Harmony asked Alice to do her magic and take another look at the county records.

"It's his land," Alice confirmed when she called back the next day. "Bequeathed to him five years ago. Seventy-six acres. Along with a house in town."

So that was how he afforded the place. "Grandparents?"

"Mother."

Harmony's hand fell away from where she was applying mascara. She felt a sudden affinity with the man she'd harassed all the way home, and an ache in her gut. Losing a parent was a rotten deal. In the hotel's hinged vanity mirror, her hazel eyes were enormous and welled with the hurt no amount of time or confident bluster could completely erase. Harmony hadn't been left a house, though. She'd faked the paperwork to stay out of the foster system and in the latest shitty apartment her dad had rented for the last years of high school. After graduation she'd slept on friends' couches while she tried to be an actress in L.A., taking terrible roles until someone recognized her talent (for both acting and smaller-time theft) and invited her to put it to use grifting for his cons. The gold ring on her pinky, an impulsive sweet sixteen gift, was the only thing she had left from her dad.

Alice was rattling off more details. "He tried to get it rezoned for residential development a few years back, but town hall rejected his application. Why would he say it's not his?"

"Dunno." Harmony finished up her lashes and capped the wand. "I need more to go on. What else you got?"

"Uh . . ." Lots of typing sounds, little info.

Harmony sat on her bed to slip on some nude sandals. "And how's Evan today?"

"Sorry, Harm," Alice said, but Harmony could hear the smile in her voice. "Jones is only a side mark. You don't usually have any trouble with these guys, I was focused on Weaver. I got the latest of the public tax records on him, by the way."

"Thanks." Her gaze fell on the novel on her nightstand that she'd unofficially borrowed from a county library in Santa Barbara and would drop at whatever branch was nearest when she finished. They at least knew something was going on with the Brookville library and upset parents—something Harmony could maybe use. "Can you get me in with his wife's friends?" Official records weren't getting her anywhere. She needed some personal insight. The inside scoop. Gossip.

"Piece of cake," Alice confirmed. "I've got one who comes in for a latte every day after yoga."

So the next morning, Harmony stopped by the coffee shop, making her way up to Alice under the soft glow of the dozens of mismatched, upside-down lampshades covering the ceiling that cast the tables and sofas in a cozy ambiance.

"So where's this Evan? Already off saving souls?"

Alice shrugged, eyes on her steam wand. "He's part of the early crowd."

"How very virtuous. Early to bed, early to rise and all that."

"Maybe he just can't wait to see me." At Harmony's smirk, she added, "Should I date someone from the biz instead?"

Harmony stuffed her change back into her wallet. "Ugh, no. Tried that with Zach."

Alice stuck out her tongue and made a gagging sound.

"Yeah." She sighed. Better to stick to anonymous one-nighters. The only person Harmony would never leave behind was right here pretending to vomit into someone's cappuccino. Alice had left her own troubled past in the rearview, getting out of her small town in central California with a guy passing through, someone Harmony knew in the business but avoided working with. Alice was too sweet for him but had clearly had no way out or anywhere else to go, stuck doing tech for his jobs, until Harmony swiped her for her own assistant.

The door's chain of bells clattered. Alice's brows shot up, and she jutted her chin toward a customer who'd just entered, a middle-aged blonde woman in Lululemon with a rolled mat slung over one shoulder.

Harmony moved off to wait beside a wall papered over with clippings from the *Brookville Bee*, until Alice gave the signal and she grabbed a tall steaming latte from the counter.

A moment later, Harmony tapped on the shoulder of the woman heading for the counter with creamer and cinnamon shakers, littered with emptied sugar packets and wooden stirrers. "Excuse me? I think we've mixed up our drinks."

"What? I thought the girl said—" The woman peered at the black scribble on her cup. "This is *regular* milk."

Harmony held out hers. "And this says oat."

"Oh, gosh." The woman's eyes widened. "You've saved me. One sip of cow's milk, and my stomach—wait, aren't you the lady who's putting on the music concert around here?"

"Harmony Hale." She beamed. "Festival promoter and averter of dairy disasters."

The woman laughed as they swapped cups. "I'm Bonnie Kelton. I'm on the Brookville PTA." She popped the lid off her latte and dumped three Sweet'N Lows into its foam. "Thanks again."

"Happy to help, I'm just fueling up before I drive out to Cranton."

Bonnie's fingers stilled where they'd plucked a stirrer from a cup. "Oh?"

Harmony sipped her latte and nodded, eyes flicking to the door. "Checking out one of the potential sites."

"You must be so busy with all of that!" Bonnie gave her latte a stir. "But, gosh, it would be so great if you settled on Brookville. We've all been talking about it. If you could hear how excited everyone is—" Harmony swung her attention back to Bonnie, crafting a warm, open, expectant smile. So often the gentlest influence was all that was required, at least with people who weren't obstinate librarians. "Oh, you know, some of the other ladies and I do a little mimosa morning—you should totally come!"

Harmony hid her sharpening smile behind another frothy sip.

A few days later, as Harmony walked into a big house in a newish development on the west side of town, she knew she'd come to the right place for gossip. Bonnie ushered her to the kitchen where chattering women, all in their forties or fifties, swarmed around a massive granite island covered in platters of fruit and cheese and long-stemmed glassware.

"And here's Harmony!" Bonnie sang out to the group, oversized cardigan trailing behind her. "Such a funny story! We ran into each other at Buzzed when they mixed up our orders."

Harmony smiled through the chorus of "No way!" and "How funny!" and one "Oh, Bonnie, you're not back on caffeine again?"

Bonnie handed Harmony a glass. "I told her she just had to come along and share more about this festival of hers with us." She introduced her to the half dozen women who were on the PTA with her, or the school board, or seemed to be there just for the mimosas.

Harmony mentally scrambled to remember each one. She set her drink down, leaned in against the granite counter, and beamed at them all. Digging up dirt on Preston Jones aside, these women were just where she needed to apply pressure next, to keep the idea of the festival alive through Brookville. Their goodwill would carry her plan forward with all the efficiency of a mother getting six children fed and shuttled to school and extracurriculars and into top colleges while she was at it. "You're all *too* sweet to let me crash your party."

One of the ladies from the school board said, "We can't wait to hear all your plans."

"It sounds very cool," a dark-skinned woman in a cute dress murmured, fiddling with the wine charm on her glass.

"It sounds," Cheryl Weaver said, "like something for sure." Harmony didn't miss how Cheryl left whatever that *something* was perfectly vague. "But I suppose we'll see." The mayor's wife took a tiny sip of her mimosa and puckered her mouth. Her friend beside her, the one from the town hall meeting with all the bracelets, immediately nodded, schooling her face to cool indifference. A couple of others dropped their gazes from Harmony to their glasses.

Fair enough. Harmony had tanked her husband's arcade to launch her festival pitch, not that either had likely figured out she'd been the true instigator at the meeting. And before they'd get on board, these women needed to see what the festival could do for them, for all their supposed civic-mindedness. People like this with more than enough were often the stingiest underneath it all. When she'd waited tables between gigs in L.A., Harmony had endured plenty of skimpy tips from these women's counterparts after long brunches. She had to hook them with something they cared about deep down. She'd used fear at the town hall meeting, but appealing to something they loved could be even more powerful.

Cheryl plucked a grape from one of the platters. "Bonnie, you got way too much food!"

"Yeah," her friend agreed. "I'm being *so bad.* Two pieces of cheese. On *crackers*," she added with a little moan.

"Oh," Bonnie said with a little wave, "Garret and his friends will finish this all off. Teenagers! Bottomless pits."

Of course with the moralistic food talk. While Bonnie was refilling someone's glass—with a blend of a decent sparkling white from Napa and fresh-squeezed juice, by the looks of the bottle and the orange peels on the counter behind her—Harmony popped a morsel of Parmesan into her mouth. "When I had aperitivo with Gaga in Amalfi, she said you should always have something salty with your wine—unless the gossip is already salty enough." She threw the woman beside her a wink.

School board lady chuckled, and the woman now on her second glass widened her eyes over its rim. "You must have so many wild stories."

"My dad was in the music business," Harmony said with a shrug—always cover an emotion you didn't want to come across with a physical gesture. "I grew up around it all. That's how I got into concert promotion." She took another bite of cheese. "How I got my name too." A little truth sprinkled in kept a grift smelling real.

"You should come to girls' night!" the woman said, her expertly messy bun bobbing as she nodded. "The Moonlight Bar has half off margaritas on Fridays, and I need to hear more."

"Of course," Harmony said, with a quick touch of her hand to the woman's shoulder. Physical contact turned people compliant. Using people's names too. "Sounds fun, Ellie. I'll be around—if Brookville turns out to be the festival's home." She didn't want to come on too strong too fast. Never start by asking for something. Dangle something for the taking, or hold something back. Make them come to you.

The gathering shifted from the open kitchen to the adjacent living room, everyone settling onto oversize couches with plates of food and drinks perched on side tables or the massive glass coffee table anchoring the room, and the conversation shifted to kitchen remodels and vacations taken and planned, while Harmony listened and waited for the right chance to draw them all in.

Cheryl was in the middle of recounting *an absolute nightmare* with her bathroom contractor—Harmony couldn't imagine living anywhere she was responsible for renovations, let alone staying long enough to need any—when a rumble came from somewhere farther into the house. "Sorry," Bonnie said, hustling to close a door leading off to a hallway. "Teenagers! Garret's band is rehearsing in the garage."

Cheryl raised her brows. "I don't know how you stand it. The noise!"

With a little smile, the woman with the great dress—Sarah—said, "It's not as bad as the other night at town hall."

Cheryl's lips pressed together while her friend clucked, and Ellie asked, "Is that juvenile delinquent still hanging around your kid?"

"We put a stop to that," said Cheryl. "Nina's got a bright future, following in her father's footsteps; she doesn't need a bad influence like Jordan DaCosta holding her back." Her blue eyes sharpened at Ellie. "I don't want her to end up stuck like some people, in the service industry." She opened her mouth wide, as if remembering herself. "Of course I don't mean your Raymond's lovely restaurant, only the DaCostas hauling groceries." She waved a hand vaguely at the others. Harmony caught the hint of a smirk. "You know I just love that little pear salad he does."

Harmony noted the swiftness and precision of Cheryl's retribution for Ellie's stepping even slightly out of line. Sarah had better watch her back, after bringing up Jordan's stunt with the speakers. Harmony filed away the knowledge that Ellie's husband ran a restaurant and might be enticed into signing up for the festival's food service. But first—

"Speaking of bright futures—" She turned to her host. "Bonnie, your boy's in a band?"

"Oh, you know," Bonnie said, with an indulgent waggle of her head, "he and his friends mess around. Libby's son plays drums. They have a battle of the bands at school every year."

Harmony swirled her mimosa around in her glass. She hadn't actually drunk any—she kept a straight head while working. "Hmm. Maybe they'd have a shot."

Bonnie cocked her head to one side. "At what?"

"Well, there will be multiple stages at the festival, of course." Harmony grabbed another chunk of cheese from her plate and chewed it slowly, letting everyone wait on her next words. "We always do a youth stage." Another nonexistent sip of her drink. "We'll have auditions, you understand, Libby." School board lady perked up, shifted the tiniest bit toward her. "But supporting up and coming talent is how we cultivate the next generation of artists."

Bonnie's blue eyes lit up. "They could play at the festival?"

The women caught each other's excited gazes. Harmony leaned in over the coffee table. "And once we lock everything in, location and paperwork and all that, you're all going to *die* when I can share the name of the headliner we're looking at. Sharing billing with someone like that?" She flopped back into the couch's pile of throw pillows with a flourish of her hand.

Libby grinned. "That's something you could put on college apps."

Nothing more motivating than a parent's love for their child. At least for moms who didn't ditch their toddlers, like Harmony's. She had them on her line—or most of them. Cheryl had her arms crossed, glass in hand. Ellie was still poking at the food on her plate after her friend's barb. Time to cast a wider net.

"So, Ellie, you own a restaurant?"

Ellie lifted her gaze, before sliding it toward Cheryl as if for permission for this to be true. Damn, Cheryl really had this crew under her thumb.

Harmony crossed her legs to mirror Ellie's body language. "I should talk to you and your husband about the festival. Once we get approval." Never too early to start reminding the town that the Weavers held all their potential profit in their hands. "We'll need to line up a bunch of vendors. Food trucks, dining tents, drink stalls." She pincered a toothpick spearing a chunk of pineapple, then let her nose wrinkle the slightest bit and let it go. Let everyone fear that feeling of judgment. "They've all gotta be top quality, though. I always like to have someone local show me around. Point out the best places to start. That's how we consistently put on a world-class event with true local flavor."

The women all nodded along. Except Cheryl, who was still not taking the bait. She was already confident in her position in town. Harmony had been right; fear wouldn't work on her. Only ego.

Harmony went on, "I often put together an early exploratory advisory group of key people from the community, to offer their local expertise and have input in the direction of some of these important choices." *Now* she had Cheryl's attention. A chance to boss around Harmony and lord more power over the town? Cheryl's straightening posture and slight bite of her plumped lip both said she couldn't pass that up. *Gotcha.* "Business leaders, stakeholders, people already dialed into the scene." Harmony hadn't forgotten Preston nor her goal of getting the scoop on him. Cheryl, with her interrupted plans to speak about the library at that town hall meeting, surely knew something about him. "Librarians," she added. "They can be helpful because they're used to putting on events for the community. Much smaller ones, of course, but still. They often know of good resources."

Ellie snorted and shook her head. "Just so long as you don't ask Preston Jones."

"No?" Harmony wore a mask of mild curiosity while the room's air seemed to flood with something toxic, like the Botox injections that kept a few of these women's foreheads smooth even as they grimaced at that name. Definitely some bad blood here.

"No." Cheryl bit off her words sharply. "You can't trust his judgment. He insists on filling our library shelves with inappropriate reading material."

Her other friend nodded. "Not suitable for children."

"Oh?" Harmony widened her eyes. "Like what?"

The woman gaped and waved a hand, bracelets jangling. "Well, you know," she said, either unwilling to say what her issue was or unsure of anything besides her support for her friend. She shifted on the boat-sized ottoman where she was perched. "Things I don't want my youngest, Asher, reading!"

Cheryl was less reticent. "People can believe whatever they want and that's their business, I don't judge." She raised both palms to the group. Some were nodding along, murmuring supportive sounds, but Bonnie only twisted a cocktail napkin in her lap and waggled her head again like Cheryl was a child to be indulged on this. Libby of the school board was stone-faced, and Sarah was staring into her drink. "But my tax dollars paid to my hometown aren't going to support these trashy books he pushes. A library should house the classics. Books that can serve as models to our children."

"Right, of course," Harmony agreed. "Like Shakespeare. *Titus Andronicus*."

Ellie leaned nearer to her neighbor to whisper, "What did he write again?"

"And Chaucer," Harmony added.

"Yes." Cheryl looked gratified.

"*The Miller's Tale* is my *favorite*." Harmony swore Sarah snorted into her mimosa, and she covered for her by loudly declaring to Libby, "Oh, I love the classics. Michael Stipe once gave me his old copy of

Lysistrata, when my dad and I were staying at his beach house. I'm a big reader."

"Me too!" Bonnie said brightly, as if hoping to steer the conversation to a less controversial topic. "Libby and I have been talking about joining a book club."

Cheryl stabbed a rhombus of cantaloupe on her plate. "Preston Jones shouldn't be making these decisions about what our children read, let alone advising on anything important for the city." She tore off a bite.

"Well, what do you expect?" Ellie asked. "His mother—you know she waitressed for us a bit—she was always hanging out with that *artist* who lives down the county route."

Artist as Ellie used it clearly carried some extra, disparaging meaning Harmony couldn't be sure of. "And he hasn't backed down about the books?"

"Or clubs." Sarah shook her head.

Ellie scowled. "I can't even take my youngest to storytime anymore."

"So he's—stubborn?" Harmony might have underestimated Preston, if he'd been standing up to overgrown mean girl Cheryl.

"He's *strange*," Cheryl said.

"Cheryl!" Libby glanced side to side, like someone could be listening in, hiding behind Bonnie's floor-to-ceiling drapes. "You can't say that—"

Why not? Harmony wondered. She was losing the thread of this conversation.

"Ask Sarah!" Cheryl said with a shrug. "She sends Mason to music lessons with him, don't you?" Cheryl had found her moment and went in for the kill. "Of course we don't judge you," she said reassuringly to Sarah. "There aren't many affordable options in town."

Sarah's face remained placid. All she said was "Mason's making really nice progress."

All right. Enough. Harmony had zeroed in on Cheryl to get to Travis, but she should have guessed anyone partnered with him was a nightmare of a person too. Time to reel Cheryl in all the way. Harmony was going to make the festival grift personal to them both.

"Well," she burst out, "it's lovely knowing there are plenty of nice folks here to help!" She picked up her drink and sipped musingly. "The hardest part is always finding people to do merchandise. We do official festival merch, of course, and the acts have theirs, but filling the rest of the stalls is always such a headache." She played with the gem-studded silver charm at the base of her glass and told the group, confidingly, "The best products for this kind of event are small, you know? So people don't mind the idea of carrying whatever it is around the rest of the day. Small but high value, to maximize the profitability of the stalls." She let her gaze fall to her glass. "Like these! This wine charm is just—" Gaudy. Garish. Something else that started with a G and meant ugly. "*Darling.*"

Cheryl's eyes widened. "But that's mine!"

Harmony played oblivious. "Oh, no, I thought this was my glass—"

"No, I mean, I sold Bonnie all these wine charms." She laid a hand on her heart. "It's my business."

Harmony dropped her jaw, like Alice hadn't found Cheryl's MLM scheme out for her already. "You mean Travis Weaver isn't the only entrepreneur in the family?"

Cheryl's mouth pulled into a pleased, humble smile, even as she drew up tall and puffed out her chest. "Travis says it's silly, but I like to do something in my free time, outside of caring for my family, of course." She nodded to her friends, who immediately nodded along. "To provide a little something extra for them."

"Don't disparage yourself," Harmony told her, waving a hand. "You're a business woman!" She held her glass up and gazed at the charm's five different colors of gemstones twinkling and its embossed—owl? Fox? Whatever. "Oh, if I had something classy like this lined up, I'd feel like we were starting off on the right note."

Cheryl raised her shoulders and held up her palms hopefully. "Would the festival like to place an order?"

"It's a cost-sharing model." Harmony launched into her pitch. "Vendors invest in stock and cover stall fees, but the profits all go to the merchants. They tend to exceed costs laid out by a significant percentage." She smirked and lifted her glass. "The power of a captive audience, good music, and plenty of wine. Shared venture, non-refundable fees, et cetera, but I can get you all the numbers on our previous events, for comparable goods." She sipped her drink for real, the tartness and fizz matching her feeling of triumph. When she put the headliner switch-up into play in a few months, claiming the star had pulled out and the festival needed a massive infusion of funds to secure a last-minute replacement or fall apart, Travis would have to face his own wife losing everything she'd paid unless he invested even more of his money in saving the festival.

Harmony would enjoy imagining Cheryl's ire directed at Travis when that went down. As for the other local businesses, well, they'd get their money back once she took it all from Travis, she always saw to that, and they'd learn an important lesson about whom to trust. Namely, no one.

First, she'd have to tackle getting that lease signed by Preston. Clearly she needed to up her game there. Pull out all the stops. He hadn't folded in the face of Cheryl's book-banning crusade, which was impressive. But Cheryl wasn't Harmony Hale.

She said, as if she wasn't absolutely confident, "Once I'm granted final approval to move forward, of course."

Cheryl preened, glancing around to her friends. "We'll have to make sure you get it."

With a smile, Harmony drained her glass.

CHAPTER NINE
PRESTON

Preston pulled up the list of active book hold requests, trying not to jam his fingers onto his workstation's keyboard too harshly, thinking how he'd love to give Harmony Hale a piece of his mind.

His boss, Katherine, had informed him he would not need to address concerns about the library at the next town hall meeting—because a special inquiry was being planned just to give Cheryl Weaver a chance to call his professional judgment into question and get his programming canceled, her list of books banned, and probably Preston fired. It had already sent him into a spiral of anxiety and sleepless nights. If he'd only had a chance to speak at the meeting, if only they'd taken the time to double-check the agenda, maybe, *maybe*, he could have diverted all this. But no, not when there were festivals to exclaim over and their unnecessarily attractive promoters to march in and disrupt everything. If that woman was here, he'd tell her what he thought of that, forget shutting up, he'd say—

She *was* here.

Sweeping through the library's one automatic door, caramel-blonde hair fluttering in its breeze, like the skirt of her teal dress over her swiveling hips as she headed past the art display cases, the carts of discarded books for sale, the flyer-covered corkboards, straight to where Preston stood behind the main circulation counter.

He braced his palms on that counter, feeling somewhat like a giant wave was about to knock him over or a train was about to run him down. "Here comes trouble," he muttered.

Apparently not as under his breath as he'd thought, because she sang out, "Reporting for duty!" with a jaunty salute.

"*Shhh.*" The library wasn't very busy this early, but that only meant her brassy voice stood out among the patrons quietly reading in stuffed chairs, studying at tables, or working at the computer stations. Not that someone like her would care about others or expectations.

Harmony looked delighted and did not lower her voice. "Did you actually just *shush* me? Classic."

Preston didn't know what to do with that, so he defaulted to his talking-to-patrons script. "Can I help you?"

"You can, and what's more, I can help you." There was that wide smile again, spread like butter over her quick words. "I feel like we got off on the wrong foot, but I really think we could have a mutually beneficial relationship." She plunked her folio on the counter and leaned forward next to it, grinning up at him.

Beneficial? Was she joking? He resisted the urge to unload on her how she'd already managed to tank his career and doom the bit of good he'd accomplished here so far, not to mention nearly running him over in the street. As professionally as he could pull off through clenched teeth, he said, "That's the idea here. We have books, you borrow them."

"I mean the festival. Can we talk?"

He jerked his head toward the next workstation along the counter. "Gretchen's actually on checkout duty, she'd be happy to help you if you need—"

"But I need *you.*" Her lips pulled into a pout.

And he needed her to go, needed a chance to calm down. His heartbeat was thrumming through his head so he could barely think, barely hear himself say, "I've got to pull requests. I'm at work. This isn't the place to discuss"—he waved a hand at her and her sexy frown and her job-destroying business offers—"whatever."

Harmony didn't miss a beat. "Then let's discuss your work. I heard you give piano lessons. If you need an extra source of income, leasing land you're not putting to any use could do the trick."

That wasn't what he'd meant at all. "This is the *library.* There's a large sign outside saying so if you're confused." There were *boundaries.* But of course she waltzed right past them, like she did stop signs.

She unleashed that laugh, strident as a trumpet, even when he shushed her again. He raised one hand toward her before dropping it back to the counter. What did he think he was going to do, press his hand to her mouth? The mouth that had pulled into a crooked version of her smile, under her glinting eyes. "I like you," she told him. She gave the back of his hand a pat and let her fingers slide over his briefly as she pulled away. Her skin was like silk, as soft as her persistence was resolute. "I really do want to help you."

Preston inhaled. Exhaled. Tried to purge the frustration that was still sending his pulse lashing through his blood. "Are you checking anything out?"

"Oh, *definitely.*" She leaned forward more, which made her back arch as she let her appreciative gaze run up and down over him. Wait—*him?* Yes, that was him she was fixing with her wolfish grin. She'd looked at him like that after the meeting, as if she'd thought *he'd* been looking at *her* like that—

Had he been looking at her like that? No. He hadn't. Not that time at least. He got his signals crossed plenty. The girl he'd dated in grad school had had to tell him they were on their second date when he'd thought they'd just been in an unusually small study group.

And Harmony might as well have stepped out of a painting by Rubens, voluptuous and lively and oh god he was *not* picturing her now as the painter's naked Venus.

So, no, not then, not now, and never again, now that Harmony's shenanigans had probably cost him his chance to save his job and everything the kids needed the library to give them. Even if—because of his height, and her totally unwarranted *leaning*—he was fighting to keep his own eyes away from the incredible view down her dress that he was absolutely, definitely, nothing halfway about it, *not* looking at.

Meanwhile, Harmony wasn't just rolling past stop signs, she was bulldozing the whole street. She cocked a brow in that practiced way of hers. "And I've never in my life said business before pleasure."

This was outside any script he could throw at a situation. He grabbed the printout of hold requests that had finally finished spewing out behind him and shoved the waiting cart forward from behind the counter. Work. The job he was desperate to keep. He'd do that. He pushed the cart into the stacks.

Harmony's voice came from right behind him and too loud. "But I *do* want to do business with you!"

Forget Rubens, she must have climbed down from a Gentileschi, the way she was so unrelenting. Maybe one with a beheading. He pitched his voice low, hoping she'd take the hint. "I don't have *time.* Thanks to your stunt at town hall, I have to prepare for an entire meeting to defend my work." He didn't even know when it would be scheduled yet.

"Stunt?" She didn't sound offended—just confused. Or worried?

"Stunt. Noun. Provocative action used to draw attention." He tried to focus on the shelves before him, but couldn't help muttering, "Fear-mongering about video games. Drug deals entirely online?" He grabbed a book and carefully placed the hold slip inside its cover. "How would that even work?" He tucked the book into the cart and scanned the next slip, then went hunting for its book. "Meanwhile, I'm dealing with an actual threat to the kids most at risk. Queer kids, kids whose parents can't afford fancy after-school extracurriculars, kids whose parents—" His throat closed up over the words. Parents who treated them not like someone to protect but a problem to solve. He'd found the book, and as he turned back to the cart, and Harmony, he held it before him like a shield, one palm flat across its cover. "This is where they can come. This is where they can be safe, and free, and travel, like other kids do every year with their families, without ever leaving their room."

And he'd failed to speak up for them. He could have insisted the other night. Probably he'd have fucked it up, if he'd been given the chance. Unlike the woman who was at last quiet—a surprised, warm expression on her face, idly drawing a book off a shelf with one finger—who'd had no problem speaking up, no problem getting them to listen and like her.

He shouldered past her and deposited his book in the cart. "And on top of all that—" He grabbed the book she'd discarded on a random shelf and slotted it back into place. "I have my own fourth grader to take care of."

He turned back around to find Harmony full-on gaping at him. "Huh."

"What?" His shoulders tightened.

The corners of her mouth turned down as she shrugged. "You have *got* to share your skin care routine with me."

"What?" he tried again. He was lost.

She dragged another book off the nearest shelf. "You must be way older than you look. I hope I have that good a glow when I'm pushing forty."

He blinked, once again at a total loss for what to make of what she'd said, for what to say. How did she keep doing that? Somehow his mouth got its act together, apparently settling on: "I'm twenty-seven."

"Wow." She laid down the book, in the wrong place again.

"*What*?" He reshelved it properly.

"Okay, no, I don't judge, even if you were—" Her fingers were flicking against her skirt. "—the Lothario of—" Was she *counting* on her *fingers*? "Tenth grade?"

Now it was his turn to gape. And sputter. "No, I don't have—I didn't—she's my *sister*." He was so used to everyone in town knowing everything about his family, he'd forgotten that she wouldn't.

"Yeah, that makes more sense." Harmony nodded slowly, as if something was falling into place. "And you're her guardian."

He took advantage of her break from messing up his shelving to grab the next hold. "And it's her land. It was left to me, my mother saw to all that when she divorced, but it was always meant as something for Lacey, in case she needs the money." He pushed the cart around to the next aisle.

Harmony was on his heels. "But it's not making her any money."

The hold slips crinkled in his hands. "Well—no." He hadn't managed to get the town to rezone it yet, and no one wanted it for agriculture anymore, with the plots around it intended for residential development soon. Preston had almost been glad—he wasn't great with change, and he loved the walnut orchard, its gentle hills and quiet and familiar trees reaching into the open sky. His mom used to take him out there when he was small and overwhelmed at parks with other kids, tell him about how her great-grandparents used to farm there, show him where they'd carved their initials into one tree. Now sometimes he took Lacey, for stargazing, or just to run around not worrying about being too much or too different.

"Why not lease it to the festival and put away actual money for your sister?" Harmony pressed.

Because change, even leasing the land, was like a towering roller coaster to him, and he hated roller coasters. So he hadn't considered this point overlong. They could really use the money, that was for fucking sure. Especially if he got fired. "But won't a festival—" He was working automatically, filling the cart with books, while he worried over this idea. "All those people, and stages. Won't you have to cut down the trees or something?" Most of the aging orchard had long ago already been sold for lumber, in a last-ditch attempt to save the farm amid rising operating costs. Preston had barely kept on the right side of county regulations for upkeep, though he'd managed to make a deal with a neighbor for lawn mowing and general maintenance in exchange for any produce the old trees still gave. And now that neighbor was selling to Travis Weaver, and around and around Preston's mind went again wondering how he was going to keep things together for Lacey. It couldn't be as simple as what Harmony was offering. No one was going to just *give* them money for absolutely nothing.

"No, those great big trees are the best part." Harmony's eyes went wide, and she held up her hands as if he could follow the gesture and see walnut branches arcing above the tops of the bookshelves. "Perfect for shade—we can set up the smaller booths and stages among them, keep the main stage to the open field. And we always clean up after ourselves. No litter." She stepped nearer, filling his vision. This close he could see her hazel eyes had streaks of gold like starbursts around her pupils. "It'll never look as if thousands of people had been there, I promise you, Preston." There were more golden flecks in their green, like bubbles in champagne.

With a sly look that seemed to send those bubbles fizzing through him, she added, "We can even do a carbon offset. And Rhythmic will—outside of the leasing fee—make a significant donation to a local environmental cause like the kid at town hall mentioned. And I'll match it. Personally."

She almost had him. How could he let his own resistance to the disruption prevent all that? Then suddenly Harmony threw her head back, fingers splayed, and, like some kind of carnival barker or game show host or a wrestling announcer starting a fight, practically growled, "Let's make this happen!"

"Shhh!" It wasn't Preston shushing her this time—though her volume did make him wince—but a patron in the next aisle. Shit. He was at work, he was supposed to be doing the job he was probably going to lose thanks to her always talking about this festival at the wrong time.

He blinked hard. Sudden noise and his routine thrown off—the kinds of things that would have sent him into a meltdown when he was Lacey's age. "I need to get back to work."

"Well, when's your break?" She was tipping yet another book from its snug place on its shelf, peeking at its cover.

He shoved it back with two fingers to its spine. "We just opened."

She smiled, already reaching for another book. "Oh, I think you're worth waiting for." At his snort, she raised her brows, exasperated. "Why do you have such a problem with someone who just wants to help you?" But she laughed, a gentle huff. As if nothing in the world was too serious.

If only. "You know what I think? I think you're nothing but trouble." He snatched the book away from her and shoved it back on the shelf. "You come in, make a mess, and move on."

She fluttered her lashes, as if taken aback by his grabbing the book. "I'm sorry, I thought this was a library."

"I—" And where the hell was his mouth now? Besides gaping uselessly?

"There was a big sign outside saying so."

"You—" He scowled. She was doing it again. Talking her way around anything and everything. "I think you actually only care about what you want. Helping yourself." He loomed over her, blocking her from any more books. "What do you have to say about that?"

She took a deep breath and opened her mouth, he was sure to unleash a tirade at him for being stubborn about the festival, for invading her personal space, for being rude to someone who was technically a library patron—

No. Instead, she released a long, heavy exhalation, fogging up his glasses completely.

"You—" He sputtered again, fumbling his glasses off and glaring.

"There you are," she said, like she'd just found him at the end of a game of hide and seek. But her voice did something funny, its huskiness catching on some emotion and going thin. Her breath hitched. It smelled like licorice. Sweet and spicy.

"You're *outrageous*," he told her.

"Thank you." He couldn't see shit, but he could *hear* her pleased smile. And he could feel her fingers on his, gently tugging the frames from his hand where he was doing a crap job trying to wipe them on his shirt. His cleaning cloths were in his bag, way back behind the counter. The blur that was Harmony shifted back, and suddenly he was extremely fucking grateful he couldn't see shit because there was a flash of pale thigh, as she must have been wiping the lenses on her skirt. He definitely wasn't disappointed. He was still convincing himself of this when she carefully slid his glasses back onto his face.

He didn't know why, but as the clear lenses brought Harmony into focus before him, he repeated her words back to her. "There you are."

She murmured, "Look, I get it. The land was your mom's. You want to do right by her. My dad, he—" She swallowed, and suddenly for some reason Preston found himself wanting to make it better, whatever was making her voice clot and eyes blink without any artifice. "He was in the music biz. That's why this is so important to me. I want to make him proud."

Her hands were still on either side of him, fingers trailing down his hair and neck and brushing over his shoulders as she drew them back.

His turn to swallow. "I appreciate that, Ms. Hale."

"Harmony."

"But I really do have to get back to work." There were others he needed to make things better for: youth patrons and Lacey. People who needed taking care of.

"C'mon, let's make a deal and piss off the Weavers. I've dug into all the real estate holdings in the county, looking at potential sites—you know they're trying to squeeze that land out of you, right?"

Probably. God, he'd probably end up finally selling to Travis, who'd made several lowball bids over the years, just to cover some of Lacey's college. And then what if she needed support at any time during the rest of her life? Autistics had sky-high rates of anxiety and burnout and depression. But pissing the Weavers off right now would be irresponsible. Not with Cheryl gunning for him. He reached for the thinning stack of hold requests. Leasing that land held too many unknowns—primary among them the living embodiment of chaos masquerading as a woman who had better not be fucking with his shelving again. "If Travis owns so much, why not just—"

"Okay," Harmony interrupted from behind him, voice suspiciously bright. But then she only said, "I'll let you get back to it."

Surprised at her sudden backing off, he turned to see her walking down the aisle out of the stacks, the fabric of her skirt swinging below her broad hips.

He adjusted his frames, not sure exactly how he'd won a battle of words with Harmony Hale, or if he was entirely certain he'd wanted to.

She grabbed her folio from the counter and, rather than heading for the doors, slid into a chair at the table directly across from his workstation. She flipped open the folio, plucked a pen from within, and tapped it against her lips before lifting her gaze and shooting Preston a look that said, clear as she'd left his glasses, *Oh, I'm not going anywhere.*

This wasn't a battle. This was a siege.

CHAPTER TEN
HARMONY

Harmony slid a finger over the white paper she'd liberated from the library's copier, pressing along a perfect crease. A few more folds, and there. When she launched it with a practiced flick of her wrist, the paper plane soared gently across the library to land among the several others she'd already thrown, littering the counter around Preston and his computer.

He pretended to ignore it. Even from the table where she'd encamped each day this week, Harmony could see his jaw tense, hear the clacking of his keyboard intensify. He'd forbidden her from the circulation counter unless she was checking out books—and she didn't bother with library cards. Records and paper trails and permanent addresses were for other people; any book she borrowed found its way home eventually, she assumed. So each missile was also a missive written before folding:

Let's talk after work.

Meet me for drinks.

Coffee before work tomorrow?

She'd figured out his problem. Or one, at least. He was dead serious about sticking to work at work. She needed to get him someplace outside the library. Then her pitch could stand a chance.

The man was so damn serious in general. Very guarded. Except that one moment when he'd removed his glasses, and suddenly looked startlingly vulnerable, even as the unfiltered force of his icy blue stare hit her dead on. Not that he was wrong to be wary—she was a con woman, after all, and he was part of her scheme. But he was also in her way.

Harmony didn't spend time worrying about her marks, though as she scribbled *Margaritas at the Moonlight Bar tonight, my treat* and began folding another plane, a twinge of—it couldn't be *guilt*, because Harmony didn't believe in looking backward. But an uncomfortable feeling pinched in her gut at the thought of conning the librarian, who was willing to risk his job for the kids he worked with. And caring for an orphaned sister. Hmm.

Harmony dragged a coral nail along another crease. Silly. She wasn't going to *steal* from Preston. (She left out of this lecture she was giving herself how she wasn't actually going to cough up all that money she'd been dangling in front of him either.) When she was done with this job, it would be as if she had never been here at all. She threw the plane.

It glided through the air and landed exactly on top of Preston's perfectly parted hair.

He slowly closed his eyes. Sighed. Removed the paper plane from his head and dropped it on the counter. Ignored the unrepentant, hopeful smile Harmony flashed him.

Though she watched for several minutes, he refused to even peek at the note. Harmony couldn't help her smile flagging. But let him try—no one could ignore Harmony for long. She was clearly wearing him down. She'd damn well better be, after all her efforts. He couldn't banish her from the entire library, so she was there, mostly pretending to work on emails and spreadsheets for the festival. But while he worked among the library's tall wooden bookshelves, he might run into her perusing titles with a tilted head. Then she could pretend he'd sought her out: "Did you want to talk more about the festival?" Or as he changed out a bulletin board display at the front of the children's section, she would happen to be coming back from the library's printer, and wave a spreadsheet and recite the benefits to the community the event would bring. He'd looked vaguely horrified when, on her way to the washroom, she'd stopped by the start of preschool storytime. She'd paused behind the rows of distracted parents and nannies and an indistinguishable and loud tumble of children on a rug tucked into a nook under winding stairs, and beamed at him as he set his shoulders and began reading *Don't Hug Doug!*

She was still right there at her usual work table today and overheard when an older woman stuck her head out of an office behind the front desk and checked that Preston would be back after his break—the last few days he'd been in early and gone after three, but apparently some days he stayed through the afternoon. So while he went off to the school, Harmony visited Alice at Buzzed.

"A kid," she said when she reached the front of the line.

Alice grimaced. "I know. I said sorry."

"An entire human child." She handed over a twenty. Cash kept you invisible.

"Your regular latte?"

"And whatever our father of the year usually orders?"

Alice nodded, her eyes flicking toward the back corner of the room for the third time.

Harmony swept her gaze over the leather couches and tables where people camped out with laptops or sat chatting. A mob of teenagers fresh out of class entered through the glass door, immediately doubling the ambient volume of the coffeehouse. "Is Mr.

Sargent in attendance today? I need to witness the face that launched a thousand distractions."

"Red shirt, at your ten."

Harmony casually leaned past the glass jars of biscotti to catch sight of a solidly built young man in a short-sleeved button-down and jeans nursing a coffee, listening attentively to an elderly lady at the next table bent forward and chattering. Except when his eyes strayed from his neighbor over to the counter, under dark lashes.

"Oh, yeah, I get it now." Evan Sargent looked like a teddy bear. Alice might fall in love more than anyone else, and she wasn't exactly *picky*, but she had some set standards. No assholes need apply. "He seems sweet."

Alice's lips twisted in a satisfied grin as she finished making the drinks. "He gets a second coffee every day now, during the afternoon lull."

Harmony raised her brows. "Decaf or regular?"

"Decaf." Alice passed the drinks over the counter with a wary look.

"He really must be smitten." She winked at a smiling Alice before turning around straight into Jordan DaCosta, the teen protester from the town hall meeting.

Drinks held wide, Harmony shifted to block the girl from moving forward. "Oh, hey! Jordan, right?"

Beneath her dark bangs the girl's gaze shifted away. Not quite an eye roll. "Hey."

Yeah, Harmony would be suspicious of herself too. This kid was sharp. Over her shoulder, Harmony told Alice, "Her drink's on me."

Jordan's gaze snapped to Harmony. "I don't need your money. I'm not poor."

"But I was once," Harmony said, setting down Preston's cup and passing another bill to Alice. Not that she had ever become actually *rich* rich, not yet, the way she blew through her hauls, just good at playing the part. "And now it makes me happy to do nice little things for the deserving."

Jordan's lip curled. "And that's me?" She huffed out a long breath, setting her hair dancing. "Can you tell Mayor Weaver that? He called my mom and said I have to do fifty volunteer hours for hacking the city's speakers, if I don't want charges brought. And he won't approve them for the club I'm in."

"That doesn't sound very brotherly and beautiful of him."

"He's just trying to make sure I don't have time to protest anymore. I've got school and clubs, plus I gotta babysit. He's a total fascist."

This kid was endearing herself more and more to Harmony. Jordan might not be poor, but she wasn't part of the clique of students or parents with all the sway in Brookville. Again, she reminded Harmony of her younger self a bit, even if she was already trying to help the world rather than just herself. And Harmony wasn't about to let Travis stomp all over anyone else's life, not if she could help it. "Maybe you could come intern for the festival." As in, maybe Harmony could sign off on all those hours and let Jordan off the hook, just like how anyone with Travis's status always got away with their youthful hijinks.

"Me?"

Harmony nodded. "I'm a big fan of your work with those speakers at town hall. We could use someone like you on staff."

Uncertainty flashed in the girl's eyes. "I don't have any real experience with, like, sound systems or whatever."

"Mmm." Harmony took a sip of her latte. Just the right temp—Alice knew she never waited for coffee to cool off. "But you've got passion. We need local interns to organize the community booths—places for people to go and keep busy between acts. There'll be merch stalls and radio stations, that kind of thing, but also community groups, health education, student groups, local colleges, volunteer organizations." She cocked a brow. "Activist organizations. Whatever you can get."

Jordan shifted in her Vans. "That sounds kind of cool."

"A lot of it can be done online, and you'd just log your hours yourself." She inclined her head. "It would leave plenty of time for whatever else you have going on. Just gets to be a bunch of grunt work during the event itself, to be honest." Or as honest as Harmony ever got. There wouldn't be any festival for students to hustle at, but the more the community bought into the idea and invested in plans, the harder it would be for Travis to say no when she pulled the headliner trick on him. And in the meantime, Harmony could help set Jordan up for success in whatever she would tackle next. Teach her how to play the game to get what she wanted. Harmony had always been able to talk her way out of trouble, but after her dad died and she'd been left to make her own way, she'd really had to figure out how to sneak into the world where people like Travis Weaver and other rich kids coasted along, instead of getting kicked back down to where they'd started with every bump. It was the only way to make sure they'd never walk all over you.

The ASB president from the town hall meeting was behind a group of girls chatting so intensely about something that had happened in math class they hadn't noticed Harmony and Jordan holding up the line. She was the one kid who hadn't shut Jordan out completely the other night, smiling at her when all the others were laughing. There was potential there. "Her usual too," Harmony told Alice.

Jordan was digging a thumbnail into the side seam of her jeans. "All that stuff you said at the meeting. I could hear you. You're, like, really loud."

Harmony smiled. "I am."

Jordan met her eyes, and there was that fire Harmony had recognized. "It's all bullshit. Civic whatever. Most of this town is bullshit. Most of the world."

"Yeah." Harmony took another measured sip and set down her cup. "It's all one big con. So bullshit them right back. You have to learn how to direct your power, though. What the bullshitters call leadership skills." She grabbed the drinks Alice set on the counter and passed them to Jordan. "Get yourself some of those and you'll be unstoppable. Now, go give Miss Future Congresswoman there her drink and see what you can pick up."

Jordan turned, drinks in hand, to follow Harmony's gaze to the tall blonde girl checking things off with a gel pen in a planner she'd dug out of her Kate Spade purse. "Um." She went rigid, eyes falling to the tile floor, blush climbing up her face.

"Can't be shy if you want to be the change and all that." Harmony gave her a gentle nudge between the shoulder blades. "First lesson: use your network of acquaintances to get ahead. That's the kind of girl who will know how to get organized." And if the class president accepted Jordan, then the rest of the kids would follow. "Ask her to collaborate on interning, I bet the two of you could work some magic together. Come on, I want to see what level of chaos you unleash on the world next."

Jordan made her way over to her classmate. "Hi. Um. Mochaccino?" She thrust one of the cups out at the other girl.

A smile lit the girl's face, then she immediately busied herself putting away and rearranging things in her bag. "You know my mom said I can't hang out with you anymore," she said softly, glancing around at the girls ahead in line, the adults seated with their coffees.

"Yeah, but she also said you can't go to GSA, but you're heading there, aren't you?" All the attitude that had drained away flooded back in the confident set of Jordan's shoulders.

Miss ASB bit her lip but couldn't hide the flush over her cheeks, her returning smile as she took the offered drink. "Yeah."

Jordan angled her head toward the door. "Want to walk over together?" And with that, the two girls and their flirty grins slipped outside, chased by a flash of afternoon sunlight.

Huh. That hadn't played out quite how Harmony expected. Something fell into place. "The Weavers' kid?" She glanced back at Alice for confirmation. Nina, the daughter with the bright future following in Travis's footsteps—not into tech, as Harmony had assumed, but politics. And the Genders and Sexualities Alliance?

Alice leaned forward on crossed arms, clearly satisfied to have this info ready. She spoke with the arch voice she always used when quoting a reference or meme she knew from being extremely online. "Harold, they're lesbians."

Well, if the Weavers got mad she'd pushed their kid back into the arms of her forbidden crush, Harmony would deal with that later. She left Alice mooning at Evan and gave the younger lovebirds space on their walk to the library, so when she arrived there they and the rest of the GSA were already disappearing through the stacks toward a conference room in the back, ushered by a small middle-aged woman in a fabulous dyed silk jacket. Preston was back at the front desk, finishing helping someone with a giant tote bag of books, so Harmony broke his rule about visiting the counter to deliver his drink.

He stared at the cup in her hand like it was some alien artifact. "I don't drink coffee."

"Good thing it's tea." He opened his mouth. "Black tea, one sugar, milk." His mouth clamped shut.

"How did you—" His eyebrows practically high-fived each other as his forehead furrowed.

"It's amazing what *some* people will do for you when you ask nicely."

"Right." His already low voice dropped like a stone to a sardonic rumble. "Because your superpower is ignoring boundaries and beguiling everyone you meet."

"Oh," she said with a pleased wiggle of her shoulders. "Do I beguile you?"

"That's not—" He frowned and still didn't take the cup. *His* superpower was being less fun than a week's worth of detention.

She set the cup beside his computer. "Your tea's getting cold."

He was already typing. "It's not my tea." He stared hard at the screen where she was pretty sure he was only pretending to work to get rid of her. His lips pursed as if in concentration or holding more words back. Which was at least an improvement from the flat line Preston often pinched them into; they were full and looked soft and perfect for—*wait*, hit the brakes.

Since when was she *attracted* to this walking, talking *OED* in corduroy and glasses?

Harmony returned to her table in a hurry and dropped into her seat, slightly affronted by the idea of being into a guy who was part of a con, a guy so unlike her normal flings. Wanting to wash away the thought, she took a quick sip of her latte, forgetting how full the cup still was, and promptly choked on it. She struggled not to cough and earn another shushing from Preston, whose penetrating gaze on her was probably because she was making noise, but which stirred an entirely different sort of turmoil through her chest.

She tried to brush his concern off—and unleashed something that came out half scoffing, half drowning in sugary coffee. A scoff cough.

Preston's eyes flared and she dropped her face back toward the speckled blue laminate of her table. This was taking forever and she was getting bored, that was all, and Alice was right, it always got Harmony into trouble. Like realizing how this table was the exact brilliant shade of Preston's eyes. She let out an annoyed wheeze. She was becoming just as bad as her friend; Harmony always kept all that separate from her jobs. The one time she hadn't, with Zach, it'd been a disaster. Harmony wasn't about to make that mistake again, no matter how many noble speeches Preston gave about books helping kids just like she'd once been; this was all his fault, for being so damn stubborn and dragging this phase of her plan out and forcing her to stare at his ridiculously glossy hair and killer cheekbones all day every day. She took a slower sip of her latte and focused on going through the documentation she and Alice had been pulling together for Travis once she got Preston locked into the plan.

A moment later, a little girl wearing a purple backpack and carrying a stack of books emerged from the children's section and stared at Harmony, then the chair next to her, then Harmony again.

Thank god for a distraction. Harmony gestured at the empty seat. "Do you want to sit here?"

The girl nodded.

"Cool." She shifted her things to one side of the table so the girl could dump her books. The girl pulled a binder and worksheets from her backpack, and was soon engrossed in homework. Harmony caught Preston still peering at her, that mouth still tense. Probably annoyed she was taking up space from real library users. Harmony pointedly busied herself with her own pretend homework (loudly typing *Preston Jones is a buttoned-up stalk of unbending bamboo* a few times), and Preston had to stop trying to stare her out of the building to help a man checking out a book and a stack of DVDs. After a rush of people checking out, he was still working on the computer, and she caught him absentmindedly reach out a hand, lift the cup of tea to his lips, and take a sip. He noticed what he was doing and frowned, setting down the cup.

But a moment later he picked up the tea and sipped again.

Yeah, he was definitely wearing down, and none too soon. Time to strike—once he was away from the forbidden desk. Harmony tapped her pen against her folio, impatient. The little girl, pretty hair hiding her face like a dark curtain, was drawing something now. A picture of a crab among stars, lines of poetry written across its wide shell.

"That's neat," Harmony said. She pulled a dollar from her purse, her fingers working as she talked. "You like astrology?"

The girl lifted her horrified gaze and shook her head. She pointed to her books, which now Harmony saw were all about space, the blue nonfiction sticker bright on each glossy spine.

"Oh, a scientist then." She tucked the paper triangles she'd made into each other.

A sharp nod.

"And the strong, silent type. Impressive." Don't talk to strangers, Harmony figured. She held out what she'd folded for the girl. The bill was just the right shape for making a paper star.

The girl took it with a grin, and immediately pulled it apart, then handed it back to Harmony. So she showed the girl how she'd made it, step by step. The girl made a lopsided star of her own just as Preston emerged from behind the counter pushing a cartload of books.

"Gotta go," she told the girl, standing and smoothing down her sweater and circle skirt. "See you later, stargazer." Harmony wrinkled her nose and waggled her head. "I can do better. Got it—" She snapped a finger and shot finger guns at the girl. "After a while, astrophile."

The girl let out a laugh, a sweet small giggle that seemed to blossom above their table.

Preston halted and shot them a startled look.

"Uh-oh," Harmony told the girl. "Mr. Grumpy Librarian is gonna shush us. It's his favorite thing, and I am definitely not. I'd better go before I get you kicked out."

The girl shook her head, a doubtful smile on her face, and Harmony knew she was right; Preston wasn't going to eject any kids from his library. His surprise was already melting into a tentative, pleased expression she hadn't seen from him before, and he was on his way again to a set of glass shelves in an open space between the front entrance and the children's section.

Harmony swept after him, but someone else waylaid him, a Black woman with a short brown bob coming into the library, a small batch of books clutched in one arm. "You were right about this series! The romance was *so good.*"

Preston nodded. "I love the pairing in book two especially, if you're still getting to that one."

"Ha, I read both this week. I need more recommendations."

"You're in luck." Preston pulled a bright blue book from his cart. "The next one just came in."

The woman's eyes lit up. "*Yes*, weekend plans set." With her new find, she made for the return drop near the checkout counter, and Preston began setting books from the cart out on the shelves, propped on little metal display holders or neatly stacked in color-coordinated groupings.

When he saw Harmony approach, his pleasant expression shuttered. "I have work to do," he said, almost to himself.

Another pinch in her gut. Why was he so cold only with her? It was getting old, keeping up her enthusiasm in the face of his frosty reception, his stiff shoulders and stern mouth. "So do I," she said to the back of his corduroy jacket while he arranged books. "Don't make me put off the mayor again—I want to be able to kick things off officially next week." He opened his mouth as he grabbed more books, and she steered around whatever objection he was about to unleash. "Let's talk about it outside work. Drinks. You and me. Tonight."

"As tempting as it is—" The tips of his ears went a bit pink, and he turned back to the display he was creating. "The idea of sticking it to the Weavers in some way, I mean. It would be reckless. Unfair to people who are relying on the library's programming." Hands full of books, he pointed with his chin toward the back of the library. "Those kids in there right now, for starters."

It had been unfair for her father to lose everything he'd built too. She *had* to take down the Weavers for him. But Preston was annoyingly *good*, with his after-school clubs and showing elderly people how to download e-books and helping young ones print résumés and reading to storytimes full of adorable urchins he'd probably hired from central casting to make her feel bad about conning him. It wasn't like she could get upset with him for standing up for the kids in his community, like she pretended to in every town she grifted, but—no, yeah, she was definitely upset. She ignored the heat rising up her neck. "The Weavers aren't going to get you fired for leasing land to the festival the entire town wants to host." Preston turned back, reaching for another book. "Come on, light a votive candle to your patron saint Dewey Decimal and take a chance."

Preston froze. Blinked. Gave her his iciest stare yet. "Please tell me you don't actually think his last name was *Decimal*."

She huffed. "Whatever!" Not only annoyingly good, just plain annoying. She was the one who never let her mask of cool slip, but now it was melting as her frustration burned hotter. And this unflappable jackass went on with his work, chilly as an ice cream factory in January. She normally didn't play too hard with the feelings of the innocents she conned, but right now she'd like to show Preston just how good she was. She'd like to see that mouth, pressed now in a thin, sharp line, kiss-swollen and panting. The careful control in his eyes flooded instead with want. That wickedly parted hair mussed, tie loosened, all those buttons at his neck and wrists undone. *Him* undone.

She sucked in a breath. Dammit, she was supposed to be working her spell on him, but somehow she was the only one who seemed hot and bothered. Preston was muttering something about Melvil Dewey being a sexist, racist creep undeserving of canonization, and she found herself interrupting, saying, "So you need to get the town on your side. Cheryl Weaver's only one person. Get out there and win people over."

"I don't." Preston stared at her blankly. "Do that."

"Oh, come on, you're halfway to being my new best friend. You got me to spend my whole week someplace I can't even make noise—do you know how powerful that is?"

"You said our wi-fi was better than your hotel's."

"Preston, I was joking."

"Oh." He gave her a deeply uncomfortable look. "The thing is—I'm autistic. Winning people over—" He drummed one hand against his thigh. "It's a statistically proven fact that autistics are judged unlikable by neurotypicals." Her mouth fell open, and he rushed on as if she was going to interrupt again. "But it doesn't matter, because I'm good at my job, and it's important to me. Did you know the therapies used to force autistic kids to act in ways seen as normal have the same origins as the conversion therapy that tries to force kids not to be queer? Some people want to erase us all. The clubs and books for every kid, showing every kid—disabled too—they say we exist. That it's okay that we do. As we are." He directed his entire intense gaze at her, piercing and earnest even through his glasses. "That's life changing. Life saving for some kids."

What the *actual* fuck? Was this what Cheryl had meant, when her friend from the school board had chastised her for talking about Preston? Harmony's entire face flushed, not with annoyance or attraction or whatever the hell she'd been feeling, but with full-out anger. That tacky bully deserved Travis. Harmony couldn't wait until she left them with only each other. No millions anymore. They'd be fucking miserable. But that wasn't going to be enough. She needed to take this censorship thing in hand. Show them they couldn't swing around the power they'd bought however they liked.

"I'm fine not being"—Preston waved a hand at her vaguely—"charming." His finger began spinning a silver ring he wore on his thumb. "Except now Cheryl Weaver's made this her mission, and I don't know what to do."

She'd been right about one thing. Her week wearing him down was paying off. He was opening up a little. Which gave her the in she needed. "Luckily for you, I can charm anyone. Well, jury's still out on you." He'd called her charming, but then why was he being such a prick to her? She scrunched her nose and gave a little shrug. "Outlier."

He glanced over at the table she'd made her own, probably imagining her hounding him all next week too. But then he said, "I saw. Lacey doesn't take to most people like that."

She looked again at the girl, seated closest to where Preston often worked, folding some of Harmony's copy paper into more stars. "That's your sister?" He was watching her fondly, and when he returned his gaze to Harmony, the fondness lingered. It sent warmth threading through her. She shook her head at Preston, before the grid of glass shelves. "Should have known. She's cute. Like her brother." With that last part she laced her voice with playful flirtation, and she didn't know if she was conning him anymore or just herself.

But the library was important to him, so it would be how they both got what they wanted. That was why she was helping. One more nail in the coffin of the high life the Weavers had stolen from her father. "I can turn the town's public opinion in your favor," she told him. "If I'm staying in Brookville for the festival. If I have a site."

"Ms. Hale—"

"Harmony."

"Headache." He was matter-of-fact about calling her that, going on with what he'd been saying: "I'm not sure even you can dissuade people from the Weavers' wishes." Was she still fooling herself, hearing some regret there? "And there's too much at stake."

Harmony often bent trust her way with mere smoke and mirrors. But she was beginning to suspect Preston was so hard to flimflam because he simply didn't have any trust to manipulate. So she'd have to prove herself.

"I'll show you. Tonight. Moonlight Bar." She reached out and smoothed down the velvety lapel of his jacket, because physical contact garnered compliance, not because she wanted to touch him. "We'll crash girls' night. Half-price margaritas every Friday."

His stupid soft-looking lips quirked. "I thought you said your treat."

"Hmm." This guy didn't let a single detail slide. But he *had* read her note, eventually. Maybe he only needed a little more reason to agree. Or maybe she'd found the one person in California she couldn't con. "I'll buy you two."

He raised a dubious eyebrow. "I'm not a big drinker."

Of course not, because that would require he ever actually loosened up. Not that she was, either. "Oh, good, then I'll buy us one, and we can sip it together with those cute little bendy straws." She mimed pinching a straw and pursed her lips.

His gaze dropped to her playacting, and he swallowed. "Okay."

"Okay?" *Success.* She'd never doubted herself for a minute.

"Yes."

CHAPTER ELEVEN
PRESTON

Why had he said yes? As Preston pulled open the heavy wooden door and stepped onto the concrete floor sticky with spilled beer, he could only assume he'd suffered the mental break Dani was always warning he was heading for if he didn't learn to relax.

Then he saw Harmony sitting at one end of the bar, long hair coppery under the red neon lights running along the shelves of bottles, a tall green drink and open book before her. She was reading pensively, as if the dozens of shouted conversations and intermittent blenders going and thudding of pumped-in music couldn't touch her at all.

Right.

A guy with a beer in hand sidled up to her, saying something lost to the din. Harmony swiveled away on her barstool, never taking her eyes from her book. Eventually the guy moved on to someone else.

Preston drummed his hand against his jeans. Going up to girls in bars was something he'd stopped doing about five minutes into college, after dismal results, no matter how much his overly confident roommate Will had cajoled him to keep trying. Harmony had invited him, Preston reminded himself as he crossed the room toward her. Repeatedly. Obnoxiously. And while Dani had been only too happy to take Lacey after the GSA for one of their regular weekend overnights (Lacey considered the stargazing away from the town's light pollution a treat), this wasn't an actual date. They were talking business. All the flirtation was just L.A. schmoozing. It had to be.

He stopped a few seats away. "Hey."

She lifted her gaze and a smile broke across her face, a gleam lighting her eyes, brighter than all the neon in the place. No schmoozing or falseness about it. It set a tingle whispering over Preston's skin: *True, true, true.*

"Hey!" She hopped off her seat, leaving the drink and book behind, but Preston couldn't remind her to take them because he was too busy almost swallowing his tongue. Harmony was wearing a clingy green dress that came down to her knees with a slit that reached up to the top of her statuesque thigh. "Let's find a table!"

He decided following while he remembered how to breathe made the most sense. Yes, very smart. They were passing a speaker on a stand near a set of busy pool tables when feedback from a guy setting up in the corner for live music screeched across the room. Preston winced.

Harmony noticed and stopped. "Is this a terrible idea? The music's going to be loud. I was looking up autism and all these sites mentioned sensory sensitivity?"

She'd leaned in a little, because it was loud, and he leaned back to answer. "No, it's fine. Just if it's sudden or jarring." It wasn't as if the library was exactly quiet most of the time. He'd probably need downtime to recover from the overstimulation, would probably veg out tomorrow until Lacey got home, but he could manage a couple of hours. "Music is actually the best, if everything's in—"

Her eyebrows perked up with delight, as they both realized what he'd been about to say. Her smile curled wider. *Go on,* the avid flash of her eyes said.

He exhaled through his nose, lips pressed in chagrin. “Harmony.”

The tip of her tongue peeked from between her teeth as she grinned. “So you *can* say it.”

They found a small table right in the middle of the jumble of people and chairs and sticky tabletops sprouting glassware and straws. Preston's knees brushed against Harmony's as he folded himself into his rickety chair.

“Speaking of noise,” Harmony said, leaning forward on crossed arms, “I think what you're dealing with at work is a very vocal minority. I checked out local social media and it's, like, the same few Facebook accounts that have made any complaints about your youth programming. And plenty of people across multiple platforms sharing videos and pictures from events who seem perfectly content. We just need to help all of those folks get louder.”

The canned music cut out and the guy in the corner launched into a blaring piano rendition of a Maroon 5 song. “Oh. Good,” Preston said. “Louder.”

Harmony chuckled through a wry grin, but waved a hand. “That storytellers event you did? Seriously cool, and like fifty posts with significant positive engagement. None negative that I could find. And it looked like you had a diverse collection of presenters for that. People just don't show up to town hall to say they had a good time, only when they want to bitch.”

She'd definitely been screwing around for much of the time she'd been staked out in the library. Putting on a show. Annoying the hell out of him. But right now it was clear she knew what she was talking about. “You found that all out this afternoon?”

“Hey, librarians aren't the only ones who can do research.” She leaned back in her seat with a toss of her hair. “I contain multitudes.”

"Walt Whitman," he said automatically. *No. Reverse. Do not start talking about poetry at this business-meeting-slash-possibly-a-date.* He knew from experience he'd ramble on too long and annoy people, and he wasn't sure if this was a date or if he even wanted it to be a date, but if it *was* a date he was pretty sure he wanted it to be a good date.

And right on cue, Harmony threw back her head and let out a groan. He'd already fucked this up. "I looove *Leaves of Grass.* 'I celebrate myself and sing myself'?" She dropped her gaze again to look him dead on, and it felt like an eggbeater stirring through his chest. "Come on. He's such a weirdo and so good at nailing, like, just what you'd been thinking but hadn't realized you'd been thinking. You know?"

What Preston suddenly knew was that he, or at least his speeding heartbeat, definitely wanted this to be a date. One where he wasn't sure what he was necessarily supposed to say but felt okay reciting a line that had stuck with him: "Wicked rather than virtuous out of conformity or fear."

Harmony made this little grooving, bobbing motion of her head. "'Urge and urge and urge.' Hot stuff. Damn, I need to find a copy somewhere and reread."

Preston could feel a smile as sincere as Harmony's spreading over his face. "I might know where you could get one."

"I don't have a card here." She made a furtive look away. "I'm gonna go get us some drinks. Not margaritas—" She dropped a hand atop his, looking into his eyes again, as if divulging an important confession. "Sorry to lure you here under false pretenses, but someone bought me one before you got here and it's not worth it."

She slipped away through the crowd, leaving Preston's hand feeling bereft of her warmth. He drummed his fingers on the table, shaking off the feeling. It didn't really matter if he wanted this to be a date. Or for there to be more dates. Where could anything possibly go with someone like that? She wouldn't be interested in anything serious with him. She was rich and beautiful and had a whole life far away from Brookville rubbing shoulders with important people. And he'd figured out in college he preferred to keep sex to committed relationships. Even if Harmony could help with his problems at work, even if they did make a deal for the festival, she was here through the fall at best. Better to keep this strictly to those matters. Easier to know where he stood, what to say, if he knew this was just business.

She came back carrying two short glasses with something amber splashed in them. But she didn't sit. "One sec," she said, looking over at the mob of people dancing nearer the guy at the beleaguered-looking piano, who had switched it up to old standards. "I see some Brookville movers and shakers moving and shaking over there. Operation: Win People Over starts now." One sip, and she settled the drinks on their table.

"What are you going to do?" There was a group of women on the dance floor he recognized as the Weavers' friends. Someone on the school board. Mason's mom, Sarah. A few others.

"I have an idea." She waggled her eyebrows. "Trust me." He trusted her to get up to another of her antics, and part of him wanted to leave before he could find out what she had in mind and how it would definitely put him on the spot. Instead he made himself stay put and try his drink, a smooth whiskey.

She walked past Cheryl's friends to stand beside the piano player, who was very good. Harmony dropped a folded bill into the glass set out on the piano, leaned one elbow beside it, and started saying something—no, singing along. The guy shot her a smile. In a minute, he cocked his silvery head, inviting Harmony to slide onto the bench beside him.

The women stopped and cheered as Harmony's voice caught on the mic angled down at the piano, and the lyrics of "Can't Take My

Eyes Off You" carried across the space. One of them, that woman with the restaurant, raised a margarita and whooped. What the hell was Harmony doing? At least Cheryl didn't seem to be here or Asher's mom. An awkward confrontation wasn't going to help anything. But neither would a sing-along. No matter how amazing Harmony's singing was, because of course it was. What couldn't this woman do?

Harmony's satisfied gaze found Preston across the room, and along with the smoky-sweet richness of her voice it sent a jolt down through him, making him insanely grateful for the cover of the table. He threw back the rest of his drink, but the whiskey washed the same flavor of Harmony's singing through him, like she was burning him up from the inside.

When the song ended, the women Harmony apparently had already made friends with during her short time in town crowded around her, gushing, and soon they were all behind the piano, singing Dionne Warwick.

Then, mouth open in song, she gestured at Preston to join them. The absolute menace. He ignored the first wave of her hand, but she kept at it, brows rising, mouth twisting in impatience. Fine. First he threw back her drink as well, because there was no way in hell he was doing this sober. He walked over with panic sloshing through him along with the drinks. Public speaking was bad enough. Public singing? Wasn't there a nice serial killer here tonight who might like to murder him before he reached the other end of the bar? He still didn't see how this was going to help. He didn't want to make friends with people who wanted to ban books. He wanted them to not ban books.

And then it seemed like a reprieve was given, as the musician murmured into the mic about taking a quick five. Until Harmony reached forward and dragged Preston over to the piano. "What can you play?"

"What?"

"Do you know more than Bach or whatever?"

"Of course—"

She steered him onto the piano bench, fingertips light on his shoulders. To the musician on his way to his break she said, "You don't mind if my friend plays something till you get back?"

"'Course not, lovely." Which might have had something to do with how people were stuffing his glass full of tips but was probably just Harmony.

Harmony leaned her face down next to Preston's, hands still at his shoulders, the soft curve of her pressing into his back and banishing his entire repertoire from his memory. "Play something they'll know."

Right. He knew plenty of songs by heart. At least one, almost certainly. It was simply difficult to call any to mind when said mind was currently occupied, studying the possibility of that being Harmony's breast resting against his shoulder. His hands hovered over the keyboard, trying not to clench. "Like what?"

"I don't know, something from the nineties?" There was no question that was Harmony's lip grazing his ear, delivering warm honeyed breath over his skin. "Quick, before the party breaks up."

There was this big songbook he used for a fun exercise with older students, full of pop songs going back to the sixties. He dropped his fingers to the keys and played the opening hook of Mariah Carey's "Fantasy."

He almost stumbled over the melody as those around him broke out in squeals. They sang off-key but enthusiastically through that song, while Harmony pretended to know the lyrics and did this incredible little wiggle-dance shooting finger guns at them all and hyping them up, and then a couple of Taylor Swift and Ariana Grande numbers he'd learned for Lacey. When Preston turned the instrument over to the guy back from his break, Harmony pulled him next to her, in a linked line with her new friends, and thank god by then even more people had swarmed around to sing and dance, because of course Harmony had made this happen somehow, had drawn people to her like moths, and in the crowd it wasn't so bad to gently sing along to songs he knew or hum while he tried not to think about her hand still on the small of his back or her hip sometimes swaying against his thigh.

Eventually someone declared they were buying the group a round, and he didn't want to seem rude so he ended up squeezed around a table drinking a shot of something sharp and a too-sweet bright green margarita.

Harmony had retrieved her book—*Girl, Serpent, Thorn*, he could see now, a young adult Persian fairy tale that was in fact one of the titles on Cheryl's list for banning—and was holding it to her chest and yelling something to Libby Reed and Bonnie Kelton, from the school board and PTA, at a nearby table. Her expression looked like she'd just taken a bite of the richest chocolate or something, eyes rolling up behind her languid lids.

He knew he should probably talk with those around him—knew he was staring instead—but soon, as always, Harmony's enthusiasm had everyone's attention, as she moved on to gushing about the twinkle lights strung around the black rafters overhead and blown-up photographs of full moons caught in tree branches lining the back of the bar. "Local watering holes like this are always the most fun," she said, reaching out to grip the arm of a woman at the next table. "This reminds me of one time I was sharing a helicopter ride out of Coachella with Phoebe Bridgers and she told me about going to a little club after Glastonbury with First Aid Kit, and, well, long story short, we all ended up in a dive in L.A. singing karaoke of Madonna songs at 2 A.M." She raised her brows. "The pilot did an amazing 'Take a Bow.'"

Harmony leaned forward, into the rush of awe from the group—wide eyes and squawking mouths, everyone talking over each other plus the music and the noise of others around them shouting to be heard—as if she could swim in it, crowd surf on it. "'Course, any karaoke machine can't hold a candle to our Preston on the piano!"

It was like she'd held up a mirror and redirected all that attention and goodwill to him. People raised their glasses and patted his arm and cheered. Preston lifted his drink in return before hiding behind a syrupy gulp of margarita.

Someone at another table started yelling about when Sara Bareilles came into her family's restaurant back when she'd lived in Northern California, and Harmony's eyes met Preston's. For one moment—only the space between beats of throbbing piano music—the bar seemed suddenly silent and empty. Nothing but the quirk of Harmony's brow and the slightly dizzy smile he felt answering it.

After that, and another round, things seemed to get hazy. He rarely drank, and never this much, not in ages. A few beers during dinners at Dani's, sure, but he was the sole caretaker for Lacey most of the time; it would be irresponsible. Besides. You weren't supposed to drink alone, that's what they said. And he was always alone.

Except now he wasn't, in this bar and this blur of impressions, listening to Harmony regale the group with more stories of the festival circuit, name-dropping celebrities to a chorus of gasps. Feeling someone pull him along when the group took to the dance floor again. Hearing shouts about how amazing his playing was, how they always knew he was fun, which was how he knew he was really drunk. Noticing Bonnie still over at the tables, tentatively flipping through pages of Harmony's book. Wondering again, as Harmony gyrated her hips at one edge of their ring of dancing, about where things might lead if he ever dared to follow that pale strip of skin revealed between the vivid green of her dress. Finding with surprise when the music slowed that green teasing against him, under his hands, as someone danced close, her own hands resting on his chest, silver light thrown from the dance floor strobes threading through her golden hair, the smell of licorice and whiskey stronger than all the tequila and sweat and noise.

Pondering, as the room began to swing in three or four directions rather than only spinning a little, if he could sit down before he cracked his head against the concrete.

Those hands gripped him hard, bearing him up. His head nestled instead against a soft shoulder and that luminous hair. "Timber," Harmony said.

CHAPTER TWELVE
HARMONY

Preston was *heavy.* Between his height and the corded muscles Harmony could feel as he leaned against her, it was like trying to haul an inebriated obelisk outside. Earlier, she'd considered suggesting he cool it on the drinks, but the man was clearly in desperate need of blowing off steam. Going from college kid straight to full-time parent of a small child? When was the last night he'd gone out and had some fun?

She had plenty of experience shepherding someone who'd had too much. And she'd insisted he come, so she would help him back, even if he was the opposite of every guy she'd ever left a bar with before and she was definitely not attracted to him or the way his voice had rumbled in her ear, beneath all the shrill singing, like a secret.

No one else in the bar seemed concerned about making sure a very drunk Preston got home safe. What the hell was wrong with this place? Weren't small towns supposed to be oppressively helpful toward their neighbors? A few people their age slapped Preston on the back as they lurched out of the bar, leering at her. One added a suggestive whistle. "Nice going, Preston." Really? They didn't know her. She could be a criminal for all they knew. Well, like a *bad* criminal. A murderer. A librarian-kidnapping ringleader.

They made it to the parking lot behind the bar. "Almost there," she told a swaying Preston. "Here's my car."

"Where's the rest of it?" He drew up tall and judgmental as she opened the door. "Cars should have *roofs*."

"You'll offend Furiosa. Come on—" She nudged him into the seat. She'd certainly never had to work this hard to get a guy home from a bar before, either. "She's a very nice car, she has plenty of room for your ridiculously tall head, you steeple."

Normally she'd let whoever looked like the most fun and fewest questions buy her a drink and that was that. The biggest challenge occasionally was kicking him out once they were done. She didn't do sleepovers.

Preston looked up at her, face shadowed from the yellow parking lot light at her back. "You shouldn't drive either. You should be safe." His words were edged with so much concern.

"I haven't had a drink since that first godawful margarita." She walked around to the driver's side and slid in beside him. "I'm just naturally this fun. Now, unless you want to ride on the handlebars while I bike you home, let's go." He was fumbling with his seatbelt, so she leaned over him to pull it straight and click it into place beside his hip. He heaved a breath, face flushed, and let his head drop back against the leather seat as she pulled out of the lot.

The cool air on the drive seemed to do him some good. Perk him up. He stared at the sky, streetlights and shadows rippling over his slack expression a few minutes. She checked on him more often than her rearview mirror, to be sure he wasn't about to vomit on Furiosa. Then he sat up and stared at her even more intently. Probably watching to call her out about going one mile over the speed limit. She stopped at the turn out of downtown and flicked on her signal. He was awfully aware of driving rules for a guy who biked everywhere. "So do you drive at all? Is that, like, an autism thing?" The sites she'd checked out had talked about executive function and spatial awareness, but she wasn't sure she'd understood all of it.

"Yes. No. I can drive." He traced his finger along the chrome edging his door. "It's a someone ran my mom off the road thing."

Oh, shit. Watching her dad fade away had been a nightmare. But to lose someone in a blink like that? She wasn't sure which was worse. "I'm sorry." She hated this part. The apologies for something no one had control over—barring Travis Weaver or the driver at fault—and then the forced *thank you* or *it was a long time ago*, as if that made the pain any smaller.

Preston blew out a long breath. "Me too."

"And you were in the car?" She was prying, and it was unfair. "Never mind."

"No. Lacey was. She worries. So we bike when we can." He shrugged. "It's better for the environment. And I like biking. Slower pace. Time to think. And cheaper."

Of course he was trying to save the planet too. Obnoxiously good. Harmony felt a little better remembering she was helping him with his problem at work and not just using his land for her con. Her grift would probably leave Preston better off in the end, she told herself. Taking out Travis would surely knock Cheryl down a peg or two, if she didn't flee town entirely.

If Preston didn't get fired months before the con finished playing out.

But justice for her dad—for those years he spent sliding into despair, for his stolen dreams—it was all worth it. Nothing was more important. Before he died, while he was sick, Harmony had sworn to him she'd get it all back, all the big-time money and what it would show the world. She was going to help Preston to help herself, and otherwise leave him the hell alone. Because all she wanted from him was the chance to ruin Weaver's life the way he'd ruined her dad's.

Time to get this plan back on track. She told Preston, "Assuming you don't die from the hangover coming for you, we'll get a real social media campaign started for the library, more than those scattershot posts someone's been doing. And you." She'd already posted from a bunch of those fake accounts that afternoon, building positive public sentiment toward the library's programming. But they could make sure the town knew everything the library was doing for its kids and that it was Preston behind it. Get him some accounts to tag, give him some armor against anything Cheryl tried to bring. Their roaring success at girls' night would come at her from the other direction. Harmony and Preston would squish her like a Botoxed grape.

She pulled up outside his house. Preston didn't move. His hands were splayed over the leather seat and door. "Did we stop?"

She sighed. "You're not going to remember anything I've been saying in the morning, are you?"

"Huh?"

Eloquent. "You'll be fine. Good thing you have brain cells to burn." She was going to have to help him inside. She tugged him by the hands and let him lean on her again. Getting to the porch only involved one near-disastrous tumble over a wobbly paving stone. "Where are your keys?"

He slumped a shoulder next to the door and dug those long fingers into the pocket of his jeans. They'd hypnotized her a bit when he'd played, quick and capable over the piano. Now they nearly dropped the keys they drew free. Harmony caught them and unlocked the door.

They made it as far as the couch. That seemed as good a place as any to deposit Preston safely. He sprawled, limbs stretched wide. A book balanced on the couch's armrest thudded to the ground. "Water," she told him. "You'll thank me later."

She found the kitchen around the corner from a dining nook past the living room. The counters gleamed when she flicked on the lights, and she saw everything was tucked neatly away in the deep-navy painted cabinets as she hunted for a glass.

She waited for it to fill at the tap, taking in all the little details making evident the life lived here: the artwork of constellations stuck onto the fridge, the ingredients for meals lined along shelves, worn cooking utensils standing in a crock beside the stove. The kind of life that huddled like a kicked dog at the rough edge of Harmony's memory, that she'd caught glimpses of at friends' houses or on cons. That she'd stolen for a little while, before moving on.

She shut off the faucet. Moving on was what she should be doing now. She'd greased the wheels of more than a few cons with alcohol, but for some reason couldn't seem to make herself try that tonight, to get the lease from the folio in her trunk and stick it in front of Preston's unfocused eyes. Proving her helpfulness to Preston would get him to sign without worse tricks. The last thing she needed was him raising a stink about it afterward to Travis or the council, she told herself.

Preston only grimaced when she brought him the water, so she set it on the side table right near him. "When you can—"

He grabbed her arm as she leaned over him. "Stop making everything spin." In the dim his glasses caught no glare to hide his eyes, big and blue and distressed, seeming to accuse her of more than the alcohol's effect. The glow from the kitchen pooled in the curls that had fallen over his brow. She brushed them gently back. He reached out with his free hand and stroked his fingers through her own hair spilling over her shoulder, sending tingles whispering across her scalp and down her spine.

She did still need that lease signed. She'd set out to charm Preston and now she'd wormed her way into his life, his house. It'd be foolish to throw that away, to not pursue what she wanted until she got it. That was what she did. That was what was tempting her.

His large hand was locked around her wrist. His arm was heavy. It would be so easy to let it drag her forward. Let this tip into something else. Grease those wheels one way or another. "I should say good night."

His eyes didn't stray from her face as she straightened, swelling black pupils drowning their blue. His thumb swept back and forth across the inside of her forearm, more languid than her pulse. His voice was gravelly with alcohol and shout-talking and singing and exhaustion, the next word he managed almost lodging in his throat. "Stay."

Worked for her.

That was all the invitation Harmony needed to settle on the couch beside him, one cushion over but still tethered by his grip on her arm. Not to take advantage. Not any more than she already had. Just to stay one night in this house with its strange sense of familiarity and safety. Just to follow through on her efforts. Just to make sure Preston was okay.

CHAPTER THIRTEEN
PRESTON

A brass band was thumping through his skull. A parade marching over his brain. Preston groaned and opened his eyes.

Soft morning light flooded into the living room, blanketing where, impossibly, Harmony Hale slept beside him on his couch. He stared, bewildered by the sight of her. Head nestled upon a throw pillow, the sun tracing the curve of her cheek, she was still and unguarded. No promises and cajoling. No sly smiles or shifting away before you could pin her down. Her long lashes rested just above that dusting of freckles, the cupid's bow of her mouth faded from last night's red. Her chest rose and fell gently. Even with her right there, somehow, strangely, he missed her.

Her arm lay stretched toward him, their fingers almost grazing each other on the cushion between them. His twitched.

Her lips parted and drew in a wakeful breath. Those lashes lifted, and Harmony stared back at him. "Good morning."

They were only a murmur, but the words rolled through his head and stirred nausea through his gut. "Ughh."

"Yeah, you had a wild night." Harmony stretched, her knuckles brushing his.

Wait. He fought to sort through drunken memories rising from the sludge his mind had become. How wild? "We didn't—?" Was he worried they had or worried they had and he couldn't remember it? *How wild?*

Harmony dropped her hand to her chest. "Excuse me, I don't take advantage of inebriated librarians, I am a gentleman."

He pinched the bridge of his nose. "You're a menace." He was dying. His mouth felt like death. That throbbing in his temples was actually church bells tolling for him. Too loudly for him to even fully take in or deal with how Harmony, sitting up, cringed at the bright smear of lipstick she'd left on the pillow, before furtively turning it over and giving it a pat. "What are you doing here?"

"You asked me to stay."

"Why would I do that?" He'd definitely been so very drunk. "Oh, god, what time is it?" His phone was jutting into his hip, because, he was realizing, he'd slept in his clothes, on this couch, and it was disorienting and wrong, and *oh god his phone said it was almost nine.* "Lacey's going to be back soon. I have to shower. I have to change." He had to throw up.

He ran for the kitchen.

"That's okay, I can make breakfast." Harmony's voice followed him. "You need some protein in you. Do you have eggs?"

He braced his hands to the side of the sink, but no relief came. He whirled on her. "You can't be here." All the parenting books he'd read after taking charge of Lacey made the importance of this rule very clear. No bringing women home unless they were long-term. Serious. It especially wouldn't be fair to Lacey, who deserved to feel comfortable enough to speak in her own home. Harmony was only in Brookville short-term and was the least serious person he knew. Or maybe the most serious? She was seriously maddening.

Like now, how hurt rounded her eyes. How he couldn't read if that was true or false. He felt sick and dangerously close to a meltdown and tried to explain the rule he was desperately clinging to. "It's the rule. We're not"—he waved his hand between them—"together."

She gave a half-hearted grin. "We could be."

No space between his pounding headache and his racing panic to process if she could possibly be serious—or how his heart got in on the pounding and racing at the idea of it. "You have to leave."

"Preston, can we—"

His hand kept waving. Both of them now. "Please, *go*."

Her voice went flat. "Of course." She gathered up her shoes from beside the couch and was out the door.

It was only after he'd dragged himself through a shower and was feeling slightly more himself, dressed and coming back downstairs with only a moderate thunderstorm flashing through his skull with every step, that it dawned on him what an incredible asshole he'd been. But it also occurred to him that he'd left his bike at the Moonlight, and he didn't have time to walk over and get it, and he was possibly still too drunk and definitely too upset to drive his twelve-year-old Civic, and Dani had to be at the gallery in Heraldale by ten, which was why she was going to show up any minute and—

He opened the front door to find his bike propped against the porch rail.

It had to have been Harmony. Somehow. Why would a steel bike lock stop her?

But as the weekend passed and Harmony failed to show up at his front door, or track him down at the farmer's market, or stop by the concert he took Lacey to Sunday afternoon, it seemed as if his behavior had. He'd tried to get her out before she could see the part of him he always, always hid, because it made people run away. But the coolness with which she'd left—it played on a loop inside his head: Harmony stooping for her shoes, walking to the door, pulling it shut behind her. Despite her kindness with the bike, ordering her to leave must have accomplished the same thing.

He'd fucked everything up. Of course he had. That door had closed for good on another person who couldn't stand to be around him.

He couldn't do this. After just *one* night trying, he'd made such a mess—there would be no more annoyingly adorable pestering, no money for Lacey's future, no help with the faction in town trying to ruin things at the library.

So he was in a sour mood on Monday, and when two women from the bar that misguided night showed up at the library and began poking around the juvenile fiction section, he was immediately sure Cheryl had sent her friends on some sort of book-banning reconnaissance mission. Until they drifted over to where he was pulling books for a cart for that afternoon's teen anime club and definitely not spying on them.

"Oh, Preston!" Libby Reed, from the school board, said. "We were hoping to talk to you."

They'd probably notice if he ran for the break room. He remembered how he'd overreacted thinking Harmony wanted to yell at him about books, and planted his loafers on the speckled carpet.

Bonnie Kelton—her daughter was always requesting those elf books—smiled at him. Was this an *I'm about to say something to crush you and I'm acting fake-nice to pretend it's not awkward* smile, or a real smile? "I couldn't put down the book Harmony lent me the other night. Finished it in a sitting. Libby's already halfway through it."

Her friend nodded. "It was so great to run into you the other night, because we've been trying to find a book club to join—"

Bonnie broke in, "You and Harmony were so cute together at the piano!"

"It's nice to see you having some fun," Libby agreed, "after, well, everything. But we wanted to ask you if you could recommend more books like that?"

It had worked. He wasn't even sure by what alchemy Harmony had managed it, but they were here because they wanted *more* books like one of the ones on Cheryl's list? "We can find the right book for everyone," he told them. "What about it did you like?"

"Oh!" Libby bent her blonde head, considering. "Well, I guess I like how it's not just about miserable people. Or women with no hope, you know? That was why I quit the last book club I was in. It gets old."

"I loved the setting," Bonnie gushed. "I didn't know how much was made up or not, but it was so gorgeous—and the twists! I could actually get through this in time for a club."

Preston walked over to the next shelf and grabbed *The Girl Who Fell Beneath the Sea*, another young adult retelling, this one of a Korean folktale. "This one's great, I bet you'll like it. I can pull more for you to choose from before any book club meeting."

"I'm not hosting," Libby said with a stern look at Bonnie, who was already flipping through her new book. "I do not have time to organize another thing. I've already got the big church fair coming up, and Evan Sargent roped me into spearheading the food drive this year, and then it's election season."

"You know," Preston offered, "we have several book clubs that meet at the library. We often showcase related books and sometimes have speakers in too. If none of those seem like a good fit we're always happy to start another, with a focus on strong female protagonists, or fantasy, whatever you like."

The women shared a pleased look. "That would be fantastic," Libby said.

"Heidi runs the adult programs like that. I'll let her know."

Bonnie narrowed her eyes at him. "Did Harmony tell *you* who the headliner for the festival is going to be? She was dropping hints at the Moonlight but wouldn't say."

"No," Preston said, firmly ignoring how his heart made a little twinge every time at Harmony's name. "I don't know."

"Well, I just wondered because she'd mentioned again asking you to help her with some local planning." Bonnie raised her brows, ready to scoop up any offered gossip. "And you two have gotten so close since she's been in town."

What did *that* mean? Trust Harmony to have done a parade down Main Street rather than a walk of shame. Not that she had anything to be ashamed of—he was the only one who did, which shadowed the rest of his day, despite the promising signs of Cheryl's circle coming around. But Harmony wouldn't be looking to him for any help, not now. She wouldn't be waiting to pounce on him when he got off work at three. She certainly wouldn't be sitting on the low wall of a planter along the steps outside the library—

But she was Harmony, and there she was among the roses, standing up and looking at him expectantly as he closed the distance between them.

"I wanted to apologize," he told her right away. "But I didn't have your number or know where you were staying."

She shrugged. "Oh, I just find a different guy each night at the Moonlight and crash with him."

His face must have done something because her eyes crinkled and she gently said, "Joking." She bit her lip. "And I'm sorry, I didn't mean to mess up your routine so badly."

"That's no excuse for how I acted after you helped me. I was an ass. I'm sorry." His thumbnail scraped over the bottom of his jacket, practically murdering the corduroy's wale. He'd sign that land lease and let her go.

"Should we have like a code word for if you need some space?" Her eyes glinted. "Tequila, maybe?"

He grimaced. "I don't intend to ever have a hangover that bad again, but sure." His hand stilled. Did that mean she intended to stick around? "I want to sign the contract. For the land."

Her eyes flared with surprise, but only delight rang in her voice when she said, "Of course you do. We'll take good care of it."

"I trust you. It's working already. What you did with Cheryl Weaver's friends." It was another of her magic tricks; he didn't understand how she managed all she did, but the force of her was undeniable. Maybe everything would be all right. "And thank you. For bringing my bike home. How did you get the lock open?"

"Are you kidding? You told me the combination when I tried to take your keys back at the bar, before I knew if you'd biked." She was digging in her purse, for longer than seemed necessary to finally just pull out her phone. "But let me give you my number. You'll need it while you make it up to me, helping me trial vendors for the festival."

"What?" He blinked. "I'm doing what now?"

"You want to help make sure the festival's a success, right?" She looked up at him with wide, bright eyes, but then dropped her gaze again to her phone. "If it becomes annual, Rhythmic will keep renting your land. Maybe even buy it outright. You'll get everything you want."

Right. The money. That was the only reason why he went ahead and swapped numbers with her. The only reason he was going along with this, despite thinking she'd come merely to get that contract. It was the responsible thing to do, really. For Lacey's sake. Not everyone had a successful dad in the entertainment industry and extra cash to throw around on impractical cars and spontaneous donations at the whims of random librarians.

Harmony popped out the grip on the back of her sparkly phone case and then flattened it again. "*And* you'll help keep Cheryl away from me. She's already dragged me to two mediocre burger joints she insists are the best in the area. One only had turkey patties." She tilted her head back and her lids dropped half-closed. "God, what I wouldn't do for one of those fig burgers I had out in Indio."

"She take you to Anthony's?" Preston asked.

Harmony looked at him with interest. "No?"

"Of course not, because it's a true hole in the wall." To be honest, he preferred carryout to eating there himself. But the food was great, and they had a catering truck that made the rounds to the local sports fields.

"Sounds promising. Wanna go with me to check it out?"

Yes. "I have to get Lacey."

"Right! No, like, another time." She tucked her phone away, downcast face pinching.

Had he misunderstood? Had she not meant now? "I have some downtime while she's in her after-school stuff certain days. If that would work. Or my friend Dani likes to have her over every couple weekends."

Harmony smiled up at him, and that he understood. That he'd grown familiar with, grown to crave. "We'll make it work. Text me that schedule. Oh!" She dug again in her bag, much more quickly. "But first." She flourished a paper from her folio. "Let's make it official."

CHAPTER FOURTEEN
HARMONY

She'd gotten what she wanted. Her plan was back on track, after a detour through Tweedland. Harmony was waiting in the carpeted hallway outside the main offices at town hall with her complete stack of documentation ready for Travis Weaver, and soon she'd have this scheme humming along again.

So why did she have that gut feeling that warned her when a con had gone wrong and she needed to get out before she got trapped?

When the secretary invited her to go through, Harmony stood and gave her shoulders a shake. Preston had thrown her off her game. She had that in hand now. While she wasn't a fan of being tossed out the other morning, he was absolutely right that she didn't belong in his neat little life. And that was fine. She hadn't come this far to make breakfast in some house in Brookville. She'd been aiming for this revenge for years, and she was the one leading this parade.

Even with the lease signed, though, she couldn't just ditch Preston. She needed to keep up the act she'd established somehow. She'd been flirting with him for weeks. Plus, Sarah Lessner and Bonnie

Kelton had commented at Buzzed that morning about her and Preston dancing, and about seeing her with his bike in the back of Furiosa (after she'd picked that lock). Small towns. That was why she'd asked him to accompany her around to vendors.

And she really could use the help, not to make the festival a success but to rope in as many locals as possible—merchants, or performers, or their parents—to really put the squeeze on Travis once the festival was in danger.

She kept this in the forefront of her mind as she marched into his office.

Travis was fussing with some papers in a folder and left her standing there in her favorite teal jumpsuit. Like she hadn't used this power move a dozen times herself. Uninvited, Harmony swung her purse onto the back of a chair and slung herself onto its cushions, crossing her legs and resting on one elbow. "Great to see you, Mr. Mayor. Been experiencing more of your little town." She gazed vaguely out the window and its view of the town square, as if not entirely sure which mayor she was meeting with, in which town. "It's darling."

Travis shut his folder. "I'd started wondering if we'd be seeing you. Or if you were just a lot of hot air flashing in the pan."

"Oh, I'm hot, but the festival is very real." Harmony gave half a smirk. Like nothing in this room was worth too much of her energy. All his diplomas and awards and commendations from local service groups hanging behind him? Real cute. But he was playing with the big girls now. "And a hot commodity itself. I took a few tours around the area, saw a few prospective sites out west of Cranton, took a few lovely dinners with its mayor and stakeholders out that way." She drew a file from her folio and glanced at it. "But ultimately Rhythmic feels the Brookville site offers the strongest potential, and we're ready to move forward with planning." She dropped the folder on Travis's desk. "Everything you'll need for permitting."

"This is still a major decision." Travis wrapped one hand over the other. "And we have to take the wishes of the community into consideration. They tend to have strong opinions about new enterprises in town." He huffed through his nose, and Harmony imagined he'd been busy putting out the fire she'd set on top of his new arcade.

"I think you'll find public sentiment is not only in favor, but will demand the opportunities the festival offers."

"True," he said grudgingly. "My wife hasn't let up about this."

That at least had gone exactly to plan the last few weeks. Maybe even enough to entice Travis into biting. Harmony wouldn't mind getting her hands on a chunk of his money upfront. Faking an event bigger than any before required laying out plenty of deposits to really sell the ruse, and her own funds would be stretched thin. Recrossing her legs, she leaned forward. "I shouldn't really mention this here, where you're acting in your capacity as a public servant, but I just have to say, if you wanted to come on board as a sponsor, Rhythmic would be happy to offer prime billing—"

Travis wagged a finger. "I never invest my own money in speculative ventures. If an idea is good enough, it'll have wings."

At which point he'd happily scoop it up in his net and take all the credit and profit. It'd been worth a shot. But fine, she'd just be sure to have plenty of people ready to scream at him when their investments were threatened, when their babies were losing their chance at performing and internships—why, *their very futures*. He was going to become the sponsor—the savior—of the festival eventually. Then Harmony would make sure local businesses who'd paid fees or done work prepping for the event were paid back thanks to that cash. Everyone would get what they deserved.

For now she just smiled at him. Gave him the focused attention she'd withheld till now. "Like your own brilliant work." She drove every drop of vigor she possessed into her gaze, locked on Travis's beady blue eyes. Daring him to recognize her. Or recognize the partner who had made his success possible.

He acknowledged only himself with a nod. "Built everything I have myself."

"A real bootstrapper." She'd like to swing a boot right at Travis's smug face. *Titus Andronicus* him. She nudged her papers forward. "Get back to me ASAP. Rhythmic is looking to announce the headliner and dates by next month."

She strode out of town hall with her fingers clenching the fine leather of her purse, her steps sure in her Louboutins. She was tall and confident and held the reins of power and knew just how to tug them. She was not the little girl who'd listened to her father begging Travis to give him a crumb of his own work for pity's sake. She was the woman who would steal it all back.

She considered taking Furiosa for a drive through the countryside. Let the wind in her hair and the music blasting on her speaker erase the bad taste of Travis. Speed away from her problems, at least for a while, like she always did.

The library beckoned from across the green. She headed there instead, past the fountain's statue wearing a Giants hat and jersey, and wandered in, looking for Preston, who wasn't at the front counter. It was an old retrofitted building, with oddly sized doorframes leading off to different collections and funny little corners and two sets of spiral stairs. Under the one near the children's section, a bench with leather cushions had been built into the curve for a reading nook. This was where she found Preston, reading *Pug on a Rug* aloud to preschoolers each sitting on a small square of carpet spread over the floor. Except for one kid, who had climbed onto the bench beside Preston, and leaned against him to see the book up close as he held it high for the group. Each time before turning a page, he angled the book to be sure the boy could see.

Preston was wearing a cream-colored cable-knit sweater today that looked so soft Harmony wouldn't have minded cuddling up against it herself, nestling her head against Preston's chest and *dammit*, yeah, she was attracted to Preston. Who knew why she'd avoided picking up her usual type the entire time she'd been in Brookville and instead settled on Mister Freaking Rogers over there, but fine. If he was game she'd take him for the ride of his life, give him a summer to remember, and he could recall her fondly once she'd left him to his tidy routines she didn't fit into.

Though the uncertainty of hitting the road again this time, once she'd gotten her revenge against Travis, was like a blur she was avoiding looking at too directly. She was grateful when the kids on the floor erupted into a chorus of woofs and acted out something from the page Preston was reading. Her phone pinged; she glanced at it to see an email from Travis already, providing initial approval of her application. For all his power-tripping, he knew the town couldn't let this opportunity pass. Victory surged through her, like the rising voices of the children reciting after each page Preston read, in zanier iterations that only ended with the book, as they howled from their spots on their rugs.

She waited while the chatty parents with books in hand gradually pulled their children away for promised snacks out on the square or nap times or whatever else you did with slightly unformed humans that size. One last little girl was still barking at Preston as he gathered up the remaining books that had been propped along the bench on display. "You're kidding me," he said in reply. "Really?"

"*Bark*!"

"That's amazing."

"*Bark*! *Bark*!"

"Well, I agree. Obviously." He held out *Pug on a Rug*. "Want to take the book home?"

The girl beamed a smile, barked a yes (apparently), and grabbed the book, then ran back over to her bemused looking adult.

Preston ducked under a mobile of flying pigs and elephants and spotted Harmony, the serious expression he'd given the puppy-girl landing on her. Not pissed or cold, she was realizing. Simply intent. Considering. Watchful. Preston had a major case of resting bitch face, but the way he squashed a smile down as he walked over to her, books tucked against his side in one big hand . . . Like how he'd waited stone-faced after apologizing, seeming to brace for the worst. She suspected now he was just extremely practiced at holding himself back.

What would happen if that studious restraint broke? If he turned all that observant dedication on her during activities definitely not appropriate for storytime?

Maybe it wasn't such a mystery why she wanted him.

"Hey," he greeted her.

"Hi. I'm checking out a Thai place Sarah Lessner recommended—got time on your lunch break to come along?" She would ignore the mystery of why her stomach swooped while she waited to see if he'd put her off again, like the other day.

That guarded look lasted another beat before his brows lifted and he nodded. "Oh, god, yes, rescue me from the leftovers in the staff fridge." Preston dropped the books on a nearby cart. "We tried making these zucchini meatballs last night and, well. There's a reason there were leftovers."

"Sarah recommended a couple things there," Harmony said as Preston grabbed his bag from behind the counter. "But looking their catering menu up online they have, like, eleventy dishes, and I've never been super into Thai so I have no idea where to start."

"I will help by ordering whatever-half-of-eleventy-is things," Preston said like a vow. "I don't really get to go anymore because Lacey's not into it either." He held the door open for her and his hidden smile surfaced a little, feeling like more of a win than the quick polite ones she'd seen him pull out for library patrons. Like the sunlight they stepped into. "But I know what I like."

CHAPTER FIFTEEN
PRESTON

As he watched the water of the town's titular brook stream past, Preston counted that he was currently jealous of three things.

One: the guy behind the counter at this Italian ice cream shop he and Harmony had come to try out for the festival. He'd called her *bella* five times despite Preston knowing he'd been born right here in Brookville, had bulging arms from scooping ice cream all day, and had insisted on giving Harmony a free waffle cone after they were done sampling half a dozen flavors of fancy slushies Harmony said would be perfect for the festival. (They'd settled on mint and limoncello.) So now they were sitting out on the shop's back patio, overlooking the brook and the little bridge traveling over it to a jogging path running along the train tracks on the far side.

It was ridiculous to be jealous of him, because Preston had absolutely no claim to Harmony, only an overdeveloped sense of romance and a tendency to build things up too quickly in his mind. Nothing halfway. And if Harmony had smiled at all the *bellas* and laughed when the guy had slammed a surprise third scoop atop the first two right before handing the cone over, well, she was like that with everyone. It didn't mean anything, necessarily. Which actually didn't make him feel better. She was like that with Preston, and he wanted her smiles and laughs with him to mean something.

So, two: people who hadn't read so many love stories and didn't romanticize every little detail about the time they spent with someone just because that someone was alarmingly beautiful and annoyingly funny and absolutely unlike anyone they'd ever met. He and Harmony had been to several restaurants and bakeries and food trucks, arguing along the way about books and music and red versus black licorice, and part of him thought that was like dating. But another part of him was currently clobbering that first part, reminding him that this wasn't like that at all. They were in business together. Sort of. Or friends, maybe? They were business-friends. Preston shifted his glasses and wiped a hand over his face. That wasn't even a thing. *They* weren't a thing. He shoved his glasses back into place.

Just in time to see Harmony wander in front of him, eating. She wasn't one to sit still, instead strolling back and forth before the water, and Preston hadn't bothered trying to fold himself into the bright-green-painted picnic table, just sat on its tabletop, feet planted on the bench, looking at the view and not at Harmony licking her way through chocolate and anise and stracciatella.

Which brought him, humiliatingly, to three: that ice cream cone.

Preston told both parts of himself to stop fighting each other and join forces to defeat the totally inappropriate thoughts any business-friend of Harmony's should not be having around her.

"Oh, hey," she said, turning on him. "Want to be first to hear who the headliner is?"

He gripped the edge of the table, steeling himself against the sight of Harmony applying her tongue to frozen cream and sugar.

His voice was only halfway to wet cement when he managed, "Sure." She'd gotten whatever clearances she'd needed from town hall, and things seemed full steam ahead for the festival.

Harmony took another lick and smiled. Preston tucked that smile away with the hundred others he'd collected so far, his insides melting a little like that ice cream. She'd be gone after getting this festival up and running, that had been made clear, and they could never be more than this, but a smile that gorgeous should be committed to memory.

"Legend Watts." Another lick, and a satisfied grin.

"You're kidding."

"I know, it's such a coup, right?"

It was such a *coincidence*, he was going to tell her, but she was already launching into a story about seeing Legend Watts at the Grammys one year and the afterparty where she was chasing some big deal and somehow ended up falling into a pool in a full ballgown and jewels.

"Wow, Harmony Hale failed at something?"

She snapped her jaw down and gave him a sharp look. "Oh, I finished the job—I mean . . ." She wiped her tongue around where her chocolate ice cream was melting, and she had to be fucking with him, right? Because she took a beat too long twisting the cone around before saying, "We signed the artist we were there to meet. And I suppose I always say I love working without a safety net. But Christian Siriano is never going to dress me again." She heaved a tragic sigh and paced again along the edge of the patio deck.

Today she was wearing this cute little blue dress that crossed over her breasts and sort of swooped out after skimming down the ample curve of her hips, and was it actually possible to be jealous of fabric because maybe he needed to add another item to his count.

Harmony scrunched her nose. "I hope it's not a bad sign this place is a ghost town. Those drinks were good, right?"

"It is kind of chilly today." The afternoon sun filtered through a mess of wispy clouds and scattered over the slate water. They'd have to leave soon to get back in time for the end of Lacey's music therapy.

"Yeah, but it's deserted out here."

He quirked a brow at her waffle cone. "No, it's *desserted*."

"Wow, did they hand you a book of dad jokes along with the adoption papers?" But she was laughing a little, and it felt like a prize. She took another bite of her free ice cream. "The chocolate is decent. But I fucking love this anise."

"Because you're a maniac who eats black licorice by the handful." She'd dug pieces out of a bag she kept in her purse when they'd waited forever at the gyro place with dry spanakopita that for some reason she still said she'd sign for the festival.

She just shook her head. "You gotta try this." She advanced on him, and he was opening his mouth to say something like *No thanks if I put my mouth where your mouth has just been that might be a little too much like kissing you and then my brain might finally fall right out of my head*, but she was too quick and before he knew it he was tasting chocolate and spice like Christmas cookies he hadn't had for five years.

She watched his face. "Good, right?"

It was fucking incredible, Harmony standing right there beside the table and insistently sharing any kind of pleasure with him.

Except she'd angled the cone forward and now as it came away a drip of ice cream fell past the reach of his tongue and rolled down Preston's chin.

"Shit." He tipped his head back, trying to slow the disaster playing out on his fucking face. "*Shit*." If he'd come out here to eat an ice cream cone, he'd have grabbed a giant stack of napkins like he always did, but this was obviously an evil ice cream cone Bicep Guy had deployed on a secret mission to make Preston have a true meltdown in front of Harmony. The drip was rounding his chin, about to trail down his neck and fall on his shirt and his face was *sticky*—

"Oh, sorry!" Harmony's eyes were wide with concern. "Um, here, hold on."

No time. His hands waved as if they could air-dry the mess before it finished destroying his life. *Go on without me. Save yourself.*

And then—

Harmony licked him.

She grabbed him by the shoulder, leaned in, and swiped her tongue up his chin, halting the rogue ice cream drip and every single function of Preston's brain.

When she drew back, he didn't move. He was watching the final flick of her tongue retreating into her mouth, trying to process the tiny, throaty sound she made as if savoring the flavor. She let out that gentle huff of a laugh. "Oh no, I broke you." And then, anxious and quick: "Sorry, was that not cool—?" She took another step back.

He stood, cupped her worried, beautiful face with its freckles like cinnamon sugar, and kissed her.

She dropped the ice cream cone with a wet thud and kissed him back and *holy fuck* the rightness of Harmony's lips against his, singing through his head like the sweetest note. Her lips parted under his and he was jealous of nothing, there was no one he'd rather be than himself, the man currently kissing Harmony Hale. She tasted better than cinnamon, tasted of star anise and sugar and something else that beckoned him to press nearer, wrap an arm around her back, and tug her closer.

She had one hand at the nape of his neck, and her other clenched a fistful of his lapel, holding him to her. His own hand threaded into her hair, fingers playing through its softness. The kiss was only overtaken by the piercing whistle of a passing train, like the white-hot cry already inside Preston's head of how this, *this*, was what he'd been waiting for.

But Harmony, hair and skirt fluttering in the train's breeze, must have felt him tense and broke off the kiss. "Oh—" A double crease appeared between her brows. Like a pause button.

"No—" he said, his tongue trying to remember that words were a thing and not just kissing, trying to explain it was only the noise.

"No?" She shifted back on her heels.

"*Yes.*" He reached for her. Only now they'd stopped, he was realizing all the reasons it should be no. What was he doing? They had a business deal together. She was only here a few months. Fear rumbled through him like that train, fear of how much more he wanted. How right kissing Harmony felt, how ruinous it would be when she left.

He let his hands drop to his sides. "It's time to go get Lacey." That was a bullshit excuse, and Harmony's face pinched as if to say she knew it, but she nodded and walked back through the shop. Preston felt like garbage for using his responsibility to his sister that way.

He simply didn't know what else he could do to avoid Harmony leaving his heart, inevitably, like that abandoned lump of ice cream on the ground.

CHAPTER SIXTEEN
HARMONY

Harmony hadn't seen Preston for four days, so when he texted just before she was supposed to pick him up to check out a wine and cheese truck at the farmer's market, she was sure he was going to cancel.

Something came up.

Yup. The coward. Harmony threw her mascara back in her makeup bag beside the sink and grabbed her reddest lipstick. She traced it over her mouth as if she could erase the memory of Preston's kiss—purposeful and thrilling and right. Until it wasn't.

It was the white lie that did it. Preston was always so direct, irritatingly so at times, and only fished out polite, meaningless small talk and false smiles for other people, she'd noticed. Adults at the library and chatty waitresses at the restaurants they'd tried together, people he didn't really care about.

Her phone buzzing again on the counter almost made her hand wobble over her lower lip.

I have to go to the library.

Sure, he suddenly had to work, the man whose schedule was planned a week in advance down to the minute. Bullshit. Just like his excuse for ending that kiss, laying the blame on his sister. Who did he think he was conning?

She stared at herself in the mirror. Her set shoulders sank forward. Wasn't she doing the exact same thing with her dad? Excusing all the lies she was telling Preston, because of her duty there, even when the time they'd been spending together made that feel kind of shitty?

That kiss hadn't been a lie.

Mirror-Harmony's perfectly drawn eyebrows rippled. Even if Preston showed up here right now looking for another, she didn't know how to resolve the fake Harmony she projected, who was always calm and confident and rolled with anything, and the real Harmony who was actually quite upset for some reason. Who couldn't stop thinking of her mouth on Preston, the taste and texture of him, sweet and creamy and rough stubble. The sudden warm press of his kiss.

It couldn't be that Preston hadn't enjoyed it. Harmony was a spectacular kisser. So it must be her. When she wasn't trying to bamboozle someone, when she was just being herself, and seeing where things went, for once, it turned out he didn't want anything more.

Maybe there was nothing more to her. Just sparkle and lies and skimming the surface. Nothing that would hold up to longer scrutiny. Certainly not Preston's keen gaze. Maybe that was the real reason why she always got in and got out.

Harmony jammed the cap back on her lipstick. This was what she got for acting like Alice. She knew better. The one time Harmony had mixed personal and professional before, it had ended with Zach serving a six-month prison sentence.

She'd worked with Zach on previous jobs, run by someone else, and so when he'd contacted her looking for work, she knew he was good at what he did. He'd seemed like he'd be good at a lot of things, so she'd broken her rule about keeping work and sex separate. But soon it grew obvious he didn't get that this was Harmony's show now. He didn't follow directions. Tried to take money off anyone he could in the course of the con. Didn't want his take reduced by Harmony paying back innocents caught up in her scheme against the main target. He got pushy about it—literally. Others had tried to shove Harmony around before, growing up how she did, living on her own so young, and she knew by now to bail out before it got bad—so she didn't warn Zach when the cops were closing in. Now he was in county jail in San Bruno, his probation date highlighted on her calendar app.

She did not feel guilty about that. Because she didn't look back.

So why did she keep replaying in her mind the way Preston had wound his arm around her, wound his fingers into her hair, like she was worth hanging on to?

The buzz of her phone snapped her out of remembering Preston's lips on hers.

Can you meet me there instead?

Harmony's eyes flicked to her reflection and away. Actually, Preston had been very up-front about his busy schedule and was clearly extremely into her. Poor thing. He'd probably been dying for his next chance to get together.

She tucked her lipstick into her purse and grabbed her keys.

It was Saturday, and the library was bustling, as much as a place where you had to whisper could be. Someone whispered for Harmony, as she wandered through looking for Preston. "Ms. Hale!" Jordan and Nina peeked over the screen of the laptop they were huddled near, chairs drawn close together.

Once Harmony had gotten the festival approved at town hall, she'd been in touch with Jordan and made the internships official (even if the corporation they were interning with wasn't technically real). Now the girls showed her what they've accomplished already.

"Two big LGBTQ+ groups out of San Francisco committed to coming," Nina said, pointing to the color-coded spreadsheet on her screen. "The outreach to our area is going to be super important for a lot of people."

Jordan was resting her hand on the back of Nina's chair, listening with a proud gleam in her eye. "And we're still making a list of local organizations," she told Harmony. "Even smaller ones who might share booth space. If that sounds okay?"

"Great idea."

"Oh, *pop tarts*," Nina swore adorably. "I forgot to add the voter registration group." She toggled between her email and spreadsheet, typing furiously.

Harmony straightened. "This is really cool." Or it would be, if it was actually going to happen. If this weren't just another example of her jerking people around with her charade. Like all the businesses she'd already signed up. Auditions for the local youth stage were in a week. Both Jordan and Nina had insisted on helping to organize that too. They'd really taken this job—which Harmony had mostly invented to get Jordan out of hot water with Travis—and run with it. Harmony suddenly wasn't so sure she was as immune to guilt as she always thought.

She couldn't even pay them, with the work counting for Jordan's volunteer hours. At least they were getting to spend a lot of time together. Jordan was playing with a strand of Nina's hair now, which definitely didn't make Harmony's chest ache remembering someone running his hand through her own hair—before pulling away. "Have you seen Preston?"

"Mr. Jones?" Nina pointed toward the main nonfiction section. "I think he was heading for the back stairs?"

"Thanks."

"We'll send what we have along to you once it's ready for official approval."

Harmony nodded and cut through the bookcases. The set of stairs over here was roped off, with a STAFF ONLY sign attached. Harmony stepped over it and wound her way up to the second floor.

Piles of books were stacked against the walls of the hallway. A box of shiny hardbacks waited at the top of the stairs, a sticky note on top reading "Crossover Book Club" in Preston's scrawl. Harmony picked her way through to the rows of bookshelves crammed with volumes.

Eventually she heard Preston talking under his breath somewhere farther into whatever forgotten corner of the library this was. "That'll be good for the library sale . . . You can go right in the discard pile, you outdated, racist relic." Harmony followed his voice and rounded a back aisle where he was crouching and pulling books from the lowest shelf and moving them to piles on the floor.

"Oh, good," she whispered. "Is this where you keep all those dirty books I keep hearing about?"

"*Fuck*." Preston jumped and steadied himself, hands gripping the shelf. His voice dropped to a library-appropriate murmur. "Sorry. Overactive startle reflex." He shoved himself up to standing. "Autism thing."

"To be fair, it is kinda creepy up here."

"Didn't you see the—" He stopped and shook his head, lips twisting away either a smile or a scowl. "Never mind. Old building. Not ADA compliant, so we just use this for storage. Hope they didn't hear me at the study carrels on the other side of that wall." He wiped his palms on his jeans, looking around at the stacks of books. "Katherine let it get kind of out of hand the last few . . . decades. I've been trying to work my way through it, weed stuff out when I can. Got distracted." His gaze returned to Harmony—or just past her shoulder, maybe. "Why didn't you text me you were here?"

Because she was worried if she gave him the chance he'd beg off. "Can you still make it? Farmer's market?"

"Yeah, of course. I just needed to bring something down. Heidi called out last second, and the new book club's first meeting is today. The books I pulled were up here, and Katherine can't manage the stairs anymore with her knees, so she asked if I could do them a favor and set up the conference room real fast." He finally stopped and took a breath. Their low voices made this seem like a more intimate conversation than it was. Was it going to be like this between them now? Awkwardly filling every moment with harmless words to avoid talking about what had happened?

Screw that. Harmony could be irritatingly direct too. *Wanna make out up here instead?* she would say, and watch that ruddy color blush over his insufferably handsome face. Then see what he did about it.

Except all that came out was "Do you want to hang out for the meeting a bit before heading over to the market?" Who was the coward now?

But that was good too. It might give Operation: Win People Over a chance to progress. The book club was real, it could actually help kids like Jordan and Nina, and she'd helped make it happen. Like a little bit of the good Preston was always doing. After all the work the kids had taken on, making sure she left them better off seemed important.

"No." Preston blinked. "Why would I do that."

Harmony shrugged. "It's for people who like books. You're a person, you like books."

"Maybe too much." You would hardly know it, the way he was picking at the ragged spine of a book on the nearest shelf, where he'd turned his stare away. "Anything I like, I like too much. So I have rules, two comments, then stop."

"Preston, that sounds exhausting." And lonely. As lonely as the way her chatterbox habit of smoothing her path to anything she needed sometimes felt. Like a wall of talk between her and everyone else, everyone she was using.

"It is." He ran a hand over his hair. "But it's better than people wandering away in the middle of you speaking to them. I don't want to screw things up with those people, not after you worked to turn things around with them." His gaze shifted but never quite landed on her, which was another thing she'd noticed him doing with the random people they encountered, people Harmony would lavish with attention and lock eyes with to better steer them into giving her whatever she wanted.

She took a step into the aisle. Daring Preston to look at her. "You don't stop at two comments with me." He'd practically retold an entire book about two grad students fighting over some scholarship or something, while they waited at the fancy doughnut food truck last week. (If the festival *were* real, Harmony would spend the entire weekend cramming *Dough for It*'s marshmallow and crème brûlée offerings in her face.)

"Well." His fingers stilled. "You're so over the top yourself, I guess I figured you wouldn't mind."

A smile tugged at the corners of her mouth. Now their low-pitched voices did sound like they were sharing secrets. "You're right." She stepped farther along the aisle. "I always want more." At least when it came to him, it seemed. The rare person who could hold his own with her.

He still didn't meet her gaze. One hand pulled into a fist resting on the bookshelf. She was sure Preston was two seconds from telling her she was actually too over the top for him, that the kiss had been a mistake.

She cast about for anything to say to cut him off and noticed a battered copy of *Howl's Moving Castle* beside the book he'd been murdering. "Oh, I loved this as a kid." She drew it off the shelf and flipped it open to a familiar title page and rich vanilla scent. "We moved around so much, with my dad—you know, the turbulent music industry. But if I opened a favorite book, it was like I was back in the same spot, with the same friends." Way to make herself sound like a total loser. But as outgoing as she'd always been with others, she hadn't been able to bring any classmates home, when they'd had a home, not when people judged her dad for needing her help so much around their messy apartment, for sleeping it off on the couch, for saying whatever was on his mind no matter if it seemed strange to them. And you could still read by the glow of the streetlights even when the power was cut off again.

Preston watched her hands turning pages. "That must have been hard." There was a softness to his words, like he was finally focused on her rather than evasive.

"Yeah, it can get old, flitting from place to place." But at least you left before people realized they didn't really want you around. She shrugged. "I get to experience a lot of different things."

His lips made a wry twist. "'Tis better to have *Dough For It* and lost than never had marshmallow doughnuts at all?"

She snorted. "If this place *is* haunted, I think Tennyson's ghost is gonna come for you."

His breath sort of caught before rushing out in a huff of a laugh. Then his smile buckled under a tensed expression. Like he was weighing a decision. "Guess it's good you're escaping back to L.A. before too long." But any playfulness had washed out of his voice.

What the hell did that mean? Why bring up L.A. when they were supposed to be going to the Brookville farmer's market right now, except he was here helping people on his day off, obviously to make her feel especially like a scoundrel—and to avoid her, it was feeling more and more like. Preston did so much real good for everyone but himself, he didn't deserve her messing up his already complicated life, and here she was ruining his rare chance to do something fun, chasing him back to work.

She shot the book back into place with a thunk, and he gave an automatic little *shh*.

"Let's just go," she almost hissed. Fucking fine, she'd drag him out of here, make him spend an hour or two relaxing and eating artisanal whatever they were supposed to be trying today, because she'd learned early she had to grab what she wanted when she could. "You take care of everyone," she told him, seizing hold of his wrist to lead him toward the stairs. "But sometimes you gotta take what you want."

He twisted under her grip, mouth set as if he'd made his choice, and she thought he was going to pull away—but he spun her around by the hand and pinned it against the shelf suddenly at her back. "What I want?" His voice had dropped an octave, almost strangled by need, and his eyes were on her now, so near and laden with electric desire. "Too much."

"Good." She crashed her lips against his.

His hand cradled her head, drawing the kiss deeper at once. She was drowning in it, under Preston's hot, unyielding mouth. Her free hand splayed against his chest, wanting to feel him there, the solidness of him, not another daydream.

His hungry kiss wrote itself over her jaw, her neck, the softness under her ear. She shivered so hard she wasn't sure she'd have been able to stand without the bookcase supporting her, without Preston holding on to her.

She almost laughed with the joy of it. "Isn't this against library rules?"

He drew a long shuddering breath, breaking the seal of his mouth from the curve where her neck met her shoulder. His voice sounded as if it'd been dredged up through an ocean of temptation, as he grazed his nose along her jawline. "Is that you asking to stop?"

In answer, she lashed an arm around him and kissed his cheek, his neck, and he wasn't wearing a tie today but his shirt collar was in the way so instead she drew his earlobe between her teeth and flicked it with her tongue.

Preston punctuated his ragged inhalation with a "*Thank fuck*" and drove his mouth back over her skin, slower this time. Intentional. He muttered against her shoulder, "It would be, if I was working." His fingers twined through her hair, gently angling her head back so he could follow the curve of her collarbone. "I'm not working, I'm providing a favor."

He sure as hell was. His tongue flirted closer to her neckline and the swell of her breast. When she gasped again, louder, throatier, he lifted his kiss to her mouth, quelling it. "We have to be quiet, though." He tugged her lip between his teeth, and he had her utterly—pinned here at her mouth, her hair at her nape, her hand under his against the books. All her anxiety about him putting distance between them evaporated beneath the burn of his gaze as he released her lip and let his hand drop to clutch her hip's curve. His fingers ran down where her skirt parted into a long slit, then traced back up, slowly, slowly, playing over her skin. His palm opened and seared heat up her thigh. A desperate sigh broke from her throat. Preston bent his head, mouth brushing her ear. "*Shh.* Or I have to stop."

That would be a tragedy. A catastrophe. A disaster of such magnitude not seen in this state since the great earthquake of aught six. So she kept her voice low, tucked between the close shelves with soft sunlight brushing through them from a distant window. "Don't you dare."

His warm huff of a smothered laugh only ratcheted up the rising temperature of her blood. His hand shifted almost imperceptibly higher. "This all right?"

"Yes." Their words lived on a shared breath as he kissed her and cupped her ass. He held her as if he couldn't get enough—of her, not some nameless bar hookup, not a persona she'd crafted with some still-promised prize to entice—and she kissed him back hard, silently declaring that she might have been a thief, but all she wanted was this stolen moment with him.

He released her hand, but she hung on to the bookshelf for dear life, since he'd only done that because apparently he really couldn't get enough of her. His hand spread wide and scorching over her rib-cage, fingertips prickling so close to where she wanted his touch.

"Okay?" he whispered.

She fought to answer, to get him to keep going, to not shout the word and make him take his hands off her. "Yes," she rasped.

He slid his hand over her breast, and his breath stuttered. He crushed his mouth again to the side of her neck, stifling whatever sound clawed in his throat like a wild animal. His fingers kneaded gently over the fabric of her dress. His thumb caught across her tightening nipple.

She sucked a breath, and god, she had been so right about Preston, nothing escaped his notice, because he did it again, experimentally, steering his thumb around in little circles until finding the teasing pressure that set her panting. She tugged at Preston's shirt and planted kisses down his neck, stirred her tongue over the muscles joining it to his shoulder. His fingers flexed everywhere on her.

His hair was falling forward, his glasses foggy, but the undiluted longing in his eyes was plain and the best thing Harmony had ever seen. "You still want more?" he asked.

"*Yes.*"

His fingers trailed like meteors across her thigh. "I fucking love this dress." Up, up, his hand traveled over the softest inner part of her leg to her trembling center.

He groaned her name against her throat, a hushed, aching "*Harmony*" that lit her up inside even as his voice rumbled through her, setting off a darker urge deep within. And he stoked it, fingertips brushing over thin silk, that touch more than enough as his attention focused on her every shiver and swallowed moan became a relentless chase to something she was sure you were not supposed to do in the library, employed there or not. He braced himself against the bookcase and returned his mouth to where he'd made her shudder, at her neck. The heel of his hand pressed hard against her pelvic bone, and she ground herself on him, rubbing his hand into her clit.

His talented fingers stole under the damp fabric as he bent toward her breast, scraped his teeth over dress and nipple, and that was all it took—one slide sent the sparks inside her shooting into fireworks, blazing through her core, along her skin, down to her toes. His kiss swallowed her cry.

They were both drawing harsh breaths like the scrape of turning pages when he dropped his forehead to hers. His hand retreated, and he was kissing her again, long slow swipes of his mouth upon her throat, as if trying to drink even more of her in.

She hooked her fingers into his belt loops. "Preston."

"*Shhh—iiiit.*" His hushing turned to a half-grunted oath as she towed him against her. His firm chest to her breasts, his hips fitting against her belly. His hardness there ignited something different in her, something hungry to know that this, between them, was real. Preston swallowed, throat bobbing. He murmured, a bit hoarse, "There's only so much we can get away with, I think."

She nodded and nipped at his jaw. "You'd really better prep that book club meeting. Or someone might come looking for you up here. And that's my move."

"It's a good move. I like your moves." He pressed a kiss to her temple. "And I do really want to go out with you. To the market. For work." He seemed to catch himself starting to ramble.

It was endearing, really, how he didn't immediately suggest taking this to her hotel. She was willing to stick to the schedule with him, now she knew how much that kind of thing mattered to Preston. She smudged away the lipstick on his cheek with her thumb. "I think we can call this a date, at this point." Not just a hookup, not for a job, which was admittedly unfamiliar territory for Harmony. But what with the evidence of how they'd both put pleasure before business all over Preston's hand that he was wiping on his jeans. He looked debauched, with more of her kisses smeared on his mangled collar, hair tousled, glasses a little askew.

"Right." He smiled, a flash of wonder in his eyes, though some of that tension from before was back around his mouth. That might only have been the other situation going on with the front of his jeans. He straightened his glasses. "Just—give me a minute, to, um, calm down. I'll find you once the club's set to go."

Harmony nodded again, fixing his shirt to hide the remaining traces of her lipstick, already planning when she could take care of him properly. Something had flared inside her ribcage at that last tender kiss. Preston took such care. She ran her fingers through her hair and adjusted her dress before heading down.

That was a tough act to follow, but the rest of their afternoon together was nearly as fun. The cheese and wine tasted incredible under the sunshine. She kept catching Preston's intense gaze on her, and every time she'd stick out her tongue or stuff a morsel in her mouth and chew obnoxiously until he rolled his eyes. When he pulled a face at the mess she made of some local honey drizzled over her Parmesan and prosciutto, she licked it off her fingers and enjoyed the blush, almost as red as his wine, that swept up his face. "You're shameless."

"And you're one to talk."

The blush deepened.

Preston suggested she come with him to pick up Lacey so they could stay a little longer, and they wandered through the market, tasting free samples of tangerines and the first fresh strawberries and talking, somehow getting into a competition to see who could name the most books with a fruit in the title. Preston had an advantage, knowing so many children's books.

"*Blueberries for Sal.*"

"*The Grapes of Wrath.*"

"*James and the Giant Peach*."

"*The House on Mango Street*."

"*Where the Watermelons Grow*."

"*Huckleberry Finn*."

"That's cheating."

"*Olive Kitteridge*."

"Harmony."

"Well, *that's* not even a fruit." She smirked. "I win."

A local folk band was set up at the front of the food stalls, and Harmony started dancing along, earning a scowl from Preston—standing in the back of the gathered crowd, because of course he was polite about his height—that she knew now to read as a suppressed smile, another secret between them like the one they'd shared among the bookcases.

One-night stands had their advantages, but it was nice to wonder, as Preston bought a box of those strawberries for Lacey, when Harmony might get him alone again. Because she'd only gotten a taste, and damn, forget the piano, the guy was talented at plenty. His *hands*. His long, strong fingers. She wanted to know how they'd feel inside her; she wanted all of him. She wanted to give him his too much and more, once she got him somewhere they didn't have to worry about being noisy or interrupted.

But otherwise she couldn't really ask for more, for a more perfect day—outside of the one when she finally brought Travis Weaver to his knees. They picked up Lacey, loading her bike in Furiosa's trunk with Preston's and putting the top up so it wouldn't be too loud or windy for her. And Harmony didn't mind at all driving away alone at the end of it, back to her hotel under the sharp golden slant of the late afternoon sun.

CHAPTER SEVENTEEN
HARMONY

What with Cheryl Weaver's sneering attitude toward Preston, Harmony would have thought the way she'd been spending time with him would be like rubbing Cheryl-repellant all over herself. But apparently Cheryl's desire to girlboss her way through everything going on in town was even stronger. Which was how Harmony found herself surrounded by the self-approving chatter of the Brookville Business Association's social hour and struggling through the chewiest bite of calamari ever, or possibly a deep-fried deflated balloon.

She gave a closed-mouth smile to Ellie Vickes, one of Cheryl's friends, whose California fusion tavern was hosting the business association's monthly meeting. Harmony made a mental note, as Ellie zipped off ordering waiters around, to keep seafood off the menu when they did the paperwork for their booth at the festival.

Cheryl had insisted on introducing Harmony to several business owners she approved of, and Harmony at least could round out her list for the food stalls and supply orders with these wealthy proprietors who would put heavy pressure on Travis when the time came.

The mayor was talking nearby with Ellie's husband Raymond, a tall, dark-haired guy with incredibly hairy forearms that made Harmony glad he wasn't in the kitchen tonight. They were discussing franchising, which apparently Travis was all about. "I'm telling you, Raymond, that's where the money is. You're never going to be big time working for yourself. Get others working for you."

"You mean besides Ellie?" They both laughed. "Profit margins are too slim."

Travis shook his head ruefully, tone turning bitter. "I hear you, man, after all those cybersex rumors about my place, investors have been skittish. I'm still doing damage control. I'd planned to launch our expansion without liquidating any of my own funds." He took a long draw of his drink, and the conversation turned to the house brew, which he and Raymond were each half a pint into. All around, men and women in blazers and button-downs and sheath dresses, expensive watches and flashy jewelry, drank the blond ale or complicated cocktails and munched on appetizers, as the evening outside the wall of windows settled into darkness.

Harmony finally swallowed down the calamari, ready to tackle another potential festival investor, but Cheryl swept back up to her where she stood by the spread, a nearly empty glass of white in hand. "Well, you seem to have met most everyone worth meeting tonight!"

"I'm very grateful for your guidance." Appealing to Cheryl was all about balance. Treating her like an inspiration while maintaining her own aspirational allure of connected and cool.

"That's what the business association is for, making the right connections." She raised her glass in acknowledgment, then added, as an afterthought, "And of course our important work giving back to the community."

Harmony let her irritation with how Cheryl really treated important parts of the community turn into a conspiratorial scrunch of her nose. "That and these amazing little bites!" She held up the plate of calamari. "You've got to try one. Absolutely worth it."

Harmony said a silent thanks to all that wine as Cheryl actually popped one into her bright-pink mouth.

Preston was busy giving lessons tonight, but Harmony wished she could see the way he'd fight the smile off his face watching Cheryl slowly realize the pickle she was in, clinging to her pleasant expression as her eyes went just the tiniest bit frantic.

Thinking of Preston *also* made Harmony wish she could drag him off somewhere she could rub a lot more of him all over herself.

Travis drifted over to his wife just then, squashing any thoughts but revenge, and Cheryl grabbed a napkin to dab daintily at her still full mouth.

Back to business. Harmony beamed at Travis. She'd still love to get him on the hook for more of his own cash. Really scrub those accounts spotless in the end. "Lovely to see everyone's excitement about the festival." She tilted her head toward Cheryl. "Excited about what we can give back as well." Like every bit of pain Travis had cost her dad.

Cheryl nodded emphatically, trying and failing not to look like she was chewing a mouthful of rubber bands.

"I don't know, Miss Hale." Travis shifted his weight, taking a leisurely pull of his drink. "I'll be very interested to see who this headliner of yours is."

"Of course, you got your start in music, so you know that the right artist is the key to hooking audiences, and I know you'll especially appreciate the caliber of performer we've partnered with, and just how important that is to the success of this venture."

Travis sucked his teeth. "I've heard the pitch from everyone in town, even over my own damn dinner table. I'm still not convinced this whole thing's going to be anything more than a giant drain on my city."

What the hell? She'd thought she had Travis squared away. She'd already been out to the festival site getting quotes from contractors for clearing the fields of stumps and setting up fencing, major expenses for making this all seem real, and tonight had set meetings with potential key suppliers, shifting into working on all the other businesses that would be drawn into the scheme and push Travis into her trap. If he got it in his head to try to pull the plug on the festival after they started actual work and she began taking vendor payments, that could leave her in a sticky position with some of the contracts she'd be using to fund the rest of the grift, trying to cover everyone's investments herself. And she never left community members holding the bag, only her deserving targets. Travis causing trouble—throwing up municipal red tape, warning friends off of investing—would ruin the momentum she needed to drive this con home and make it that much harder to get him on board in the end.

For a split second, Harmony debated laughing Travis's concerns off, but decided if he was still dragging his feet on the festival, he'd respond better to the serious touch. "Now, Mr. Mayor, the documentation of our past successes should reassure you—"

He shook his head. "I've been checking over everything you've supplied, and went looking online at some of your festivals."

Thank god for Alice and her expert internet fakery. "And so you must have seen how our events are anchors of the communities where we've worked."

"Anchors can drag a ship down, Miss Hale. There's still time to pull the brakes before this train leaves the station, if you don't live up to all your promises."

Lips pursed, Cheryl made a noise of protest and flapped her napkin.

Harmony refused to be deterred, despite Travis's questionable and mixed metaphors, giving him her savviest smile. "I get it, you didn't get where you are today by doing anything by half. I'd be happy to reach out to representatives at some of the municipalities where Rhythmic has done events, ask them for letters of recommendation as it were—"

"A meeting."

"A meeting?"

"Video call. Let's hear it direct."

"Of course, excellent idea!" She tilted her head at Cheryl. "That's why they made him mayor, right?"

"This week should work for me," Travis said. "Call my girl at the office."

By "girl," Harmony assumed he meant the fortysomething mother of three she'd chatted with while getting some details about traffic regulations nailed down the other week, who was clearly the one actually keeping the city running. Harmony's smile was tight over her teeth. "No problem. I'll get my best intern on it." She cast another knowing look to Cheryl, who choked down her calamari to gush about Nina's leadership and organizational skills and all the colleges she'd be applying to next year and all the plans Cheryl and Travis had for her career in politics. That let Harmony spend half her mental focus thinking through how she was going to pull off Travis's request.

It kept her busy the next few days, planning with Alice, putting together an online profile for a city councilor—who looked remarkably like an older, stuffier Alice—whose little city outside Indianapolis hosted a family folk fest. They seeded the information artfully online, in case Travis decided to do any more digging. Thanks to Travis's demands, Harmony didn't get a chance to see Preston, but that was the business, always putting out one fire or another. This was nothing compared to the time she'd had to hire a gospel choir last second to show up and sing to convince that handsy pastor to trust her with his church's investment in the Christian music festival. Or when she found an overnight veterinarian to put a cast on her arm because the millionaire real estate bro she was charming out of his portfolio had decided they'd discuss business details after skydiving. Something about bonding through adrenaline. Too bad Harmony slipped in her hotel's bath and couldn't make it after all! She still managed to close the deal and put an end to the guy's illegally evicting entire communities from their gentrifying neighborhoods. Hiccups always came at some point in a job. Harmony did not panic—and that was partly because Harmony never did stupid shit like jumping out of freaking planes.

Alice, however, was panicking just a little as Harmony did her hair and makeup over at her place before zipping down to Travis's office to take her call from Indiana. "You know I'm not the greatest at the lying stuff." She fidgeted in her desk chair near the window under the slanted roof. Alice had rented a furnished studio above a game store at the fringe of downtown, its entrance up a flight of stairs tucked into the garden alley behind a line of small shops and offices.

"Please." Harmony brushed some more eyeshadow over Alice's lids. With the boring color and her usual cat's eye swoop tamed to a conservative line, plus the updo Harmony had already pouffed her hair into, she'd gain ten years on her twenty-three. It would be convincing enough over video, especially with only the indirect sun at the window for lighting and the poor connection Alice had devised. "I've seen you go all in with a pair of fives and scare an entire table of grown men into letting you get away with their money."

"Poker table's different. And background support for you, sure. That's not what I mean. One on one with Travis? I can't steer things the way you can." She kicked her sneaker against the chair leg. "Conversations get away from me."

"You know this stuff inside and out. You just have to tell him about it." Harmony dabbed some staid maroon lip matte on Alice's tense mouth. "Plus, you won't be alone. I'll be right there beside Travis."

A knock came at the door.

Harmony frowned at Alice. "Does anyone even know you live here?"

She shrugged, the shoulder pads of her blue business suit shifting. "Maybe it's Gary from downstairs? He mentioned inviting me to his D&D campaign . . ." She rose and went to check the peephole. "*It's Evan.*" Alice spun, wide-eyed. "What is he doing here?"

"Stalking you, apparently?" Harmony wiped her pigment-stained hands on a tissue. "Get rid of him!"

"But—" Alice pouted. "Biceps. And that adorable belly of his. I just wanna curl up and take a nap on him. After I wear myself out doing other things on him. Which I'll never get to do if I brush him off."

"Alice! I have to be at town hall in fifteen minutes. And you have to be in *Indiana*!" The one full-height wall across from Alice's desk would serve as an office backdrop, with a few framed pictures of park events and commendations they'd slapped up earlier. Her bed wouldn't show in the frame.

"Alice?" came a rich baritone from outside.

Alice wrung her hands, looking ready to run in circles. "He must have seen me!"

"Maybe he's canvassing for souls or something." Harmony raced for the bathroom. "Tell him yours is already saved. Backed up to the cloud. Just get him out of here." She pulled the bathroom door halfway shut to block herself from Evan's line of sight just as Alice turned the deadbolt.

"Evan! Hi!"

There was a pause before Evan said, "Hi. You look—awfully nice today. Got a date?"

Alice patted her hair with a grimace. "Job interview." Which started in like ten minutes.

"Oh." Harmony could hear the relief in Evan's voice. She peered through the bathroom door hinges to see him dressed in another nice button-down and shorts, holding something in both hands. He did have a cute belly, and sheesh, the man had legs like tree trunks.

"So," Alice said, wedged in the doorway. "Fancy meeting you here."

Evan winced. "Hope it's okay I stopped by. Gary mentioned at service last week you were renting in the building." Small towns were going to be the death of Harmony. "And the other day you mentioned you were still settling in and didn't even have a corkscrew yet. So I thought—"

Alice grabbed the offered corkscrew. "That's super nice of you, thanks."

"I thought maybe we could . . ." A bottle of wine dangled in his other hand, but Alice was inching back inside, the door still hiding most of the apartment, and he stiffened. "Sorry. Do you have company? I should go." Harmony thanked whatever saints this man prayed to for giving Alice the perfect out.

But Alice shook her head hard enough to put the structural integrity of that French twist in jeopardy. "No, no company."

Evan made a sheepish shrug, running a hand over his short dark hair. "I thought I heard you talking to someone."

"Just practicing. It's a really important interview."

His mouth pulled into a smile. "So you're thinking of getting out of the coffee game? What kind of job?"

"Public works."

"That's amazing." Evan's eyes lit with a twinkle of true enthusiasm. "You'd be great. Helping people. Do you need a ride there or anything?"

"It's a video interview."

He grinned down at Alice's sneakers and suit. "I'm surprised you have pants on. I mean—" His gaze jumped back to Alice's face, his own flushing. "I meant, I'm surprised you put pants on. Suit pants." He swallowed. "Your pants look really nice."

He looked like he was considering cracking open that wine right now and guzzling it. Harmony could certainly use a drink watching this train wreck.

"Yeah," Alice said after a moment. "It's in Indiana."

"Indi—so, like, back east?"

"Yeah," Alice repeated, before offering, "the Hoosier State." This conversation was definitely getting away from her. It was making a break for the state line. Approaching the outer atmosphere.

"So maybe not settling in after all?" You didn't have to be an expert at body language like Harmony was to tell how crestfallen he was at the idea.

"Oh, you know," Alice said like she'd just murdered his puppy but was trying to make light of it. "I move around a lot."

Evan's brow flexed with thought. "Must be late there."

Alice gave a weak laugh. "Which is why I'd better get to it!"

"Of course." Evan stepped back. "Good luck!"

"Thanks. Thanks for stopping by. And for this." She waggled the corkscrew, almost stabbing Evan, who took another step back. If he fell down the steps, Harmony was going to give herself away when she screamed out of frustration.

"Okay, bye." Finally Evan turned and disappeared down the stairs.

"Goodbye!" Alice carefully shut the door. She walked over to Harmony, emerging from her hiding place, and dropped her head against her shoulder. "Goodbye, dream of using Evan as a giant Totoro nap pillow."

Harmony patted her back affectionately. "You are so weird." She gave Alice a bracing shake by the shoulders. "But the show must go on." Alice groaned into her blazer before raising her head and nodding.

The curtain went up at Travis's office, where he and Harmony took Alice's call at the conference table to one side of the room. Alice had pulled herself together and was perfectly in character. Despite her worries about directing marks without them catching on, she was great at playing a part, and they'd rehearsed their opening. "Hey, there's our superstar."

Harmony beamed at Travis's screen. "Melissa! How's the outdoor gear game?

"Not bad." Alice pitched her voice lower than her typical chirp, and even managed a Midwest accent that only veered a little into Canadian. "We just opened a new flagship in Indianapolis."

"Congratulations!"

Alice tapped her pen and nodded. "Franchising hasn't slowed down."

Travis perked up from where he'd been resting his chin on a propped fist. "Franchising?" They'd let him stew, ignored him just long enough to feel excluded but not to sink into complete irritation. And dropped this bait to get him to come to them.

But they weren't going to come on too strong. Harmony waved a hand. "Oh, sorry, we should get to city business. Mayor Weaver here is very strict about keeping his public duties and private work separate."

"Very noble of you." Alice smiled. The barest trace of a smirk. Let him worry he was missing out without making him angry. This had to be his idea. "Well, I'm certainly happy to share with you all about our experience working with Rhythmic."

"It's been beneficial to your town?"

Alice let out a convincing surprised laugh. "Oh, yes. I can definitely say that. I had my girl pull together the numbers from this last year—" She rattled off a few key figures. "That last one, the wider impact survey, really shows the financial snowball effect. Though I guess you don't get too much snow out there, huh?"

Harmony made a polite affirmative laugh. Travis, though, barely flashed a brief smile. More like baring his teeth. Normally Harmony would've gotten a guy to speak with him, because he was more likely to take men as trustworthy and knowledgeable, but she didn't want to reach out to her networks, not with Zach's probation coming up and the need to keep invisible heightened. Besides, there'd been no time.

She could only wait and see how Alice managed. Councilor Melissa's expression turned pensive. "We have to make do during our nice months. It means a lot, having an event like this, not just as a draw for the city, but for the sense of community it's built." And dang, she was doing just fine, because even Harmony felt convinced—and again wondered if she was doing enough to pay back all the people, all the kids, whose hopes and efforts were the engine of her scheme. Normally her cons prevented real harm by taking down their targets, and Travis and Cheryl *were* real dirtbags with too much influence, but this was also personal. She shook off the thought as Alice cocked a brow. "Though the economic boost is nothing to sneeze at. I admit, once Miss Hale started working her magic here, I figured, everyone else in town was getting a lift from the festival, the real unfairness would be denying my business the same. My employees. My investors."

Travis tapped his knuckles against his lips, before saying, "I've had some interest in taking my virtual reality arcade wider."

"You should jump on that if you can," Alice advised. "Franchising's turned my business into a self-running moneymaker. Left me so much more time to focus on my public service."

Travis shifted in his seat. "Wish I could. Things weren't helped with the recent questions going around about the nature of the entertainment." He shot Harmony a dark look.

Harmony met it with a thoughtful smile of her own, as if they were ruminating on a problem together. You had to let negativity like that glide right past you. "You know, our festival would be the perfect opportunity to showcase your business to investors. You could have a whole tent, let people come in and experience what you offer, let the money men see the engagement. Good family fun. Just like the festival."

Travis dropped his arm to the table and leaned forward. His graying brows rose. "My own tent?"

Harmony kept the smile she felt locked away, deep inside. It was a smile between her and her dad. "A big one."

She let Alice feed Travis more metrics about partner businesses' sales, but she could already read her success in the mayor's body language.

As Travis might say, this ship was leaving the station, with him on board.

CHAPTER EIGHTEEN
PRESTON

Preston's phone rang right at the end of dinner out at Dani's, and she insisted she'd get the dishes and then show Lacey what she'd been working on for her upcoming show. He took it out on Dani's porch, because only one person besides her or spammers actually called his number.

"Will."

His college roommate's British accent was tinny. "Hey, how are you doing?"

That was a bigger question than it usually was, whenever Will checked in every six months or so, and one of the reasons Preston had reached out earlier that week. He tapped the mezuzah on the wide doorframe and sat on the top step, looking out at twilight falling over the wild garden, littered with Dani's sculptures. "Complicated."

"Interesting."

"Where are you?"

"In transit, heading to Japan." Will had majored in music like Preston but had gone on to make a career of it, which took him around the world. He'd call at random times while waiting for planes or stuck on a bus. Even if they played phone tag for the better part of a year, with a few texts here and there, Will never let it drop, like most of Preston's friends from college had once they'd graduated or the rest had once he'd disappeared back home.

"Nice."

"It is. How's it going over there?"

"Oh, lots of excitement. Legend Watts might be playing this new festival here?"

"Huh, I had not heard that."

"Really?" Preston scraped his shoe along the edge of the step. "The festival promoter was saying the announcement was coming." He actually hadn't seen Harmony for days; she'd gotten buried with some request of Travis Weaver's and they'd only had a chance to text a few times—leaving Preston plenty of chances to mentally replay the hottest time in a library since Alexandria burned. And, of course, because his brain was a nightmare that couldn't simply let him enjoy that, worry about it.

"Eh, people throw big names around a lot. Building hype, to get interest from whoever they end up signing. It's all part of the process."

"Yeah." That did sound like Harmony.

"Or they're still talking with management, early stages, that kind of thing. Wouldn't hear about it yet until it was more official. You know what a nightmare handling those big name artists is."

"Egos the size of elephants."

"Legend Watts especially," Will said.

"Yeah, that guy sounds like a jerk. But you can't deny his talent."

"That's what they say. So—" Will's voice turned curious. "What's complicating things?"

I finally met someone, Preston thought, *and I think I like her too much so I was going to break things off but instead I made out with her in the library and I think I'm heading for a heartbreak even an album of Legend Watts ballads won't heal.*

Will was used to Preston sometimes getting caught up in thought. "Let me guess. A woman."

That seemed insufficient to describe Harmony somehow. "Less a woman than three schemes in a trench coat."

"*Very* interesting. That does sound complicated."

It had seemed very, very simple the moment Harmony had touched him, in the upstairs stacks. And afterward, when she'd looked absolutely radiant at the market. He couldn't stop staring, knowing what had put that extra glow all over her, that pink in her cheeks. The way she'd danced like she didn't give a shit a crowd was watching. She always danced to any music—even without noticing, rocking her head along with whatever was playing at a restaurant or even someone's ringtone.

The last rays of sunlight were slipping through the branches of the oaks and lighting up the redbuds' petals like lanterns. The brambles were already bathed in dusk, with rabbits venturing out from their cover toward the grass. Creatures that would race away fast as soon as Preston made a move.

The better things got with Harmony, the more he felt like he was waiting for the axe to fall. Like when he'd come out here with his mom as a kid, on days she and Dani would talk and bake or can fruit together for hours. He'd be able to relax, be himself. But then it was always that much harder going home and facing his father's expectations.

And like when he'd finally gotten away for good, gotten the scholarship and spot in the music program, and thought things might be all right, building a life for himself, seeing his parents only occasionally, while they had their clean slate, their new baby—that was when everything fell apart worse than even his worry-prone mind had really ever imagined.

He and Will talked for a bit longer, catching up and discussing some recent releases they'd both liked, before they said good night/good morning and Preston went to find Dani and Lacey. The rabbits scattered when he stood.

Dani had a show planned at the big gallery out on the coast, and her studio out behind the house was filling up with more half-finished pieces than usual, small vases shaped like roses and pinecones and large ones Lacey could probably crawl inside, tall sunbursts and writhing metal vines with ceramic leaves. Lacey, of course, was already poking at a pile of clay at one work table, and Dani was at her wheel, slurry all over her hands and something forming under them. They were so predictable, for all Dani's eccentric artist reputation in town.

"Thought you were cleaning up, and yet." He angled his head pointedly at the drips falling on Dani's stained sneakers and the smudges already on Lacey's T-shirt.

Dani smirked at her clay. "Oh, there's time to hose Lacey off before dessert." She could probably use it, after how she'd raced around the garden playing some pretend game while he and Dani had been cooking. There was still a puff of cottonwood seeds stuck in her hair.

Lacey looked back and forth at them both, intently. "You are not being serious right now."

"I'm always serious." Preston mugged a frown at his sister and walked into the spacious old barn. "I seriously want to know what you're making."

"A crab." Lacey began rolling out a noodle of clay that looked like the bucatini they'd had for dinner.

"Can't wait to see it." He settled on a stool near Dani.

"Process above product," Dani sang out like she always did, before asking, in a low voice that didn't carry above the whir of her electric pottery wheel, "How's school going these days?"

Preston fiddled with the end of a clay wire cutter on the stand of tools beside them. "Seems better. No more reports of trouble." Lacey was being left alone at lunch. And recess. And in class. And that was the current worry rolling around his head—not bothered, thank god, but not befriended either. Her therapist insisted her social skills were coming along just fine, but Preston was sure there was more he ought to be doing—setting up playdates? Yet every time he suggested it Lacey always said she wanted to go home after school or the library. He was literally the last person to know how to help. He still didn't quite know how he'd stumbled into things with Harmony. He still didn't know what he was going to do about how that entire situation was like a joyride heading straight for a cliff.

Like the shape Dani was pulling from centrifugal force and the sloping movements of her hands. He knew from years of watching her work it could either come together as a new, expanded thing or suddenly *flomp* over.

Preston watched the walls of wobbling clay, feeling caught in the same moment of uncertain balance.

Things had been so, so bad. And then, slowly, they were all right. He'd been hanging on to all right so hard, he didn't know what might happen if he reached for anything more.

Maybe that was why, when he met Harmony for lunch out in the gazebo that week, he greeted her, "Hey, Trouble."

Of course she only preened, flourishing a deli box stuffed with a couple of wraps, bags of chips, lemonades, and a pile of about a thousand napkins.

It was a full week—he'd had extra meetings with Katherine to discuss the impending, still unscheduled inquiry into the library from town hall—and Harmony had suggested lunch so they could see each other, but it occurred to him this wasn't for work, like when she'd always insisted on using her expense account for everything.

"You have to let me take you out," he told her between bites of his turkey and avocado. "Properly."

"Properly," she agreed in a ridiculously fancy voice. She smiled and stole one of his chips. "Sounds nice."

"Dani's taking Lacey this Saturday, if that's good?" She'd caught wind over dessert of how he'd been spending time with Harmony, and Preston suspected she'd asked to have Lacey again as part of her ongoing campaign for him to get a life. At least she hadn't entirely given up on the idea of romance, if not for herself—for all her putting her hand in, Dani had never moved on from whatever disaster in her past had put her off relationships, the barest details of which she'd only shared after too many Negronis a few Thanksgivings ago.

"Sure," Harmony said. "You should come to the auditions that afternoon too. Give your expert opinion."

"I'll still have Lacey, Dani's at the gallery until evening." And he had to be careful here—he never wanted to make Lacey feel like she was a burden or an unwanted package being passed around.

"Bring her along." He must have looked dubious, because Harmony laughed. "She's one child, how disruptive could she be?"

Lacey was admittedly pretty chill most of the time, but storytime with some kids could turn into World War Three. "Have you been around children much?"

"Not at all," she said brightly. "But I have the advantage of actually having been one, versus you, I assume, having emerged from the womb wrapped in tweed and a scowl." He was still fighting the resulting aggrieved scowl off his face when she added, "And, like, mortgage papers."

That was unfair, he'd inherited his mortgage. Thank god for the absurdly low property tax rate that had come with it. Another reason if, despite their efforts, things went wrong with that inquiry and he got fired, relocating would be a supreme, budget-destroying pain in the ass.

He didn't want to think about all that right now, when he had to get back to work in just a bit. So he sniffed and told Harmony, "I like this jacket."

"So do I." She leaned over and smoothed his lapel, which was not in need of smoothing.

He wasn't above finding an excuse to touch her either, slipping his fingers through her hair and tucking it behind her ear. "You sure?"

She made a low, considering hum. "Nerd chic, I must have a kink for it."

He tugged the lock of hair. The scowl was definitely back. "About Lacey."

"Bring the kid! It's going to be a bunch of teenagers already. It's not the board room, it's the music biz. Halsey brought her baby backstage at concerts, this one tour—"

She rattled off stories of other musicians who'd done the same, reassuring him, but he was already thinking that Saturday night would be a good time for the talk he knew they needed to have before things went much further. He'd already taken things faster than he normally would, and that should be addressed. Yes. He was going to do this right and have a very adult conversation with Harmony about what he wanted out of a relationship, and her plans—namely, leaving—and all that. Properly.

* * *

When they arrived Saturday, the auditorium at the high school wasn't exactly giving off a rock-and-roll vibe. Dozens of teens from all over the area were unloading instruments in the parking lot under the watchful eye of the giant Bobcat mascot painted on the building, warming up voices in the halls, and standing around in the aisles of the theater where Harmony had set up a long table in the open area before the low stage. She had interns running around with clipboards, handing out numbers to each group or performer.

"We'll get started in just a bit," Harmony said as they gathered at the front of the house. She was wearing a bright red dress today and stood out even in the half-dimmed space. "It's a great turnout. Here—" She dug in her bag on the table. "Lacey, I brought snacks. Granola bars, candy—"

"Oh, no," Preston warned his sister. "You don't want that."

Harmony froze and looked at him. "Because you shouldn't take candy from strangers?"

"No, just you." He made a gagging face at Lacey. "Because it's probably black licorice." Which he actually liked a little, but he liked seeing Harmony screw up her face in that indignant little pout more.

"How dare you. That licorice is *mine*." She laid a protective hand on her purse and tossed a pack of strawberry gummies to Lacey. "No stealing my delicious, perfect candy." She winked. "Unless it's to hide some in your brother's Wheaties. That'd be funny."

"That would be a felony." He went on, even as Lacey smiled and Harmony waved Jordan over from the front of the stage where a couple of bands were already waiting. "No. A venial sin. At least."

"Just a joke," Harmony clarified to Lacey. "Never listen to me."

Jordan ran up, a few other interns trailing her. "Keyboard and drums are set, and all the amps and mics. We're going to have the first group do a sound check, and then it should be pretty fast getting through each."

"Great. You guys are doing spectacular. Jordan, you're gonna emcee for us."

"What? No."

"Yes. Come on, you got up in front of that whole town hall meeting."

Jordan lifted her clipboard, hiding half her face behind it. "I was running mostly on sheer spite and adrenaline." She cast a desperate look to Preston.

He held up his palms. "I'm with you." He could only hope Cheryl Weaver proved a consistent motivator when it was time to speak at his upcoming meeting.

"Okay," Harmony said, pulling Jordan farther away from the other kids with an arm around her shoulder. "Here's my secret."

Jordan groaned. "If you're about to tell me to picture everyone in their underwear, I promise that is going to make it like a thousand times worse."

Lacey, digging into her strawberry gummies, let out a little snort.

Harmony shot her a stern look but with a glint in her eye. "Eat your second-rate candy and let me bestow my wisdom." She turned again to Jordan. "Look, you just need to understand: people want you to do well. No one wants to see someone flop. Any audience is rooting for you. Even if there are haters, they don't want that funny feeling in their stomach or under their skin of seeing someone mess up. It's awkward, and no one wants any part of that. People want to believe in you, they want to agree. Well—" Harmony glanced at Preston. "Maybe not Mr. Jones because he's prickly and uncomfortable all the time." He couldn't even glower back at her, because Jordan was taking deep breaths in through her nose and starting to nod along. "But otherwise. It works with a big audience or one on one. You remember that when you're out there working to make the world a bit better."

Nina, as always, was not far from Jordan and hustled up to her side now. "List is checked off, except we need the stage lights angled to the front of the stage. The spring musical tech crew left them pointing at the ceiling because those pop tarts think they're hilarious. I couldn't reach."

Harmony dropped her head to one side, casting an imploring look at Preston. "Do you mind?"

"On it." He had a feeling he'd do far more if she asked. Sins venial and mortal. Possibly high treason. How the hell was he going to talk to her tonight? It was going to be harder than speaking in front of town hall.

Some parents had come and were already sitting, waiting for acts to start, or clumped along the aisle chatting. Sarah Lessner, who'd matched him drink for drink at the Moonlight last month, came walking past where the stage lights hung along the wall, currently illuminating the top of the proscenium. "Hey, Preston, have you seen Mason?"

"I haven't." He reached up and adjusted the first light. "Joey playing today?" Her older son had taken lessons for a while before quitting for varsity baseball.

She nodded. "Keyboard with Bonnie's and Libby's kids." She blew out a breath and scanned the theater. "Mason's running around here somewhere too. They both have done just great with you."

"Thanks. I'm glad Joey's keeping it up." He made his way along the strip of lights.

"Yeah, well, being in a band is how you get girls, apparently. Not regular showers without your mom and dad yelling at you."

He laughed, pulling the final light down as a chord of music blared through the theater. *Shit.* He dug in his pocket for the case with Lacey's ear plugs, turning back to see Harmony already popping expensive-looking headphones from her purse onto his sister's head.

Harmony must have felt Preston's warm gaze on her, because she glanced over her shoulder and caught him looking. She'd been bending over toward Lacey, and as his sister ran off to sit in the front row, he realized it looked like he'd been staring at Harmony's ass. She flashed him a grin and shimmied a little, swinging her hips along with the band's warm-up song and sending another kind of heat flushing over Preston's face.

Fuck it. Forget the serious talk, that was the last thing he wanted to do with Harmony. He wanted her, so much, more, all of her—but he'd take whatever he could get. For so long he'd wanted *someone*, the idea a shadow that seemed now more like his own loneliness, while Harmony was bright as a sun and abundantly herself. She was so much, extravagant in her liveliness and kindness and, yes, that body, holy hell. His hands clenched at the memory of those curves in his grip, hungry for more, and now, as she turned back to the stage, he really was transfixed by her gorgeous ass.

Surely whatever little bit of her he was allowed would have to be enough for him.

He fixed the lights on the far side of the stage, thinking how the slivers of time they'd spent together had already filled his weeks with so much more than he'd imagined dating around his schedule might. He refused to spend any more time worrying about how it would feel when it all eventually ended.

It was almost impossible, sitting in a folding chair next to her for hours of student acts. She'd lean over to whisper about one band that was incredible, or do that grooving little chair dance of hers, or meet his eyes with a perfectly blank expression when he knew she was dying to grimace or laugh at a particularly out of tune performance. She took notes in her folio, and Nina wrangled acts, and Jordan did fantastic introducing each as parents and other teens cheered in the audience behind them.

He checked on Lacey a couple of times, who seemed content watching the show, her backpack with the books she'd packed still flopped over on the floor by her feet. But during a ten-minute break midafternoon, as a couple of the bands who had already performed gathered around Harmony and she recounted some stories of the music industry that rivaled Will's, Preston suddenly realized Lacey had wandered on stage, over to the keyboard.

He started to get up, but Harmony grabbed his wrist. "She's fine."

Lacey began playing an arrangement of "Mercury" from one of his lesson books. He'd taught her, of course. Sitting side by side at the piano had been one of the only ways they'd spent their time in those first weeks as they figured out their new normal together. But she'd never wanted to join in for student concerts. She stumbled over the opening but kept going.

Harmony's fingers slid down and squeezed his. "She's really good."

"Well. Her brother's an asshole taskmaster." Who had to swallow down a lump of pride seeing his sister brave even this semipublic performance. Kids were talking, more voices echoing from the hallway, but some of them stopped and watched Lacey, hair fluttering as she leaned over the keys. And when she finished, a bunch of them clapped.

"Watch out, Legend Watts!" Harmony yelled as she applauded.

When Lacey sat back down, Preston saw Mason join her in the front row, asking her something. Before long they were whispering together, heads close over the bag of candy, and Preston had an entirely new distraction through the end of the auditions, as he tried not to turn around too many times to convince himself Lacey was actually making a friend her own age, and make sure she was still doing okay, in Harmony's headphones again, listening to music with Mason beside her.

By the time they got through everyone, it was almost dinnertime. Kids streamed out of the auditorium, hauling instrument cases and yelling and generally being teenagers. Sarah Lessner came up while Harmony was talking with the interns.

"Mason's asking if Lacey can come over to play tomorrow afternoon? I know it's last minute; it's okay if you're busy."

Preston looked to Lacey, who nodded. "No, that'd be great. Text me?"

"Sounds good. Come on, Mason!"

He took Lacey out to the parking lot to find Dani, who was picking her up here.

Dani grabbed Lacey's backpack as she climbed into the Jeep. "I was going to come inside to find you."

"You were going to come inside to spy on someone." Dani wasn't satisfied with what he'd shared so far about Harmony.

Dani cackled. "Humor an old lady."

"You're not old!"

She hopped into the driver's seat. "Have a nice night, babe."

God, he hoped he would.

When he got back inside, the place had cleared out and Harmony was slinging her purse over her shoulder. "It has been *a day*." She walked up the aisle, mischief playing around her mouth and effervescent in her eyes. "I feel like a mess. Do you mind if we stop by my hotel so I can freshen up before dinner?"

She was such a liar.

"Not at all."

CHAPTER NINETEEN
HARMONY

Harmony opened the door to her hotel room and gave it a quick scan. Bed made by someone else every day. Clothes and dry-cleaning bags in the open closet space on hangers locked around the rod, shoes lined up below. She'd hoped they'd end up here tonight, so that morning she'd dumped any other clothes laying around into the dresser across from the foot of the bed.

The bed that waited in the room like the answer to a question brewing between them the entire drive over, as she let Preston pretend to fix her dress's hem when she scooted closer at a red light, and his fingers pinched and played with the fabric the rest of the way. The air had thickened between them on the walk up the covered stairs, Preston's big hand steadying at her back.

No more pretending. Harmony turned and reached past Preston to grab the do-not-disturb sign, hung it outside the door, then shut it with a click.

Preston's eyes were on her, their blue charged like the sky before a thunderstorm. "Dani will have Lacey until she drops her at Mason's tomorrow."

She slid her bag gently to the floor, without breaking eye contact. "That's nice. You won't have to be up early." It felt like Preston promising not to rush her off like the last time they'd spent a night together. He was giving her his full attention, and she knew how precious that was.

He took his time now, shifting a small, deliberate step nearer. Leaning in toward her. Like a magnet attracted to his mouth, she swayed forward, and he dipped his head down, pressing his lips to hers.

At the library he had seemed like a starving man, desperate for each kiss before what he wanted could be snatched away. Now he savored her, sipping gentle kisses from her mouth, running his hand over her hair.

But soon the intensity built. Slow and sweet kisses became the play of their tongues together. His hands ran down her back, and the way he was holding on to her, his height cradling over her, made something catch inside Harmony. She slid her hands from Preston's chest to clutch around his neck, hooked her fingers through his hair, and pulled herself against him.

There was no pretending he wasn't as excited for this as she was, not with the hardness that met her fluttering stomach. He clasped her tight and kissed her until she was breathless. But when one hand skated up from her ass to find the pull of her zipper, she shifted back.

"Right," Preston said, hands skimming to tentatively rest upon her shoulders. His eyes brimmed with yearning, pupils blown black against blue. He wrenched their gaze from her mouth to meet her own. Swallowed hard. "Right. Dinner."

"No." She could have laughed, because, ha, *no*, except something was making her stomach twist into enough knots to rival a pretzel stand. The wild urge to tell him, before this went further, who he was really kissing.

Her heart raced even faster than Preston's touch had set it pounding. What was she thinking? She couldn't torpedo her con. Preston's rule-following must have been rubbing off on her. That was the last thing of his she wanted rubbing off on her tonight.

It was the uncertainty that shivered over Preston's features that snapped her out of it. He looked lost. She'd done that to him, when they were supposed to be having fun, finishing what they started last week in the library. He wanted more but not that much.

So she stepped back, in her nude heels, and reached for the zipper herself.

Preston's gaze on her now was something palpable, hot as a spotlight, as she drew the dress open and peeled one shoulder down, revealing the strap of her plum lingerie set. She always did love putting on a show. She slipped the other sleeve off, and with a small shake of her hips let the dress fall to the floor. "You ready to get into Trouble?"

He didn't even scowl or roll his eyes at that. For a moment he looked as drunk as he had that night at the bar. Then his stare snapped back up to her face, full of intention. Like he knew he was indeed deeply in trouble and meant to enjoy every single second of it.

He strode across the room, somehow tugging her against him and backing her toward the bed at the same time. His hands were back on her, thank god, running over her bare skin, playing with the lacy edge of her underwear. He kissed her deep and hard, tongue sweeping over hers, teeth raking her lips.

When they hit the side of the bed, she let herself fall under his rush of kisses, which traveled down her neck now, as Preston braced himself above her, knees brushing her own. She toed off her shoes and kicked them away.

She couldn't wait to get more of him and impatiently kissed his jaw, along his ear, loosening his tie and drawing it away before working the front clasps of her bra open one by one.

He leaned on his elbow so he could spread a hand over one freed breast and *yes god* his touch was warm and firm and made her immediately feel like some kind of treasure, discovered and secured by his penetrating stare.

"*Fuck*," Preston breathed over her skin.

She managed to say, around her insides clenching and the instinct to gasp, "For a guy who works with books"—a shiver escaped her lungs—"your vocabulary's awfully limited."

His lips twisted wryly. "Sorry, I left my thesaurus at home." Then he applied that smirk to her skin and there were no words needed at all, none that might possibly describe the heaven of Preston's mouth stroking over her breast, slowly, gradually, *agonizingly* honing in on her nipple.

She grazed her fingers over his back, up through his hair.

"Do that more firmly." He spoke into the wide hollow between her breasts. "It feels wrong unless—"

"Autism thing?"

"Mm-hm." He had already moved his mouth to her other breast, and it was no problem at all for Harmony to dig her fingers into his back, to claw them through his curls, over his scalp.

Preston slid back, hand still massaging her breast as he kissed down her side and sank to his knees.

"*Preston*."

"Let's see how articulate *you* are in a minute." His fingers snared the lace and dragged it free from her hips. He shifted back on his heels, removing his glasses and folding them before carefully placing them on the bedside table.

When he leaned forward it was to spread her thighs, looking for all the world like he was opening a book he was *very* interested in studying. His eyes had a slightly unfocused look that didn't quite catch on Harmony's face as he asked, "Okay?"

"I'm gonna give you a late fine if you don't hurry up."

"We don't give late fines anymore. They're inequitable."

A swell of feeling for how sweet he was, how sincere, washed through her. Preston never bullshitted.

But she was immediately distracted by another feeling, because Preston certainly wasn't bullshitting now as he laid his mouth down between her thighs. There was only heat and the perfect balance of soft and insistent he learned quickly from her sharp inhalations and how her hips bucked, especially when he swept his mouth down and circled her clit with his thumb, chasing it back with a swirl of his tongue. She writhed under him, holding on to fistfuls of bedsheets. "Fuck."

He laughed, breath warm over her sensitive skin. His hand stilled. "Can I—?"

She scoured her hand through his hair again. "I've only been imagining you inside me all damn week."

Preston groaned at that, sending a gratifying vibration up through her pelvis as he kissed her. He dipped a finger inside her, and soon another, delivering delicious friction he played in counterpoint to the velvet glide of his tongue. When he hooked them upward it set off red sparks through her, and his mouth sucked at her clit, and she moaned "*God, fuck, yes, Preston*" as her orgasm lit and rolled through her like lightning and thunder at once.

Preston kept working his hand in her, tasting her, while she floated back from where he'd sent her. But like she'd told him, she always wanted more, and it seemed like every taste she got of him only drove her need for another. She tugged on his hair until he drew over her, and then she grabbed him by the belt loops and pulled him down to kiss him slow and thoroughly while she worked his buckle open and the fly of his pants.

He'd been dressed up for their dinner, clearly, and now he shrugged out of his jacket and began unbuttoning his shirt. Not fast enough. She helped too until their hands met in the middle of his heaving chest.

He captured her fingers and pressed a kiss to her knuckles. "You're so fucking gorgeous," he murmured against them. "And I've wanted—" He interrupted himself with another kiss, to the flesh between her finger and thumb. "I thought so the minute I first met you."

"You thought I was Cheryl Weaver's minion and yelled at me to go away."

He ducked his face to her hand, hiding a smile. "It was a very confusing minute." He reached to kiss her on the mouth. "Thank you for staying long enough for me to see how wrong I was."

That flare of something inside her ribcage again made Harmony's breath hitch. She got what she wanted plenty with her looks, but knowing he'd only acted on that attraction once he'd grown to know her, once he'd seen through so much of her facade she threw at the world, made her feel a little bit like she'd been turned inside out—and like she was still safe, even exposed like that, with Preston. Maybe because he spent so much time masking himself from others too.

She pushed his shirt off his shoulders. "Well, obviously I wasn't going anywhere until I got to see your tits."

He rolled his eyes so hard his head actually drifted backward a little. "You—"

"Yeah?" She scraped her fingers through his dark chest hair.

But Preston's only answer was to drive his mouth against hers again. She worked his pants down over his narrow hips, and his boxers, and oh lord, she was not a patient woman, but Preston was a tall man, and this had been worth the wait.

When she wrapped her hand around him, he pressed his forehead to hers. "Fuck. *Harmony.*"

No one said her name like that. No one cried it out or groaned it or whispered it reverently like Preston. She was always Claudia or Trish or Megan or whoever she was that month, and whoever she was with didn't often bother to remember those aliases anyway. Zach knew her real name, but he wasn't one to whisper anything sweet in your ear.

Preston did, as she pumped her hand over his erection and brushed her thumb over the head of his cock. His hands clenched on either side of her head and he breathed her name again. *Harmony. Sweetheart. Please.* He kicked free of the last of his clothes and she pulled him down beside her, head to pillow, and climbed on top of him.

"Wait, in my wallet, I have a condom—"

"So do I." She leaned over to grab one from the bedside table drawer. "In my purse too." She hadn't been about to let another chance at him pass. And, damn, all that biking must have paid off in the lean, toned muscles under her now.

He grinned up at her. "You brought treats for everyone." He caught her breast and licked it before she sat back to open the foil.

Once he was set, she shifted up from his thighs to slide herself along him. He hissed with pleasure, so she rocked along him a few more times before falling forward, braced on the headboard, to guide him inside her. They were both gasping as she worked herself down his length. Her hand clenched the headboard hard.

She gave herself a moment and felt Preston, hands splayed hot over her thigh and ass, straining not to take this too fast. Harmony pitched against him, chest to chest, kissing his shoulder, nipping where it met his neck, teasing his ear. His turn to have someone take care of him. She moved slowly, and god he felt so good, there was no need to rush; she reveled in the sensation as she eased forward and sank back down against the base of his cock for an eternity or two.

His hips jolted up against her, all that restraint slipping at last, and it was too good, she wanted more, so she sat back to drive herself over him. She looked down and Preston was smiling an utterly blissed-out smile, wide across his sweat-sheened face, dark lashes low over his blue, blue eyes. It might have been the truest, most beautiful thing she'd ever seen.

Then he swiped his tongue over the pad of his thumb and took hold of her breast, rubbing circles over her nipple and pinching gently. Everything she was feeling dialed up to fucking eleven. She clenched hard around him, and his thrusts sped.

Preston's fingers dug into her hip, holding her in place. He was crying out her name again, shuddering so hard and *oh god* she was always in control, could always get ahead of whatever was coming for her, but right now a relentless tide was crashing over her, pulling her tight, drawing her onward to break against a climax that seared her vision white.

Undone, melting forward, Harmony could only remind herself to breathe as Preston kissed her and kissed her, slow and deep. Sink into the bedsheets as he pulled her down to him and stroked his fingers along her heavy limbs. Enjoy far too much how he cuddled her against his chest, where she could hear the steady, brisk drum of his heartbeat.

She was in so much trouble.

CHAPTER TWENTY
PRESTON

It didn't mean anything.

Not when Harmony came clenched around him and Preston thought he might actually die from how spectacular it felt. Not when she insisted they stay in, order Thai food, and afterward pulled him down on top of her again. Not when she dozed off in the middle of talking nestled against him and he was so fucking content, even knowing he never slept the first night in a new place. Not when he actually slept great, not when he woke to her arm flung over him, not when she stirred and smiled up at him a little sheepishly and kissed him like it was the only thing on her to-do list for the whole day.

Not even when he'd almost let it slip, the night before, how it felt like he'd wanted her for even longer than he'd known her, how she made him gladly ready to break all his rules.

And certainly not when she rose from the bed to shower, bare assed, and over her shoulder asked if he was coming.

She was such a menace and she knew it and he loved it. But, he reminded himself as he climbed out of her bed, this was still only for now, short term, until she left. He was going to get that through his head. And while he worked on that, he was going to enjoy the best goddamn shower of his entire life.

She was drying her hair when he went to put on his glasses, resting beside a thick book on the bedside table. "You know this is from the Santa Barbara Library?"

Worry pinched her brow. "Sorry, this too loud?" She wasn't using the small hotel dryer still clipped to the wall, but her own that looked sleek and modern and probably expensive, like a spaceship.

He waved *The Oleander Sword* at her. "This has got to be overdue."

Harmony gave a vague, bright smile and half-shouted, "Yeah, be my guest!"

He gave up and was halfway through the second chapter, sitting on the edge of the bed, when she was done getting ready. "There's yogurt in the fridge, if you don't want to wait." She invited herself into his lap. "Or we could go get breakfast?"

"I think we're firmly into brunch territory at this point." He set the book down, because Harmony was kissing his neck and he intended to savor every moment with her and also his brain might have sort of shorted out when her tongue slid into his ear. He cleared his throat. "Where should we go? Do you still need more places for the festival?"

She stopped kissing him, which was too bad, and rested her forehead against his neck. "I have a confession." That sounded worse. Preston tensed, trying not to dig his fingers into Harmony's back and thigh where he held her. "I did need to find vendors, but I may have asked you along, after you signed the lease, because I wanted to keep seeing you and wasn't sure how to ask." She started kissing him again, quickly.

He exhaled, half sigh of relief, half reaction to her touch. "Ah yes, Harmony Hale, famous shrinking violet." More like a Venus flytrap, the way she was drawing his earlobe between her teeth. His fingers definitely clenched into her a bit.

A puff of breath warmed his neck as Harmony made an embarrassed sound. "I don't actually date that much? Too busy with work. I guess I'm not very good at it, outside of, like, work functions."

"I think you're good at everything. Especially—" He turned his head, capturing that wicked mouth of hers and drawing her into a long kiss. When they broke apart for breath, he could feel her smug smile against his lips. "—annoying librarians." Her eyes glinted, and she fucking licked his face.

"Oh, my god!" He shoved her off him, tackling her onto the bed.

"What?" She laughed. "You liked it last time!"

He planted a kiss to her temple. "If you're that hungry, then, yes, let's go to brunch." He was certainly going to spend any time he could with her.

They stopped by his place so he could throw on some clean clothes. He and Harmony had tried so many different restaurants in the area, they had never just gone to the diner on Main Street. The normal hum of conversations and clatter of silverware greeted them, along with a waitress carrying a tray through to the back. "Hey, Preston. Any table."

He led Harmony to one near the windows, far from the noise of the kitchen.

Harmony sat across the little booth from him. "It's weird how everyone knows everyone in a small town."

He shrugged. "Jules worked with my mom."

"Here?" At his nod, she raised her brows. "Guess there are a lot of reminders of her everywhere."

Preston glanced around, thinking of afternoons doing homework at an empty table, his mom ruffling his hair as she rushed past. "Memories."

"That's nice." Harmony twisted her napkin. "I've kind of kept on the move, since my dad, well."

"Oh. I didn't know." The urge to somehow help, to ease the hurt in her voice, kicked in, but there was nothing to say to make that better.

"Yeah. When I was seventeen." She smiled weakly, drawing in a long breath through her nose. "Too much hard living." She seemed to notice she was destroying her napkin and dropped it. "But I have this to remind me of him." She held up her pinkie, where she always wore a gold ring delicately formed like three notes stacked up on top of each other, beside a sharp symbol.

"For Harmony?"

Her wavery smile grew. "Yeah. No one's ever noticed that."

Jules swung by then for their drink order, and Harmony reached for his hand and gave his fidget ring a spin. "I like yours too. Makes me think of you. I feel like I can always see your wheels turning."

He stared at her hand holding his over the table. It was such a simple thing, something everyone was always doing at other tables, but felt almost unreal happening to him after so long.

"Even when you're quiet," she said. Then her fingers contracted. "Oh, sorry, do you not want to, like, be public?"

He grabbed her hand back. "Don't be silly. Also, we've been going out together for weeks, the small-town gossip ship has sailed."

She squeezed his hand. "Good, don't want anyone else trying to move in on my territory."

That sort of lit him up inside to a dangerous degree, and he covered by joking, "Yeah, women were knocking down my door before you scared them away."

Her eyes narrowed. "Are you questioning my excellent taste?"

"You're right, watch out, one's behind you right now with a butter knife!" Her low chuckle was so familiar already and far too soothing.

He scratched at his stubbly jaw with his free hand. "Small towns." Where everyone knew him—as the odd one, or the sad one, or if he was lucky, the helpful one. Not the one they wanted to date. "Hard to meet someone who doesn't remember your awkward stage."

Harmony blinked innocently. "Oh, were you planning on growing out of it?"

He made a *very funny* face and gave her hand a gentle shake as Jules came back with their coffee and tea and a pointed, maybe pleased, look at their hands and took their order. While they waited, he told Harmony, who was still playing with his ring, "It's for stimming. Helps process sensory overload. Worries. Whatever."

She looked up at him, considering. "What are you worried about right now?"

So many things. That he was falling far too fast to catch himself. That he liked it when she said or did ridiculous things she didn't mean, that snapped him out of worrying and let him just be in the moment. With her. But he couldn't tell Harmony, pouring packets of sugar and creamer into her coffee now, all of that. It was too soon, he knew. You didn't tell women stuff like that after one night. And there wasn't even going to be a later for them when he might get to. "Lacey." That was always true. "If she'll do okay on her own today."

Harmony nodded and blew on her coffee. "Do you think she wants you there? I could drop you off."

"No." He ripped open a sugar packet and dumped it into his tea. After years of pretty serious clinginess, Lacey wanted friends her age, not to have her brother always hovering around. "Mason's a good kid and Sarah's great. Lacey's just had a rough time at school and can't always get across what she needs to." He added milk and stirred. "I might pace a trench in the kitchen floor until she's home. Fidgets can only do so much."

"Do you want to hang out till then? I'm very good at distracting people."

"No shit." He took a sip of his tea, thinking of the week he'd spent trying not to ignore all his work because she was there. "You should put that on your résumé."

She tossed back her hair. "There's no room after listing all my other talents."

"Right, because you contain multitudes. Distracting librarians. Inspiring local youth. Stealing library books."

Harmony lifted her mug like she could hide behind it. "Oops. It was too good to leave when I headed up here from the Santa Barbara Bowl. Good thing late fees are passé. I'll mail it back." She sipped her coffee. "Guess I picked up some bad habits, growing up the way I did."

"Rich people are weird."

Her coffee must have still been too hot, because she coughed a little. "Right."

She set it down, looking a bit uncertain, and he realized he hadn't actually answered. Because of course he wanted her to stay, as long as she could. "What do you want to do this afternoon, then?"

So after bacon and eggs and a comically tall pile of waffles and whipped cream, they went out on the town green and collapsed in a food coma on a blanket from Harmony's trunk, and eventually Harmony decided they would scroll through each other's playlists and share a memory about any song the other asked about.

"'Atlantis'?"

"Studying my brains out first year of grad school. 'High Hopes'?"

"My first job."

"Which was?"

"Stressful." Her finger didn't stop scrolling as she looked down at his phone, lying on her stomach beside him. "'Master Pretender'?"

Preston dropped his forehead to the blanket. "Trying to learn it on piano to impress a girl. My turn," he said over her chuckle. "'Thunderstruck'?"

"My dad blasted AC/DC while he worked. Why are all of these titles in Italian?"

He smirked and said (because by now he suspected Harmony wouldn't give him shit about it, or at least would give him shit while doing something surprising herself, which he was definitely interested in seeing), "È la lingua della musica."

Her mouth fell open. "Stop it. You speak Italian."

"Certo, un po'. Da mia madre. Ma principalmente perché lo usiamo nella musica."

Harmony narrowed her eyes. "Hmm. I'm gonna assume that was something incredibly romantic."

Preston's brain scrambled for any scrap of the Merini he'd read the past winter, but Harmony was muttering over his phone, "And why do you have so much Taylor Swift on here?"

"Lacey's obsessed."

"Okay, but 'All Too Well'?"

"What about you, with all these show tunes?" He nudged his shoulder into hers.

"I was a theater kid."

He looked out over the grass, where others were picnicking or skateboarding or falling asleep with open books shading their faces from the sun. "That explains so much."

She rolled onto her side, propping her hand on her hip like a lounge singer on top of a piano or Cleopatra carried on a palanquin or something, even in her jeans and T-shirt. "Star of my high school musical."

"Well, I don't believe that," he said flatly. "You simply lack the presence." She kicked him gently in the calf and rolled back over, a strip of tantalizing skin showing where her shirt rode up.

It wasn't his turn, but he wanted to know more. Sometimes she was so effusive with stories, but they were often about rock stars or music execs, not so much herself. "Who'd you play? Sandy in *Grease*? Maria in *Sound of Music*?"

"Ha." At his questioning look, she explained, like it was obvious, "They don't cast the fat girl as the ingenue."

"That's bullshit. Your voice is incredible."

"Which is why I played Mama Rose." She sighed dramatically. "Always the mother, never the future burlesque star."

He was about to tell her no one could compete with her striptease the night before when something on her playlist caught his eye. "Oh, no. Harmony. I'm so disappointed."

"What?" She actually sounded worried, and he fought the smile off his face as he held up her phone.

"Not Andrew Lloyd Webber."

She tsked. "*Superstar* is the exception."

"All the Sondheim redeems you."

"Such a snob. God, yours is just, like, half classical music. What's so great about Beethoven, anyway?"

"I mean, if you want to know, I got an entire degree that would allow me to explain."

"Please don't. Hold on, you didn't major in, like, books?"

He snorted. "Saved that for grad school. Hence the all-night study sessions." Undergrad had been easy compared to that. He'd spent as much time helping Will, who was dyslexic, pass his heavier classes, as studying himself.

A breeze played across the lawn, drawing a strand of Harmony's hair across her face as she scanned his playlists some more. "And a ton of obscure British singer-songwriters. Wait, you have, like, *every* Legend Watts album on here—oh!" She held out his phone. "Text from Sarah."

He dropped her phone on the blanket to grab his.

"Everything okay?"

He scanned the message. "Yeah." His shoulders relaxed. "She says they're having fun, and can she take them for ice cream before dropping Lacey off."

"Sounds like a success."

He texted Sarah back that it all sounded good. "Better head home soon." The wind ruffled through the red and white streamers taped to the fountain's statue to celebrate the Bobcats' win against Heraldale. Preston slid an elbow out so he could lean over and brush the hair back from Harmony's face, and left his hand there, cupping her cheek, thumb stroking over her cinnamon-sugar freckles. Because that was something he was allowed to do now. Because they were dating. "Dani's getting busy prepping for her show. Not sure when I'll have the chance to take you to dinner—"

"Oh, you *took me to dinner,*" she said with an eyebrow waggle.

"Is that supposed to be an innuendo? What does that even mean?"

She turned her head and kissed the edge of his palm. "I just say stuff, see what sticks."

"But I hope we can still see each other, even for a quick bite or something—" She nipped at his thumb before he could pull away. He shook his head, resigned. "Should have seen that one coming."

She rolled onto her back, arms bent behind her head, basking in the sunshine. "I don't mind mini-dates, even if it's not for the festival."

"Yeah?" The sunlight gilded the fringe of her lashes, illuminated her skin until she glowed, and that warmth seemed to spread right through his chest. She was so goddamn lovely.

"It's been fun."

"Yeah." Fun. They were having fun. And fun was good. Really, really good. Much better than bad, or even all right.

Even if part of Preston knew he simply wasn't built for it. That the fact that he'd gone to her hotel meant he already felt for Harmony far more than he'd admitted even to himself, that he felt more, too much, growing within him every time she touched him or made him laugh or shared another precious piece of herself.

That it all meant entirely too much.

To him, at least.

CHAPTER TWENTY-ONE
HARMONY

Sometimes Harmony imagined her life was a movie. A technicolor spectacle with chorus dancers backing her up as she walked down the street, just for an extra boost, or when she pulled off a tricky bit of grifting, swelling music celebrating her win.

If her life was a movie, then right now it would be a montage of her passing time in Brookville—meeting up with Alice for coffee or the *Bridgerton* marathon she'd nagged her into, giving Jordan impromptu lessons on persuasion as they signed on more participating groups and suppliers, keeping all the balls in the air for the festival, and whisking Preston away for lunch or a quick but highly enjoyable stop by her hotel. Sometimes afterward she'd pick Lacey up with Preston, but just like that day after the band auditions when she'd dropped him off ahead of Sarah arriving with his sister, she always left before she could be asked to leave. And that was cool. She was getting what she wanted, and she wasn't here to complicate his life further.

She'd come as clean as she could, she'd told herself. Let Preston know—once she'd admitted it to herself and without revealing her con against Travis—that this may have started with her angling for the festival site, but he'd been so damn stubborn about it, by the time he'd signed the lease her interest in spending more time with him had become genuine. Not that it really mattered, when the con would put an end to things soon enough, and Preston wasn't looking for anything too serious anyway. He'd as good as said so that awkward morning at his place.

But carpe diem and shit. Grab what you could when you could and run.

The sky was overcast when she arrived at the library one Friday a little early for Preston's lunch break. He was at the counter, and his eyes flicked up at her approach. His frown of concentration curled like an S, halfway into a smile. "Almost done. Last of the new audiobook orders." He kept typing and moving the mouse. His nails on his right hand were painted purple.

"Nice look. Very punk rock."

He glanced down, following her gaze. "Oh." His hand flexed. "Lacey's been practicing. Except we forgot, um—"

"Remover?"

"Yeah. That. Hence her moving on from her nails to mine. I'll have to pick some up this weekend."

"I've got some extra. Want me to maybe bring it by?" Unless he still didn't feel comfortable having her at his house. "Or next time I see you." Except that would be after this weekend, what was she saying? "I know you're careful about Lacey."

He finished whatever he was typing, and his mouth softened. "That would be great. Dani's coming over for dinner tonight? You could join us?"

There was a trace of uncertainty in his voice. "You sure?"

"If you'd want to?" His eyes lit with amusement. "It's one Harmony. How disruptive could she be?" He pursed his lips and tilted his head. "Actually—"

"Shut up," she said affectionately. "Come on."

* * *

It was raining by the time she got to his house that night, and she waited in the shelter of the porch until the door opened and Lacey stuck her head out.

"Hey." Harmony held out the bottle of nail polish remover. "Heard you need some of this."

Lacey took the bottle. "Hey. This—" She peered at the label. "Isopropyl acetone. Awesome."

"Harmony?" Preston's voice carried from inside. "Come in!"

Lacey didn't take her eyes off the bottle as she stepped back. "Please come inside."

"Thank you for having me." Preston had explained about Lacey not talking around others much, and how it was more about feeling overwhelmed than shyness, but it still shook the chill of the rain off Harmony to know Lacey felt okay around her here at home.

Preston leaned around the corner from the kitchen. "Hey."

"Hi." Harmony held up the red wine she carried in her other hand. "I also brought another kind of bottle."

"Thanks. Treats for everyone."

Harmony suppressed a snort, but stayed there standing a bit awkwardly in the entryway. She wasn't sure going in for a hello-kiss was appropriate in front of Lacey.

"Dani's running late. The rain." Preston ducked back into the kitchen, and Harmony came a little farther inside, placing the wine on the dining table, so she could see where he was chopping something at the counter. Whatever was already going on the stove smelled amazing. "She says. More likely she lost track of time in her studio. But we're aiming for dinner in about thirty minutes."

"Do you need any help?"

He scraped the contents of the cutting board into a steaming pan. "Didn't you say you don't cook?"

She shot finger guns. "I said I'm a terrible cook and burn everything."

"Um, I've got it, thanks."

Harmony turned back with a shrug to Lacey, who shot a finger gun at her. She was one cute kid. "Want me to do your nails?" Harmony knew her strengths at least.

The girl nodded. "We should take this upstairs. Steam and open flames and acetone don't mix. Or they *do*, but they *really* shouldn't."

So Harmony followed Lacey to her room, which was covered in more of the artwork Harmony had seen stuck to the fridge before, and a few perfectly folded paper stars. At the desk near an impressive-looking telescope she carefully took off Lacey's globby purple polish and showed her how to do two coats without gumming them up, and listened about pulsars and constellations while they waited for them to dry. Then she took off her coral matte she was going to redo that weekend anyway and let Lacey practice on her.

Harmony was blowing on her manicure as they came down to the sounds of Dani shouting hello. She'd seen Preston's friend in passing at the library, petite and with a mass of graying curls, but now Dani swept into the house with the presence of a much taller woman, holding a covered casserole dish sprinkled with raindrops, and pinned Harmony down at once with her stare. "Hello. I'm Dani."

Lacey ran up to Dani to show off her nails and received plenty of ooh-ing and ahh-ing. "Very nice, bunny. Go wash up?" Preston came out of the kitchen with a bowl of salad and placed it on the table. Dani thunked the dish down next to it. "Tiramisu. Sorry I'm late, babe." She gave Preston's shoulder a squeeze.

"Glad you could make it. I know it gets hectic before a show."

Dani turned back to Harmony. "I couldn't miss a chance to meet your lady friend."

"Oh, my god, don't call her that."

Harmony vamped down the last few steps. "Are you saying I'm not a lady?"

"Did you all want to eat or just gang up on me or . . .?"

Harmony stuck out a hand to Dani, who shook it with a wiry-strong grip. "Harmony."

They gathered at the table around salad, crostini with cheese and tomato, and pasta in a red sauce with chunks of squash, and dug in, except for Lacey, who Preston dished up a plate for with everything separate. After they ate, Dani insisted Lacey play for them and plopped down in the upholstered chair beside Harmony's, glass of wine in hand. Dani watched Lacey a while, Preston turning pages for her, before murmuring, "He's happier than I've seen him maybe ever."

Something played through Harmony's chest at those words, light and dancing, like the melody Lacey was plinking out.

Before she could say anything, Dani went on. "Don't fuck with him." She turned to Harmony, tone still conversational. "My kiln goes to two thousand degrees. There'd be no evidence."

Harmony's brows shot up before she could stop them. She'd heard a fair number of death threats before. It tended to happen when you emptied terrible people's accounts and ruined their cushy lives. But those were always full of bluster and impotent anger. Dani's words were laced with a fierce protectiveness.

"I like you," Harmony told her, a smile spreading across her face. "I'm glad someone in this town is watching out for him." Someone would be there for him, at least, when Harmony was far beyond the reach of even this slightly terrifying woman, and Preston found out Harmony had been lying this whole time.

"Hmm." Dani's eyes narrowed, assessing, and her mouth pulled into a crooked grin. "Yeah. I figured I'd like you too, if Preston did. He's an excellent judge of character."

That sat funny in Harmony's stomach. So she shoveled a plateful of tiramisu on top of the feeling to bury it, once Lacey asked if it was time for dessert (Dani had made half of the tiramisu without coffee). Harmony asked about Dani's show, and what kind of art she did, and admired a piece of hers framed on the wall behind her, a patchwork of green and black tiles stamped with patterns of leaves and seeds. Then Dani, simultaneously engaged in a thumb war with Lacey, interrogated Preston on whether he'd written anything lately.

"Written?" Harmony looked to Preston across the table. "Like books?"

"Composed. And no, not so much lately." He shoved the last bite on his plate into his mouth.

Dani lost to Lacey, which Harmony didn't believe for a minute. Dani was a secret softie. Even if she was also pushy, demanding, "Preston, play for us."

"Oh, come on, I'm eating."

"You're finished."

"With my *first* piece." He leaned over the table for the spatula. "It's just that good."

Dani rolled her eyes but laughed, and soon said she had to get home. "Loading up early tomorrow for a run to the gallery." She hugged Preston and waved goodbye to Lacey, who Preston told to go up to get ready for bed. Lacey then proceeded to drag bedtime out for several more minutes, bargaining with him to invite Mason for a playdate the next day. When his sister finally shot finger guns at them in farewell, Preston staggered back and dropped onto the couch, clutching his chest. Lacey laughed her way up the stairs.

Preston reached for Harmony's hand and pulled her down beside him. "Ha, she got you too." He wove their nail polished fingers together. "Now we match."

"You gonna do the other hand now she's getting good?"

"Eh." He lifted her hand to press a kiss to her knuckles. "Nina already immortalized the look in a video on her TikTok or wherever."

"Really?"

"She thinks she's sneaky. I'm pretty sure it was her last year who started a GoFundMe to buy me new shoes. The GSA kids linked it all over. Not because I needed any, they just thought mine were ugly."

Harmony snickered. "What a brat!" She seemed like such a goodie-goodie, with her fake swears and ASB work.

"No, I feel for her." He was playing with Harmony's hand, turning it one way and the other. "It's not easy, living with a parent who doesn't accept who you are."

Something about how he said that made Harmony think he knew from experience. But she wasn't pushing, she reminded herself. So instead she said, "You're a really good brother. You know that."

He raised his brows and blew out a breath. "I don't always know what I'm doing, but at least I know what Lacey's going through. Except for the beauty routine. Thanks again for the help there. I've been stumbling in the dark."

"But you're trying. You're staying and trying. She'll be okay." Maybe it was the coziness of the house under the soft patter of rain, the good food and familiar joking of the evening, that made her say, "My mom took off before I knew her, and I turned out fabulous."

Preston's gaze lifted from their hands to her face, eyes gentle but with that focus that made her feel as if he could see right inside her, and that was okay; all her hidden parts were safe with him somehow. "You really did," he murmured, and she knew he didn't mean her face or anything like that, with his words as tender as the kiss he pressed to her mouth.

It wasn't a kiss pushing toward anything more, or to forget everything but that moment, like so many. It felt like being known, and home, and belonging right here.

Where he'd asked her once to stay, and woken up to realize his mistake.

Preston leaned back, and she whispered, "Good night," and stood. It was harder than it should have been to leave, to head back out into the rain. But she did.

* * *

It rained all week, and she barely saw Preston. She had another wave of paperwork to throw together for Brookville's town hall, and he had a special weekend storytime event coming up. They grabbed lunch once, but otherwise she spent the rainy days reading, working on some social media posts, and going over festival contracts with Alice in preparation for taking vendor payments.

When they were wrapping up one evening at her apartment, Alice's face pinched as she hunched over her laptop, sitting cross-legged on her bed.

"What?" Harmony asked, knocking a sheaf of contracts into an even stack on Alice's desk. Rain sheeted over the window it stood under. "Is someone wrong on the internet again?"

"You got a ping on one of your old business emails."

"Someone has work for us?" Harmony slid the papers into her folio and stuffed it in her bag. She didn't take jobs with her old crews anymore. She liked doing things her way.

Alice chewed her lip. "No. It was Zach."

Harmony's hand stilled halfway zipping her Gucci tote closed. Alice turned the screen around, and she sank to the side of the bed to read the email, which featured an impressive amount of cursing and threats for one message. "Oh, darling, you're as romantic as ever," she muttered flatly. "He hasn't learned any manners in jail." Zach had never limited himself to the more artful techniques of persuasion Harmony preferred, resorting all too often to harsh words and twisting arms.

"You were right to leave him to the wolves."

Harmony sighed. "Maybe I was the wolf."

"I never liked the guy," Alice said, shaking her head, "and you know my asshole detector is finely tuned. Especially for men who put their hands on people without permission." Her dark expression fell on Harmony's hand rubbing one elbow. "He got what he deserved, just like every other jerk we run jobs on." She pulled her computer onto her lap, worry creeping back over her face. "If he's out, it's not safe to stay in one place too long. Not till he cools off."

Harmony hugged herself tighter, as if she could hide from the anxiety she'd been ignoring like a champ since Zach's release popped up on her phone that week. *No panicking.* She stood. There was no reason to freak out. She'd never used the name Hale before. Never told Zach about her plans for Travis Weaver. He had no way of finding her here. "Using the old email I handed to him is as far as Zach is likely to get trying to pin me down."

Alice nodded, seeming to relax. "And we'll be gone soon enough."

"Right." An unease Zach's email hadn't created brewed in her gut now. She fiddled with her bag's strap. It was good to keep moving on, she told herself, to keep things short and sweet. Before they turned into Zach twisting your arm. That was all she got trying for anything more.

Alice tilted her head up at Harmony. "It's still pouring, do you want to order in some egg rolls and watch Anthony Bridgerton discover the glory of Kate Sharma's bare thigh?"

"Again?" Harmony brushed aside thoughts of how very sweet things with Preston were and rolled her eyes. "You're such a sucker for fictional assholes."

Alice clasped her hands together under her chin and gave Harmony an imploring look. "Come on. I have a cheesecake in the freezer. Maybe this time Anthony's shirt will actually dissolve when he falls into that lake."

Harmony dropped her purse back on the desk and grinned. "Guess I'm a sucker too." She settled on the bed as Alice arranged her laptop and cued up Netflix. She would always have Alice. No matter how many times her friend got distracted by guys with dimples or ridiculous biceps and cute bellies or translucent shirts, Harmony would never cut her loose. She was like a sweet little baby duckling following her around—a sweet baby duckling who ran illicit online gambling sites in her spare time. One who was far too grateful for how Harmony had taken her back to her little hometown and put an end to the church and the reputation of the man who'd given that sweet baby duckling that world-class asshole detector and a hard edge beneath all the fluff. Alice flopped back to the pillows with a sigh as a string quartet and Julie Andrews's soothing tones drowned out the thrum of rain on the studio's roof.

* * *

Saturday the clouds moved off, and everything was that unreal bright green against the retreating gray, so the town square was swarming with people finally getting outside and enjoying the patchy sunshine. Harmony met Preston and Lacey for lunch out there before the special storytime, which was going to feature a drag queen along with several "real live princesses" and a parade through the library, according to Lacey. She'd taken about two bites of the BBQ Harmony had brought before the excitement made her jump up and was currently racing around the fountain—its statue wearing a rainbow bikini top and swimming goggles today—with Mason, whose family was picnicking a few blankets over.

"Everyone's worked up about it," Preston said while he and Harmony ate and caught up. "This seems to have tipped Cheryl into demanding they set a date for the special inquiry. On the schedule for next month."

"Because of one drag queen? It's not like you invited Hayley Kiyoko for a book talk and she's bringing the entire cast of *All Stars* to lip sync for their lives in the stacks."

Preston dropped his chin, shooting a serious look over his glasses at her. "First of all, that would be amazing, can you help us book her?" Harmony snorted. "And we've had Rosey do smaller storytimes before! It's a great program, she does antibullying messaging with some of the books. But once a month we try to have different bigger weekend stuff for all families, and this must have gotten enough attention." He took the most resigned bite of corn pudding in human history. "Straw, camel's back, et cetera, et cetera."

Shit. Harmony had half-hoped that the meeting would take long enough, she'd have wrecked the Weavers' reputations and wiped out the threat to Preston's job with her con before then. That wouldn't quite be in time, though. "Well, you're gonna grind that camel's bones to dust at that inquiry."

Preston's fork paused in midair. "That's a little more violent than what I'm picturing."

"It's a metaphor. For saving democracy itself." She popped a hush puppy in her mouth and chewed meaningfully.

"Is this one of those times where you're just saying stuff?"

She sipped her lemonade. "I mean, any time I'm talking, basically."

"Hmm. How could we possibly solve that?" He leaned forward and kissed her. "Want to come inside while we get started? If I can boost my head count at any of the contested events, it'll help prove we're serving the community and fulfilling our mission. A bunch of the GSA said they'd come just for that, but I think they're actually excited about all the sparkles."

"Um, yeah, I'm not missing out on drag queens and real live princesses parading through the library, who do you think you're talking to?"

"My very own"—he dropped another kiss on her lips—"real live"—and another—"one-woman parade."

She chuckled against his lips before leaning back on one arm, soaking in the sun that had emerged more fully. "Then I have to run some paperwork over to the town offices before they close." But Dani was coming from the gallery to take Lacey that evening, so she and Preston would have a chance to catch up properly. And hopefully improperly after that.

Lacey went chasing past, Mason not far behind. Jordan and Nina and a bunch of their friends were crowded around a bench. A game of frisbee took up one corner of the lawn. Harmony recognized several of the families out here, because she'd been in town so long and visited more than even her usual number of local businesses for the festival grift, from wanting to leverage them against Travis, and from wanting more excuses to see Preston.

She pulled out her phone and snapped a picture of Preston with the backdrop of families and sky breaking into blue. Tonight she wanted to show him what she'd gotten done with the social media accounts they'd set up. She could take a few good shots at the storytime too, more for the main library account to tag him in, so everyone knew that when someone attacked him, they were attacking the person behind the storytimes and summer reading programs they loved so much. An important part of their town.

Taken by surprise, Preston frowned at her as she checked how the picture came out. He was centered there among neighbors, the Brookville gazebo to one side, the carpet of green in the foreground. A sudden longing struck Harmony—to belong somewhere as he did here. A wish to not have to drive away again and again, to another hotel room she'd move on from before letting any memories settle in. To stay and be part of a community.

It was a ridiculous thought. The people here enjoying their sunny Saturday would hate her if they really knew her, if they knew she'd been lying to them all. They *would* hate her soon, once the con played out, just as much as she was trying to make them hate Travis. That never mattered before. Her lying had never bothered her before.

Preston was squinting in the sunlight, watching Lacey run over the grass with her friend.

Harmony's hatred for Travis seemed balanced on a scale against this strange urge for—for home. For more memories she'd never get to make with Preston.

Even if she wanted to, there was nothing she could do to tip it back now. Everything for the festival had been set in motion. She'd been conning everyone in town for months. Never mind that Harmony would pay them all back, or that she was only helping them by exposing Travis for the greedy monster he was, by removing some of Cheryl's sway. She was conning herself if she thought there was any way out of all the lies she'd spun.

She tamped down the feeling, drowned it in the perfect sunshine, stifled it in the grip of Preston's hand holding hers, muffled it in the sound of Lacey's shrieks as she and Mason raced for the library once it was time to head inside.

Preston went to set things up in the community room and let the special guests in at the side of the library, so when the doors opened to the crowd of kids and parents lined up, it was to a surprise of color and ballgowns and music.

One woman dressed as Rapunzel was set up for face painting, with a long line quickly forming behind her easel displaying designs kids could choose from. Cinderella was helping kids pick out dress-up items. Tiana had an assortment of noisemakers for kids to try out.

The drag queen swept through the room in a gown with flowers attached all over and a headpiece with more spilling around her light brown face, welcoming kids before ensconcing herself on a low stool surrounded by carpet squares and folding chairs. "Rosey Bloomgarden is going to read all you delightful children a story!"

Still feeling a bit unsettled and at sea, Harmony wandered back toward the doors, where Preston had been counting attendees with a clicker in one hand. "I have to go grab another cart of chairs," he said. "This is a huge turnout. People came from all over. Someone mentioned seeing it on social media? We don't normally have this much reach."

She gave half a smirk. "If there's one thing I do well, it's building buzz."

"I told you," he said as he moved off, "you do everything well." At least she was helping him do good here, a little, in a real way. To that end, she got out her phone to take some pictures.

Preston unstacked more chairs as people mobbed around Rosey. Kids with glittery flowers and unicorns and butterflies painted across their foreheads and cheeks or plastic tiaras perched on their heads squeezed in to hear *You Don't Want a Unicorn* and *When Aidan Became a Brother*. Lacey, earbuds in, was playing with rhythm sticks while Mason went to town on a drum slung around his neck. Nina was draping a sparkly scarf around Jordan's shoulders and laughing at her girlfriend's grimace.

A little girl, or possibly an animated mass of sparkles, ran up to Preston and stuck a glittery sticker to the back of his hand. "You need this. Now you're perfect."

"Thank goodness." Preston automatically crouched to be closer to the girl's eye level, as he always did with kids. Harmony hung back and snapped a picture. "You must be a fairy godmother."

"I'm five." Preston only nodded seriously, as if this followed logically, while the girl slung one of the three feather boas she was wearing over his olive jacket. "Pink looks good with green."

“You really know your colors.”

“I do,” she agreed solemnly, before running off to grab a maraca and join in with the other kids playing their instruments on command every time Rosey turned a page in a book about singing churros.

Nina, half hidden behind Jordan and giggling into her ear, was definitely, surreptitiously, filming this exchange on her phone. Maybe Harmony should see about her tagging Preston’s new accounts.

When she looked back at her phone, she saw a text from Alice, who was bringing the paperwork they’d been preparing for the next phase of the scam. She was outside, where they’d agreed to meet. So, as the crowd settled in for more stories and jokes, Harmony slipped away.

Alice was waiting in the gazebo, and they spent some time going over the details of the vendor agreements. Before Harmony walked them over to town hall, she relaxed back on the bench. It was nice to talk with Alice, someone she didn’t have to keep up the sheen of lies with. “What are you up to this weekend? Getting in some time with the church boy?”

“After that performance at my apartment?” Alice groaned. “He still hasn’t asked me out. We’re going to be gone before he works up to it.” And while Alice was all about taking big risks when they felt right, Harmony knew the purity culture she’d grown up with and mostly shaken off still made her too shy to do the asking herself.

“Yeah.” Harmony sighed, stacking the papers up neatly. “That’s the game, though.”

“Oh, don’t you talk, with all your sniffing around that library like a lost puppy.”

“Do—” Harmony wrinkled her nose. “Do libraries take in lost puppies?”

Alice pounced on this like she’d just broken a star witness in a murder trial. “They do not! Which is the point!”

Harmony resisted the urge to hide behind the sheaf of papers. Or swat Alice with them. "It's just some fun until we move on." That was all it possibly could be, no matter what she might have wished. And she wasn't even certain what she wanted or if she wanted to ask herself that. Why bother if she might not be able to get it? She'd focus on what she could get. Like making Preston into her very own real live ice cream cone tonight.

Her friend nodded, brows raised and lips pursed dubiously. "You always watch out for me. I just wanna watch out for you. You don't deserve to get hurt."

Harmony made a face probably as uncomfortable as one of Preston's scowl-smiles, dubious right back. She flopped sideways and nuzzled her shoulder against Alice's. "Come on, keep me company, since coffee boy is too foolish to snap you up." Harmony had been in town plenty long enough to weave making friends with Alice into the rest of her web of lies. So they popped across the square together and then wandered back into the library.

The party had dissipated. They'd already seen the princesses driving out of the parking lot together, and Preston came out of the community room followed by Rosey and carrying a box overspilling with shiny scarves and flower crowns and trailing boas. He nodded hello to Alice, who Harmony introduced.

"Ah," said Preston, "you're the one who revealed the secrets of my drink order."

Alice grinned. "You must know better than anyone that Harmony is impossible to say no to."

Rosey threw back her head in laughter, the flowers of her headpiece shaking. "My kind of woman."

"How was the parade?" Harmony asked.

"Resplendent," Rosey declared with a flourish.

Preston adjusted the box in his arms. "I'm going to walk Rosey to her car. Lacey's in the kids section with Mason, but Dani's on her way."

"I'll keep an eye on her."

This earned her a warm smile Preston didn't even bother squashing down. "Thanks."

They were barely to the library door when Alice tilted her head. "Do you hear that?"

"What?" Harmony didn't hear anything but the usual Saturday murmur of the library, the beep of the checkout machines.

"Is that"—Alice dropped her mouth open in mock surprise—"the opening riff of 'Careless Whisper' playing?"

"You're the worst," Harmony muttered.

"It is! Huh. Weird. Does that play whenever you two are in the same room? Or only when you've been making googly eyes at each other? Or are you *always* making googly eyes at each other?"

Okay, time for the big guns. "Costa. Mesa." The location of Alice's greatest blunder, when the cute bartender she was working beside while they targeted the bar's owner turned out to be a con man himself and made off with their score.

"Sorry," Alice stage-whispered. "I can't hear you over that saxophone."

"At least Evan's a good wholesome church boy."

Alice flicked her eyebrows up suggestively. "Until he finally asks me out."

Harmony was trying not to cackle when a commotion at the door made any effort to stay quiet beside the point. It slammed open to a shouting Rosey and Dani ushering Preston back inside.

Harmony's hands fell slack to her sides. "Preston?" Her voice was barely above a rasp. Because as the door swung shut against the late afternoon sunshine, she could make out that he was clutching his face and his white shirt was covered with a technicolor spectacle of red blood.

CHAPTER TWENTY-TWO
HARMONY

"What happened?" Heart drumming, Harmony followed as Dani steered Preston to a tall stool behind the main counter.

He banged his shin into it before settling, tipping his head back and pinching the bridge of his nose, which was not stemming all the fucking blood streaming from it. "Shit. What happened to my glasses?"

"What happened to *you*?" Harmony was trying very hard not to yell, even as Dani spoke over her.

"I got them, babe, but you're not going to want anything touching that." Dani grabbed about half of a box of tissues from behind the counter and handed them to Preston.

"That *awful* man *punched* him." Rosey dumped the jumbled box of dress-up clothes on the counter. "In the *face*."

Harmony had gathered it was in the face. She looked back toward the entrance, where Alice still stood, wide-eyed. "What man?"

"Raymond Vickes." Preston's voice was muffled by tissues and horribly wet-sounding.

"Ellie's husband?" Brewer of pale ale and peddler of the world's worst calamari? The contract he'd signed was among those she'd just turned in for the festival. "Why the *hell*—"

"The Vickeses have complained in the past about my storytime," Rosey said. "He confronted me outside. Blocked me from my car."

Preston pulled the mass of bloody tissues tentatively away from his face. "He took a swing at her. Who punches a woman?" His eyes were watering, and his nose was still bleeding. A lot. He clamped down on it again.

"He *tried* to punch me. Preston was very gallant." Rosey pursed her lips. "Should've punched him back, though."

Through his mountain of tissues, Preston growled, "I'm a *pacifist*."

"Where's Raymond?" Harmony asked, her voice charged. At some point Alice had come up beside her. She slipped her hand around Harmony's, which she realized now was shaking.

"He took off," Dani said. "Probably knows assaulting a cis white guy from town looks worse to the cops."

Rosey huffed. "Coward."

"The Vickeses are out of the festival," Harmony blurted.

Alice tugged her back, murmuring just to her, "Hon, no one's actually in—"

"*I don't care*." She'd find some other way to strike back at him, she knew plenty of scams. Her heart was still racing, her heated blood chugging through her like a steam train.

A crowd was gathering, a couple of the library staff and others looking on with concern. Dani was emptying the tissue box. "Here, babe."

Trading out tissues, Preston looked down at himself. "Oh, fuck," he said low, with feeling. "Don't let Lacey see this. She hates blood." Harmony wasn't too fond of it herself, not when it was Preston's and all over his pressed shirt instead of safely inside him where it belonged and she was going to *destroy* Raymond Vickes.

Dani took the bloodied tissues and tossed them. "I'll get Lacey—"

"Take her home. Don't tell her anyone's hurt. Oh, and she didn't eat, she'll need—"

"I've got her, Preston. And I'll make sure Rosey makes it home safe." Dani held out Preston's battered glasses to Harmony with a questioning look.

"I've got him." Harmony took the glasses. With a sharp nod, Dani went off to find Lacey. Finally there was room, and Harmony was at Preston's side. She wrapped her hand around his shoulder. "Come on, you need ice on that nose and pain meds. Let's get you home."

Alice helped her get him into the car. She shut the door after Preston and gave Harmony a quick hug. "Call you soon."

Harmony settled everything into the back, tucking Preston's glasses carefully into her purse. When she slipped into the driver's side, her hands gripped the steering wheel hard.

"Harmony?" Only when Preston spoke did she realize she'd been sitting there, trying to breathe. "Worried I'm going to get blood on your leather seats?"

"Nope. Because you're not going to." She started Furiosa. "You can't see, but I'm narrowing my eyes at you very hard." She was, in fact, checking her mirrors and half wishing Raymond would wander back into the parking lot. Definitely not so she could run him down. Though she did have three fake passports and knew where to find a kiln that would leave no evidence. With a deep breath that was more like a shudder, she backed up carefully. Preston was going to be fine. It was ridiculous for her to be so upset.

Except when she caught her own eye in the mirror, it hit her that of course she was deeply upset, because she cared deeply about Preston. Far more than she'd admitted to herself, even while she stole into his life and made his problems hers, while she told herself it didn't matter because it could never go anywhere.

Lucky for her, he was busy not bleeding all over the car, so while she took him home she managed to compose herself and not think too much about the dead end she'd driven her heart into.

She guided him straight to the kitchen, where he dug an ice pack out of the freezer and wrapped it in a towel. He leaned back against the counter, wincing, as Harmony found him some ibuprofen and a glass of water.

When he set down the smudged glass, he grimaced, and went to wash his hands.

Harmony chased him with the ice pack. "Hey, get this back on there."

"*Not now.*" His outburst was loud in the quiet kitchen. He shook her off and kept scrubbing, his strained voice growing more intense than she'd ever heard him. "Need to clean up." He took off his jacket and slung it over a chair at the little breakfast table, then reached for his first shirt button. "*Ugh.*"

"Preston." She pressed the ice pack into his hands. "You hold this; let me help." She took over unbuttoning. "You'll be glad you iced it when your face doesn't turn purple tonight."

She swore she could feel his heart hammering under her fingers. "Thanks." He sagged back against the counter, sounding more miserable than he had when his nose was still bleeding everywhere. At least the ice was back on his face, though his eyes peering over it were ringed with stark worry that she was sure hadn't been there before—anger for Rosey, concern for Lacey, that was all. "And sorry. I'm sorry." His other hand was shaking, drumming the air.

"It's okay." She helped him out of the ruined shirt. Maybe it was like a delayed reaction. "You got punched. You're allowed to be out of sorts."

He inhaled, and the fear in his eyes melted away at her reassurance. "Thanks. The blood."

"Yeah." She tossed the shirt in the sink to deal with later.

His bare shoulders shrugged, almost a shudder. "Fucking messy."

A relieved laugh cracked from her chest. Except it was something more like a sob.

"Hey." Preston's free hand stroked up and down her arm.

What was wrong with her today? Harmony did not panic. But Harmony didn't catch feelings either. "I'm glad you're okay." She hid her face against Preston's chest, hugging him. "I was really scared for a minute there at the library," she admitted.

His hand paused on her arm before wrapping around and holding her. "Yeah, I was right there with you, about a split-second before Raymond's fist made contact."

"I can't believe someone was that upset over a storytime."

His hand on her back made little soothing circles. "This has happened at other libraries. Places have had full protests or had to cancel because of threats. I always walk Rosey in and out."

"You always take such good care of everyone." She wanted to be one of those people he cared for, because she was a terrible selfish monster who just took whatever she wanted and was making Preston comfort her when he was the one who'd just been hurt. "Like worrying more about Lacey than your own actual face. She's lucky to have you."

"No." He tensed against her.

She leaned back, wrinkling her nose up at him. "Of course she is. Oh, come here, I'll wash that sticky blood off your face if you promise to hold the ice on as much as possible." He wasn't going to feel better until he was all cleaned up and put back together. She sat him at the table and grabbed a wet paper towel before pulling a chair up facing him.

"I don't think it's that bad, actually," Preston said. "Just a lot of blood. He wasn't aiming for me, at least at first."

Harmony pulled away his hand holding the ice and dabbed gently. "He's still on my shit list."

"A fearsome prospect."

"You just take care of that beautiful face of yours. Doctor's orders." She let go of his hand, and he applied the ice again.

"And where'd you get your medical degree, Doctor Harmony?"

"Mmm." She turned to toss the towel in the sink too. "Bar fight I got caught too close to once." Right in the middle of it, actually. She'd been eighteen, still in school and partially surviving off drinks and bar food she could get people to buy her, plus swiping cash from drunks as the night went on. They normally didn't notice till she was long gone.

Preston's eyes crinkled gently. "Bet you won."

"I always win." But then, she'd made a habit of only playing games she could rig. Everything had somehow gotten so much more complicated lately. "There's going to be some bruising. You'll have to explain something to Lacey."

He sighed. "I just don't want her to worry. She has nightmares sometimes, still."

"She *is* lucky to have you." Harmony bit her lip before adding, "Anyone with you in their life is."

He shifted uncomfortably in his chair. Those pain meds better kick in soon. Unless Preston's discomfort was with the idea of Harmony being in his life for longer than a few months. Now *she* was uncomfortable, with a sensation like snakes slithering all over her skin, into her gut. Shit, feelings were the worst. But this was not the time to demand more or invite rejection. Preston needed taking care of right now. She reassured him she wasn't pushing her way in, laying her hand over his on the table beside them, bringing things back to Lacey. "A kid could end up a lot worse off, both parents dead." At least Harmony had been old enough to watch out for herself by the time she'd been left alone. She had always been fine alone.

"My dad's not dead."

"What?" Harmony sat up straight. She'd assumed— "Then where is he?" This was one too many shocks in a single afternoon. She leaned near Preston again. "He's not dead?"

"He's an electrician in Sacramento."

"Sacramento? That's like—" Preston was doing that thing where his voice went very flat and hollow, and she knew he must be tired and in pain but *what?* "Then why the hell isn't he here?"

Suddenly Preston's voice wasn't empty at all but steeled with anger. "I don't want him anywhere around her."

Shit. She wasn't going to push, but then she goddamn pushed, and it was none of her business. "You don't have to tell me."

"Lucky," he huffed, with a ghost of bitterness. Face half hidden behind the ice pack, casting his gaze down at the tablecloth he was practically shredding with his thumbnail, Preston said, "I'm the reason Lacey doesn't have anyone else."

That was just ridiculous. "You ran your mom off the road?"

He shook his head, still staring at the tablecloth. "My father would jump straight to the strictest therapies for Lacey, he'd be on her case about how she is. Make her change." He swallowed. "I was kind of a handful, growing up. Meltdowns. Screaming. Not the son my father envisioned. Like that just now—" He jerked his head toward the sink. "Losing it over mud, or grass, or a shirt tag, whatever, he'd hate that. But yelling only made it worse."

Harmony squeezed Preston's hand.

"My parents fought over what to do. They were young. A year out of high school when they had me. They put me in this one therapy the state offered, hours and hours every day, but then my mom pulled me out. And they fought over that. She saw how miserable it was making me, spending all my time training to act—not so different. He said that was good." Preston cleared his throat. "But I sort of figured out how to manage, and I was going to go to college. So they had another baby. We were all going to get a clean start."

About a thousand choice swear words were battling to get out from behind Harmony's teeth, which she clenched hard.

Preston lifted his unfocused gaze to her now. "My father left as soon as Lacey showed signs of autism. He wasn't sticking around for that again, didn't even stick around long enough to find out she's brilliant and not at all the same deal. She's going to do amazing things, I just have to keep getting her what she needs—" He frowned, dropping the ice pack to his lap. "You rolled your eyes. I can see that much. Why did you roll your eyes? She *is* brilliant—"

"I know."

"She *is.*"

"Preston, I know she is, just like her brother when he's not too busy being a fool." She lifted the ice pack back to his face. Why were the best people so hard on themselves, when plenty of jerks ran around completely thoughtless of the damage they did?

Preston screwed his eyes shut against the touch of the ice. "I fucked everything up for her. If I hadn't been the way I was, who knows what her life might have been? I just don't want to fuck it up for her any more than I already did."

Harmony had never been very good at holding back, and words spilled from her now, burning in her throat. "This was not your fault. Sounds to me your dad left because, unfortunately, some people are trash and betray everything they should be to you." Like Travis had done to his business partner.

Like Harmony was doing to Preston, lying to him. Her stomach pinched. But, she realized, she wanted to be better. Even if she wasn't sure how. "Sounds like Lacey is a lot better off with you," she told him. "And I like you the way you are." He opened his eyes. The trust in them made her think of the worry they held before. "Wait, is that why you were apologizing for no reason? Did you think I was going to mind that the feeling of blood bothered you more than actually getting hurt?"

His head listed to one side. "It's an old impulse. Not to let people see that."

Because they'd taught him to hold himself back. These were the same therapies he'd mentioned at the library once, trying to—to *erase* Preston. She set aside the fury that stoked in her. "You're supposed to say tequila," she reminded him. His brow rippled. "The code word? If you need space." She brushed her thumb over the back of his hand. "But you don't have to hide yourself," she murmured. "Not from me."

He set the ice pack on the table and gathered her hand up in both of his. "Harmony, I think I—" He seemed to swallow down whatever he'd been about to say. "I'm really glad you're here."

If seeing Preston hurt had sent fear and anger marching through her, the way he was looking at her as he said that filled her with a fizzing, swelling happiness that almost made her chest hurt and spread a smile across her face. Maybe feelings weren't so bad. "So am I."

"Oh, shit." His face fell. "I was going to take you to Café Marotta tonight."

She held the ice out. "Foiled again."

He sulked as he returned it to what was looking like not too bad a bruise running from his nose under his left eye. "It's really romantic."

"I like the sound of that. We should go when you can enjoy it." She stood and dropped a kiss to his sweet forehead. "Properly." She went to wash the glass. The bloody fingerprints were grossing her out a little bit too, honestly. "But I like hanging out with you at home too."

"Yeah?"

"Yeah." She left the glass in the rack and turned around with a grin. "I don't get to see your tits at fancy restaurants." She wanted to make him laugh, which he did, but in fact Preston's torso, narrow but defined, made her want to run her hands all over him.

"There's no dress code at my house, if you want to take advantage of that too."

She laughed now, low and appreciative. "Don't you think you'd better take it easy there, mister?"

He slumped on the table, resting his head on one propped elbow. "I got punched. Be nice to me."

"Oh, I'll take care of you."

He took her up on this, in a decidedly unsexy way, insisting on stain treating the shirt Harmony had figured was a loss and tossing it in the laundry. She allowed him to direct her through the steps as long as he kept icing his poor face. Once it seemed like it had been long enough, she dug out his glasses, which were scuffed a bit around the frames, and he went upstairs and showered.

She was exploring one of the bookshelves when he came down in a soft T-shirt and sweats that Harmony was pretty sure were his pajamas. He answered a text from Dani, checking in and letting him know Lacey was good, and wandered over to the piano, where he seemed to just play around, until he grabbed a pencil to jot down notes between running through a silvery melody taking shape, again and again. Christ, this man.

Eventually Harmony danced her way over to him, the volume of Millay she'd picked out balanced on her head, making that musing, dreamy look of his turn on her and grow into a smile. They cozied up on the couch together, each with a book, sharing lines they liked or that made them laugh, while the windows went fully dark and they waited for the pizza they'd ordered to arrive.

Preston, predictably, made them eat at the dining table rather than the couch, and so it was there they opened the box to find their thin-crust Neapolitan cut into farcically large slices.

"This isn't a slice of pizza," Preston declared, lifting a slice bigger than his head. "This is a *bedsheet*."

"Big as a continent. At least Australia."

Preston's eyes flashed. "Your ego."

Harmony almost choked laughing. When they'd finished, she took the leftovers to the kitchen. Preston was leaning in the doorway, arms crossed, as she closed the fridge. Her purse was still on the table. She asked him, "Do you want to get some rest?"

"Yeah." Made sense. He'd had a rough day. She nodded, while he fidgeted with the hem of his sleeve at his bicep. "Stay?"

"Yeah?" Another rush, like golden sunlight through her veins.

"Yeah." As Preston padded across the tile floor toward her, Harmony thought maybe his wanting her here made her so happy because it meant she was a part of that same feeling for him that he created for her, that he felt safe and cared for and okay being himself with her. He trusted her.

And as he slid his hands over her hips and up her back, pulling her into a hug, tucking her head under his chin, for once she didn't see that as a sign of a sucker. Maybe it was because she'd earned that trust. Maybe it was because it meant she was actually someone deserving of it.

When he leaned back and tilted his head down to kiss her, she realized that wasn't true. But maybe it could be. "Hold on." She wanted him to be honest with her. She couldn't keep lying to him.

"I knew it." Preston sighed dramatically and eased off. "I'm too ugly now to kiss."

"Back to being a fool, I see." That was a horrible way to start off. She pecked him on the cheek, safely on his unbruised side. He angled his head to brush his lips over hers. "Only—I need to tell you something." Oh, god, why was she doing this when his hands were back on her hips and she could be kissing him by now? "I've been bullshitting. Not about us—" His brows had shot up, and his hands dropped to his sides. Hers wanted to pull him back against her but clenched against her stomach. She stared down at the black and white checkerboard tiles.

Preston lifted her chin with one finger, like he was holding back from touching her as much as he wanted until she gave him permission again.

If he still wanted to after she said this. "The festival."

He heaved a little relieved sigh. "I know."

"You—you know?" She swayed a little, anchored only by the barest touch of his finger on her jaw.

He squinted a steely stare at her. "I have a master's in library and information sciences. I know how to research." He dipped his head to one side as if admitting something himself. "Plus, a lot of my undergrad classmates are in the industry. I know all about the headliner. Funny story—" He must have seen the anxiety on her face, because he stopped and said, "It's all right. I understand."

That didn't make sense. "You really don't have a problem with it?" Jeez, she knew she was hot but she'd seriously done a number on him. Though she supposed he had every reason to hate the Weavers too.

His finger traced up her jaw. "Harmony, the only thing bothering me right now is that I don't have my hands all over you."

That should have been good enough for her. She wanted those hands. "What do you understand?" Stupid rule-following all over her.

"That you have to spread a big name around to drum up interest, even if they haven't actually signed on, until you secure a good headliner and all the acts." His fingers feathered through her hair. "Work your magic."

"Right." She swallowed and said, "Right, exactly."

It had been foolish to try to confess. What did she think would happen if he actually knew? She didn't want to be some fake Harmony anymore with Preston, but if she told the truth she'd only be a liar to him. She'd only hurt him. What she needed was to figure out some other way to stop lying. She couldn't tell him everything right now, but she could promise that.

The idea of there being no more faking between them excited her nearly as much as Preston's gaze searing into her. That trust beaming down from his poor bruised face made her believe she could somehow do it. Like he said, she was good at everything.

And Preston was very good at winding his hand through her hair and caressing that spot just behind her ear, making it hard to think, making her go fizzing and golden everywhere under his touch and through her blood.

"Well. I just wanted to be sure to tell you." She leaned into his hand, seeking out more of that touch. "Because I'd pretended before. And you should know—" His knuckles grazed her cheek. "What I feel for you is real."

His hand slipped around the nape of her neck, drawing her into a kiss she wanted more than she deserved, and was determined to find a way to be worthy of.

CHAPTER TWENTY-THREE
PRESTON

Stay, he'd said, and she'd let him lead her upstairs, and somehow, despite his head aching, today had turned into possibly one of the best of his life. His hands were impatient for her, and she hadn't made him wait, lying across his bed and untying her wrap dress and, *yes*, this day was like his birthday and Christmas in one. They took it slow, because he had to be careful of his face, and it was exquisite torture having to hold off from kissing Harmony with the abandon she drove him to, but so worth it to hear those gasps of hers drawn out as he tried to show her what he'd almost said downstairs, what he put into every touch, that he wasn't falling for her, it had happened too quickly, too decisively—he already loved her.

Irresponsibly, hopelessly, doubtlessly. She couldn't feel the same, not so soon and not before she left—likely not ever—but it didn't matter. He was gone for her.

After, he'd found her a new toothbrush and let her wash up first, and now he finished brushing his teeth and came out of the bathroom to find her sitting on the edge of the bed in an old T-shirt he'd gotten at a book festival that had always been too baggy for him. It fit snugly over her curves, leaving her thick, dimpled thighs on full display as she stood. "Did you know your blanket weighs, like, eleventy pounds?"

"Twenty-five," he said automatically.

Her brows flexed, then she nodded. "Autism thing."

"Autism thing," he agreed. He hauled the blanket and bedsheets back, and she climbed back onto the bed. He slipped in beside her and only pulled up the regular blanket over them both.

"Don't you need it?" Harmony snuggled onto his chest.

"A lot of the time." He wrapped his arm around her shoulders. "Takes some getting used to, though." He appreciated how she took these things in stride, not questioning them but not fussing either. Like when he'd almost melted down in the kitchen. So much of the time he shoved down all the little things that bothered him, the ways his body wanted to react to them, and it was manageable—he'd described it to his therapist once as a low-level hum, like bees in a garden you were aware of and giving space. But sometimes it got to be too much, the air was more and more full of stingers to avoid, then *one more thing* and suddenly you were drowning in bees. Which obviously had to be dealt with right away and maybe not calmly, because, you know, bees in your lungs.

When he'd snapped at her, his dread had been like a physical blow as much as the one he'd taken to the face today. His stomach had clenched, waiting for the confused, annoyed look, the walking away. Instead, she'd helped him through it. He squeezed her against him now, holding her hand on his chest, and pressed a kiss to her temple.

She gave his ring a spin, which was probably why he imagined she sounded anxious asking, "Do you need to get up by a certain time?"

"No, Dani will drop Lacey off whenever she's stuffed her full of enough pancakes and let her get dirty in the studio or garden. I should probably work on prepping for the library inquiry, but there's plenty of time to worry about that in the afternoon. Do you need an alarm set?"

"No." She lifted her head, smiling, but her eyes fell on his bruised face and she pouted. She kissed him gently. "Is this going to complicate things? For the inquiry?"

He blew out a breath. "Not sure. God, Katherine might want to file a police report."

"Do you want to?"

He shrugged. "Not really. But maybe we should get a restraining order against Raymond on library grounds." It was stressful just thinking about it, the kind of thing he could let run around and around through his mind until it pulled him down into hours of sleepless anxiety. But between the lingering relaxed state of his body and having Harmony here to talk to, it didn't seem as bad as it could have. "We can't have him disrupting another storytime. People need to feel safe at the library."

"So what you're saying is, you *can* ban someone from the library, if you really want?"

"Yes?"

She snuggled back down, using him as a pillow, sounding smug. "Which means you liked having me around when I was hounding you about the lease."

Nope, not much room for anxious thoughts with Harmony's Australia-sized ego around. He reached to leave his glasses on the table and switch off the lamp, and smiled into the softness of her hair. "You're welcome to trouble me whenever you like, Ms. Hale."

* * *

The soft curve of Harmony's shoulder, where he'd rolled over with her in the night, was the first thing he saw waking. A moment later, he felt Harmony draw his arm up from where it was draped over her stomach and kiss his hand. She murmured "Good morning" against his knuckles.

He kissed a trail along her arm, over her shoulder, and up her neck, wondering if she'd been awake long. "Do you want breakfast?"

She locked his hand in both of hers, and he was glad he hadn't rolled too near her in his sleep, because, well, it was morning, and she was beautiful in the light filtering in through the curtains. She was always beautiful. "No. Nope. Not getting out of this bed. Forward my mail to this pillow." But then she sat up—to yank the weighted blanket up over them. "Not my fault, no escaping from this." She lay down again, on her back. "Oh, my god. This is amazing. It's like my entire body is being hugged."

The way this woman made him jealous of fabric. "That is a service I also provide." He tugged back the blanket and slid on top of her, bracing himself by the elbows, pressing just past gentle against where she shook with laughter. "No getting away now."

"Good." He was so focused on the bright gleam in her champagne eyes he didn't realize she'd already got her hand between them. He only noticed when she grabbed him through his pajamas.

He dropped his forehead to hers with a sharp exhalation. "I suppose there are benefits to staying in bed a little while longer." Mindful of the bruising around his nose and cheekbone, he kissed her, and, god, he would never grow tired of that, not if the festival and Harmony leaving were a hundred years away. He kissed down her jaw, her neck, to where he knew he could draw a shiver from her.

Her legs opened under him, and when he shifted to work his own hand between them, she arched her spine, pulling the shirt over her head and happy birthday and merry fucking Christmas to him all over again, because her skin was golden in the rising sun, radiant as her grin. He was pretty sure he was muttering her name and maybe a few other incoherent things against it, but all he could focus on was the weight of her breast in his hand, softness that somehow threatened to break him, and the rasp of her breath as he delivered a first kiss to the pink bud of her nipple.

She gripped him by the shoulders, hard, as he swept a hand between her thighs. *God*, the heat of her, wet enough to easily coat his fingers before he circled her clit. Harmony writhed beneath him, her hand carding through his hair. When he thrust his fingers inside her, though, both her arms fell against the mattress.

She'd gone breathless when she reached for him again, hands stroking up his abdomen. "More," she panted. "Preston. I want you." Her words shone through him like a supernova. Her hands slipped under his waistband, pulling him to her. He fumbled at the side table for a condom and sank into her and, *fuck*, he must still be asleep, he thought wildly, because this was too good, this had to be a dream.

He felt it everywhere when Harmony laughed. "Full body hugs for everyone."

"Menace." He rolled his hips back, then slid deep inside her again, breath stuttering. "Sweetheart." Hitching himself up on her, he found that angle that always made her thighs tremble and her gasps melt into a deep moan, sweet and low. His hips snapped against her again, again, and she was kissing his throat, his collarbone, hands raking down his back.

If this were a dream he could tell her everything. All the feelings she inspired in him, all the ways he wanted to provide her the same, somehow, someday. Instead he thrummed his finger over her until she tensed and shook apart beneath him, her cry driving a piercing sweetness through him that set him shuddering, everywhere, into her.

It wasn't a dream; it was real and perfect and he was so goddamn lucky, even as his heart echoed Harmony, thudding *more, more, more*. As each slow press of his lips to her temple said *stay, stay, stay*.

* * *

"I like it when you call me sweetheart." Harmony had in fact refused to get out of bed while he showered and was lounging still as he dressed. He flushed a little, pulling on a clean shirt, because that had sort of just slipped out again. "I could get used to this dating for real thing."

"Me too." At least that was fully honest. "I would say I wish I'd made time sooner, but I'm glad I waited for you."

She beamed at that, then her eyes narrowed. "If you've never had time to date how are you so good at this? Wait, have you secretly been bringing home women from the Moonlight every night? Have you got a bunch of 'sweethearts' lined up somewhere?"

He ignored her attempts to fluster him and adjusted his shirt collar. "I haven't had time to date *recently*. It's not like you forget how."

"Oh," she said, with a wicked look in her eye. "Would you say it's like riding a bike?"

Fighting to keep a straight face, he told her, "No, of course not. My bike's a much better kisser." She laughed, and he leaned over and kissed her before sitting on the edge of the bed to finish buttoning up his shirt. "Dating wasn't exactly easy, even before having two jobs and Lacey. But I was seeing someone in grad school, until—"

"Until?"

"I got the call." He cleared his throat. "Came home."

"And?"

He shrugged. "And?"

She nudged him with her toe. "And she checked on you, right?"

"Of course. She called. But it fizzled out."

Harmony's voice lost all of the levity it had carried earlier as she sat up. "She dumped you because your mom died."

No more buttons to button, so he fiddled with the cuff of his sleeve. "I wasn't much fun to be around then."

"Aw." She made a sympathetic pout. "Does that mean you think you're fun to be around now?"

Her grin flashed when he shoved her over, scowling and laughing. "You're so mean."

"Yeah," she said as he attacked her forehead with kisses. "I'm terrible. And you love it."

God help him and his heart that wasn't quite his anymore, he did. Every outrageous thing she said, that wiped away the emotion clotting his lungs and clogging his throat—the truth that people always left him—and made him laugh right now instead.

He was reheating the last enormous slice of pizza in a skillet when Lacey got home. She said hello to Harmony, who was reading one of the five or so books she'd pulled off the bookshelves, and dumped her overnight bag at the foot of the stairs. "What happened to your face?"

"Someone forgot to use their words instead of shoving. But I'm okay. Harmony took good care of me. Want pizza?"

"No, I had pancakes." She went back into the living room.

"And some fruit or eggs or something?" he called after her. There was always more to worry about messing up raising a child, though he was probably too anxious about Lacey—seeing people hurt used to send her into meltdowns, and she was clearly fine today. Then again, maybe he ought to be worried about what she and Harmony were talking about because had Lacey just told Harmony he had so many love stories on the shelves because he liked "mushy stuff"? "Lace Face!" he yelled in an attempt to retain some of his dignity. "I'm cutting you up some carrot sticks."

It worked, at least. He heard Harmony saying to Lacey, "That's a cute nickname your brother calls you."

"Oh, he has lots for me."

"And what's your nickname for him?"

"He doesn't have one."

"What?" Harmony thumped her book shut and looked over at him, aghast and delighted at once, as he brought the first plates out to the table. "We have to think of one, then!"

He set down the carrot sticks. "Please don't."

"A really good one." Her smile sharpened.

Lacey ran over and sat. "Nothing rhymes with Preston anyway. Harmony, why are you wearing the same dress as yesterday? You're supposed to wear clean clothes every day."

Chair pulled out halfway, Harmony froze and looked at him. *This is your show.*

Preston grabbed the last plates from the kitchen because time to think was always good. "She spent the night to make sure I was okay after getting hurt. But she might stay other nights, if you're comfortable with that, because we like spending time together." He dared a hopeful glance at Harmony, who smiled back as she took her seat.

Lacey's face pursed with serious consideration. "Can I have a sleepover too?"

"Um. Maybe?"

"I showed Mason's friend Courtney how to make paper stars and she wants to see the real stars in my telescope. But she'd have to come at night."

That thankfully led to plenty of discussion over lunch about if sleepovers meant you were friends, the Beehive cluster, and whether fourth graders should be allowed to bike places on their own, until they finished and cleared the dishes and Harmony said she was going to take off and let them have some downtime.

"Exciting weekend all around," she said when he kissed her goodbye. "See you soon," she told Lacey. And with a glint in her eye as she went out the door, "Bye, Presto-Chango!"

Oh, no. But from Lacey's little grin he knew that was going to stick, probably for a lot longer than Harmony would even be in town or his life, reminding him far past then of the brief perfect time it was.

CHAPTER TWENTY-FOUR

HARMONY

Harmony didn't have a lot of practice *not* lying, so she struggled to think of how to clean things up in the whole honesty department with Preston while she began collecting payments from vendors for the festival and putting in orders with the local printers and other suppliers she'd signed on. This only made her feel worse, when she was already stewing over having woven such a skillful web of lies, which she now had to figure out a way to untangle—truly, she was her most formidable opponent, the only one she'd ever feared losing to.

Because as she went around Brookville now, people kept asking after Preston—word of Library Fight Night had gotten out—or sharing about how their kids who'd made it into the youth stage program were practicing regularly, or shouting *Go, Bobcats!* as if she might cheer back, or inviting her to their cousin's big birthday party that everyone was coming to (this from the owners of the Thai place, and she said yes, and asked if she could bring Preston). She was going to pay everyone back with Travis's money, but that same feeling of not wanting to lie was spreading to her interactions with the community she'd stolen into the past couple months. Was this how other people felt all the time? Ugh, no wonder Preston was so stressed out.

She hadn't gotten anywhere with ideas when it was time for Dani's show, and she, Preston, Lacey, and Alice drove out to the coast to support her. They made a tour around all of Dani's pieces shown off perfectly in the big white gallery, looking rich and mingling as Dani had instructed them ahead of time, ending at the table set out with hors d'oeuvres and champagne. Lacey took one look at the plates of tiny sesame cakes, mushrooms stuffed with cheese and walnuts, and squares of dark chocolate, and immediately made for the gallery's outdoor sculpture garden.

"At least we can all agree on this candy and its being the worst," Preston said, passing glasses of champagne to Harmony and Alice. The bruise along the side of his nose and under his eye was a mostly faded yellowish-green.

Harmony sipped her drink and nodded. "Dark chocolate tastes like dirt and dashed hopes."

"Like the void," Alice agreed.

"Like adulting."

Preston bit into a sesame cake and smiled. "I dare you to eat a piece."

"No way, Presto-Chango." Harmony poked him in the lapel of his houndstooth coat.

He grimaced, with a gleam in his eye. "When did you get so picky about terrible candy? You love terrible candy."

"Black licorice is *supposed* to taste like anise and shoe leather, that's how you know it's the good stuff."

They mingled a while longer—Alice wandered off nearer a guy who was exploring the gallery solo. Evan had better watch out, she was about due to fall in love with someone new again. When there was a lull in the clump of people surrounding Dani, they got to congratulate her. Before getting pulled away by some more patrons,

Dani turned to the baby grand piano in the corner of the gallery and said, "Preston, I think some music would really add an 'I'm feeling so rich I think I'll buy this sculpture' element to the ambiance, don't you?"

"Fine. Because it's your big day." He gave Harmony's hand a squeeze. "Didn't mean to abandon you."

"You're going to be happier over there rather than making any more small talk, right?"

"Absolutely."

"I've got Alice, go make Dani happy."

"Always the wise choice."

Soon the gallery was washed in his playing, something gentle and classical. Harmony played her part, in her sage green A-line and Louboutins, looking interested in pieces and making small talk carefully aimed to drive a sense of urgency for snapping one up into anyone within hearing. Keeping Dani happy seemed especially smart if she'd ever threatened to make fired pottery out of you.

When she wandered back over from a far corner to deposit her champagne glass, she couldn't help pausing to watch Preston play, because damn it really was impressive how he just did that, though of course he didn't just do that, he'd practiced for years because he was dedicated and talented and, yeah, she was pretty much just staring at his hands now.

She also couldn't help catching Preston's eye when he glanced up, through the crowd mingling between them, and doing a subtle dance to whatever he was playing by Beethoven or Bach or whoever that other guy whose name started with B was. Preston's mouth twisted in a smile as he looked back down at the piano, and the music shifted to a soft instrumental version of "Everything's Coming Up Roses."

Something hitched in Harmony's chest. He'd remembered her starring role. Played one of her big songs just for her, like a secret between them in this crowded gallery, because he knew her, the real her, and liked her enough to hold on to that little detail she'd trusted him with.

Oh, no. Feelings. Welling up in her, only growing more inescapable when Preston went on to play some of the other show tunes from her playlist. Even Webber. Harmony clutched her champagne flute and blinked back tears. Because she'd just realized two things.

Alice sidled up to her. "Oh, sweetie, you okay?"

"No," Harmony sniffed. "I'm in love with that total dork over there."

"Aw, *hon*." Alice put her arm around her shoulders.

"What am I gonna do?" She knew, though. Exactly what had to happen. And it scared her so, so much. She'd been fooling herself, trying to avoid the truth.

Alice drew a deep breath and looked over at Preston. "Well, maybe if you got him to do his hair different and lose the tweed—"

"Not that!" She turned to Alice, biting her lip. "I think I need to make the festival real."

Alice's face drew long with shock. But no one was more surprised than Harmony. She was trying not to think too hard about her dad. She was just going to have to find another way to make things up to him, to give Travis what he deserved.

She grabbed Alice's hand. "Will you help me? Please? I know you've been stuck working at the coffee shop for months so if there's anything at all that comes from this you'll still get your cut—"

Her friend's shoulders went slack as she sighed. "Of course. Don't worry about that. You know I've always got your back."

But it wasn't going to be easy, not even with Alice's expertise with all the permits and paperwork. They got together the next day at Harmony's hotel to go over everything. Harmony stared down the documents spread over her bed while Alice dug around on her computer. There had to be a way to pull this off. "No loopholes?"

"Hon, *all* your funds are going to be tied up with this thing, beyond what you've already laid out in deposits. You always said it was the biggest play you'd ever make. If we actually do this, we'll need trailers and stages and lighting . . . And it's going to cost more to put a rush on the paperwork we need pushed through fast."

Because they'd been faking it before and were running out of time. Harmony resisted the urge to flop on the bed, on top of all the useless papers. "Withdraw everything from my emergency savings too."

"I *have*. Maybe if you didn't have such a habit of giving most of your hauls to your marks' victims . . ." Alice frowned at her screen. "With what's left of the booth fees, and if we could sell streaming and sponsorship rights, I think we can get the last of it in order for permissions and supplies and hiring on staff, but it's not going to mean much without, you know, actual music at the music festival."

The problem was the headliner. They could rope in smaller acts with a big name, but Harmony had no money left to get someone with that kind of draw last minute. She stifled a laugh. This was her own con playing out against herself. "I'm going to have to ask Travis still. To cover the headliner." And then hire one for real, which Harmony didn't actually know how to do. That probably was going to mean needing even more money.

She was going to have to tap dance for her life when she went to Travis. Fuck.

Sinking into a chair, she told Alice, "Thanks for doing what you could."

Alice gave her a weak smile over her laptop. "You've got a lot of the work done already, hon. Like, it was fake, but you're really good at this, it's all put together. I'll keep working on the rest, ticketing and all that. You go get that money."

So on Monday Harmony called the mayor's office and made an appointment. Then she called Café Marotta and made a reservation, because she'd realized one more thing: she needed to make things real with Preston too. If this was all going to be worth it, she had to see if he was even interested in her staying around longer. Obviously Harmony was a catch, but while she'd tried to make it clear she was in it for real now, they'd started things all wrong with her grifting and maybe Preston was happy to have something uncomplicated in his complicated life for a while, assuming she'd be jetting off to the next event to plan, the next concert to promote. But maybe he'd be open to more. Harmony definitely didn't pace around her hotel room while making the reservation wondering which it was.

Plus, Preston liked mushy things, according to Lacey, and had missed out on the dinner he'd planned twice. And then played all those stupid romantic songs and activated her conscience and ruined her life, basically. So she got in touch with Dani about taking Lacey home after one of Preston's later shifts on a day he didn't have lessons to give, and showed up at the library Wednesday evening to surprise him.

His brow furrowed when he saw her. But then one eyebrow rose, along with one side of his mouth, in a pleased, surprised smile, when she explained the plan. After they said hi to Dani, who'd come in to find Lacey, they headed outside and Preston told Harmony, "I thought maybe I'd forgotten we were meeting."

"Nope." She gave his arm a squeeze. "This is a librarian kidnapping. You've evaded us twice before, but there's no escape this time." She dug out her keys while walking to Furiosa's driver's side.

"Oh, no," he said flatly, sliding into the car next to her. "I surrender." He leaned over and kissed her cheek. "But I'm paying."

And what with her plan to no longer ride off into the sunset with Travis's millions, Harmony couldn't exactly argue. "Well, yeah, kidnappers don't pay the ransom, don't you know that? It's like you've never even been kidnapped before."

Café Marotta was pretty nice, with an outdoor patio full of potted trees and twinkle lights strung between them, and a large fountain in the middle, which they were seated near. As they ordered wine, she noticed Jordan and Nina at a table in the back of the patio, tucked behind a tall fern. Clearly this was the place for couples.

Which was what she and Preston were. For now. For longer? Harmony wiped her hands down her thighs, over her circle skirt. And then, for some reason, she reached out to Preston, smiling at her across the table, and tapped his nose.

He blinked. "You booped me."

"I did."

"On the nose."

"That's traditionally where boopings occur." Yup, this was going great so far.

Said nose wrinkled. "Like a dog."

"Like an adorable, infuriating librarian." She wanted to say *boyfriend* because she had never been more impatient in her life, but that had to wait until her meeting with Travis, until she'd magicked all the lies between them to truth. Soon. "I'm just glad to see that bruise is clearing up."

"Same, although it might have made for good theater at the inquiry."

"How's that coming?"

He waited while their server brought a basket of bread and poured their wine. "I have all the data gathered on circulation of the contested books, attendance at the events, plus any relevant info from the ALA, the town charter, state law. I'm putting it all together now."

"You're going to do great."

"I hope so." He glanced over at the teenagers holding hands over their table. "Everyone likes to say how kids are going to grow up and save the world, but it's kind of bullshit. We should try at least to make it better for them now."

Harmony nodded, glad she was making the festival real—that she wouldn't have to disappoint the kids, who'd been working so hard. She peered at Preston over her wine glass. "If you get nervous you can always picture me in my underwear."

He lifted his own glass. "Oh, I already do that at all times, anyway. But thanks."

She smiled, waiting until he'd taken a drink to say, "You include the underwear? Honestly, I'm offended."

He snorted into his wine. Setting it down, eyes crinkling as he smiled wide, he said, "I've never met anyone like you."

"Of course not. There's only one me." She tossed her hair. Then she twisted a finger through one lock and swallowed. This was the perfect chance to talk about what she wanted them to be. Or maybe it was the perfect chance to grab a bread stick and shove it in her mouth and not say anything at all because feelings were stupid and relationships were scary but bread—bread would always love you. *Don't be a coward*, she told herself. Ugh, why was she so fabulous and brave? Fine. "You're different from anyone I've been with too," she began.

"Yeah." He looked at where his fingers played with the edge of the napkin spilling from the bread basket. "Different."

That had obviously come across wrong. "Like I'd fall for anyone who wasn't exceptional?"

His gaze lifted to her face, that little surprised smile back again. "Fall for?"

She opened her mouth and was definitely going to say something more, but right then Travis Weaver came hustling through the patio, followed by his wife. They marched over to their daughter's table, where Travis leaned over Nina, saying something low and sharp. Harmony couldn't hear quite what, or Nina's reply, and exchanged a concerned glance with Preston until their voices rose, and Cheryl joined in, saying through her teeth, "Why do you have to make things so hard for everyone?"

Travis was almost yelling now, while Nina stared into her lap. "You said you'd be at the school, yet here you are, hanging out again with this delinquent."

Preston shoved his hand to the tablecloth, as if he was about to stand. But before he could move, Jordan threw down her napkin and jumped to her feet. "We are not! We're not hanging out. We're dating. Because, like she's tried to tell you, Nina is gay. And we're in love."

Nina's head snapped up.

"This is just a phase," Cheryl huffed, glancing around at all the diners with forks frozen midair, gaping. "It's trendy now."

Travis shook a finger. "But it's going to tank her options for political office."

Nina seemed to erupt, standing beside Jordan, stamping a foot, hands clenching the air. "Fuck!"

Her parents' jaws dropped. Jordan actually gasped.

"Who cares! Maybe I don't want to be governor or whatever! I just want to be who I am." Nina grabbed Jordan's hand. "And stop calling my girlfriend names."

"Come on, Nina." Travis smoothed down his suit jacket. "We're going home."

"I am not."

"Well, I am not paying for your credit card if you're going to run around town like this. I paused it on the drive over. So unless you want to wash dishes for your meal, it's time to go."

Nina's jaw trembled. She turned to Jordan. "I'm sorry," she said quietly. "I guess we have to leave."

Oh, hell no. Harmony was already standing before she realized it. "Mr. Mayor." She crossed the courtyard, sucking her teeth. "If you'd be so good as to let everyone get back to their dinners, I'd be happy to pay for this nice young couple's meal." Might as well throw around her last few dollars for a good cause.

Travis barely looked at her. "You stay out of this. This is family business."

"No, this is a restaurant. And this is my intern. Who has been doing an excellent job for a world-class event. Who is nearly an adult." She really should *not* be pissing Travis off, not ahead of their meeting with everything riding on it, but like Preston had said, they needed to help these kids out right now. And she'd been waiting years to lay into this guy. "What, do you have one of those tracking apps on her phone or something? Or just good old-fashioned small-town friends spying for you? Nina is an outstanding young woman and a hard worker and deserves more trust and respect than that. Jordan too. She has an admirable spirit for social justice and a bright future, and, as far as I can see, treats your daughter with more respect and love than anyone."

Harmony shot her gaze to the manager, standing a few tables back and looking like he possibly wanted to drown himself in the fountain. "Their meal's on me. No need to kick out anyone who's dining here tonight." She swung her head back at the Weavers, pointedly. Homophobic trash cans, that was up to him.

She didn't really think that manager was going to force the mayor to leave, but Cheryl had clearly had enough of their family drama being on display. "Travis, let's go. She'll have to come home eventually and we can talk then." She tugged on her husband's hand.

Travis, red-faced, pressed his lips together hard but followed Cheryl out through the restaurant.

"Thanks, Ms. Hale," Nina murmured. "I can pay you back from all my Christmas cash at home—"

"Not necessary, you two just have a good time if you still can. Order some steak. And dessert." Why not, Harmony had probably screwed everything up for the festival anyway. If she couldn't give the girls real internships, she could at least give them some cannoli.

Jordan's eyes gleamed as she sat back down across from Nina, who settled into her chair with a slow pleased smile overtaking her pinched expression. Jordan smirked fondly. "You said a grown-up swear word. I'm so proud of you."

"*You* said you're in love with me."

Deer-in-the-headlights Jordan was back. "Um. Yeah. Yup."

Time to leave them to it. Harmony turned on her heel, realizing she'd also messed up romantic evening attempt number three with Preston, who was watching from where he stood beside their table. She walked back over, thinking how this might even make his inquiry harder, since Cheryl surely knew they were together, and, god, all she'd wanted was to ask Preston if they *could* be together, for longer term—how had she managed to fuck everything up? "I'm sorry—"

He bracketed her face with his hands and kissed her. Forehead pressed to hers, he said, "That was the best thing I've ever seen."

* * *

Furiosa's headlights shone into the blue twilight, just far enough to illuminate the next bend in the country road. Preston had offered to drive, because after her face-off with Travis, Harmony had thrown back the rest of her wine fast. Her nerves still hadn't settled—too many people were glancing their way, and while normally she'd feed off the attention as much as her butternut ravioli, she was not about to ask Preston if he might be interested in her sticking around after the festival with an audience.

Even now, alone as they drove out to Dani's, the question seemed to slosh around in her stomach. All she managed was, "Thanks again. For dinner. And for driving."

"Sorry we couldn't hang around and let you sober up over some dessert. School night."

"I promise I don't mind." She never would, about Lacey. "I get it. I had to be there to take care of my dad a lot toward the end." Shit, was it the wine letting this slip out? She tried to play it off. "No time for homecoming dances." Preston's eyes didn't stray from the road, but she could tell he was listening. His brow flexed, and she found herself saying, "When his business went under, he kinda did too, with the drinking and everything."

"That must have been a lot."

"Yeah." And she didn't even have to explain, because Preston knew, he knew everything that came with something like that—the horrible details like coroners and the mundane ones that were almost worse, keeping track of bills and shit and making sure the person you were looking after had eaten something, when everyone around you still got to just go to school and think about totally normal, stupid things. And she'd give anything to have her dad back to take care of again. "So, like, I get it."

She'd never talked about this, not even with Alice. And it felt like maybe, more than asking anything about her staying, this was enough, for tonight. She'd wait to say the other words after she fixed things with the fest, but sharing this part of herself felt almost like the same thing. Like telling Preston she wasn't holding anything back anymore.

He must have sensed something of that, eyes forward but focus flowing her way, asking softly, "What was he like?"

"Oh, big dreams and bigger feelings." The old pain scorched through her chest, but she smiled as she remembered something about her dad she could tell Preston without changing any details. "He'd do this thing, where he'd make us a picnic on a hotel room floor, and the only rule was you had to imagine you were anywhere else. Because a hotel could be anywhere, right?" He'd tried to make it fun when they'd had to leave another apartment, everything packed into their car, not knowing where they'd be the next week. "We had picnics in Central Park and on the shore of Lake Geneva and at the top of an Amalfi hillside."

He'd tried his best. Harmony couldn't fail him now. She'd been focused on the festival, but she still needed to figure out how to keep her promise to him.

Preston's mouth curled gently. "Sounds like he was really creative."

She nodded. "That was Iggie—Hale." It was wrong, the lie of false Harmony clanging against her father's name. Like everything she was doing. It was starting to feel like the cons were never going to heal his memory. But she didn't know what would.

"Know what?" Preston flicked on the turn signal. "We have a little more time." He steered them off the main county road, down another cut through fields going dim and soft in the gloaming.

"Where are you taking me?" She shot thinned eyes at him. "You're the one that's supposed to be kidnapped."

He grinned. "Quick stop."

They pulled up alongside a low metal gate barring yet another gravel road, this one running between lines of trees. The orchard. Preston opened her door for her and climbed over the fence easily. "I know you've been here for work, but sometimes we haul Lacey's telescope out here, and this time of the evening, it's—" He turned around to help her over, and his gaze and words caught on the sight of her above his eye level, ballet flats hitched up on the metal slats. "Beautiful."

Harmony beamed down at his slackened expression. "Oh, good, I see the Stockholm syndrome is kicking in." Holding his hand, she tucked herself up on the gate and swung her legs around. "My evil plan is working."

He helped her ease down. "To recruit me to your ring of library book thieves?"

"I've already got you stealing in here." The orchard's remaining trees spread before them, evenly spaced trunks breaking into wide green crowns under the purpling sky.

He made an affronted noise. "I'm not trespassing, it's my land."

"Oh, now it's yours."

"Are you arguing just so I'll do this?" He tugged on her hand and pulled her into a kiss. She felt his smile against her lips before he leaned back. "Come on."

They left the road to walk under the trees' canopy, sloping scrub-covered ground as soft as the shadows. The furthest hills smudged the horizon with purple, below the rising moon, beyond a line of cypresses edging the main road. The last walnut blossoms drifted down in the evening breeze.

Preston squeezed her hand. "Good place for a picnic?"

She nodded. "Next kidnapping, for sure."

"Here. I want to show you something." He led her over to one massive and gnarled trunk. "My great-great-grandparents farmed here when they immigrated from Italy." He pointed out a rough *RM + LM* cut into the bark. "That's them."

She reached out and traced the letters. "I love that. We did something like this too, at my high school, in the theater. Carved our initials into the greenroom wall." She splayed one hand. "*Harmony was here.*"

"No one could ever miss that you were." He laughed, his gaze on her tender. "At least yours would be easy." At her confused look, he raised a brow. "All straight lines?"

"No, the *G*—" She barely stuttered before smoothly continuing, "Geniuses at my school said we were only allowed to use stage knives." She really needed to find a way to stop lying to this man, because it wasn't the wine—whenever she was around Preston, she wanted to be her true self; everything wanted to come spilling out of her. She was in love with this feeling of sharing and being seen.

But, she realized, suddenly struck by the evening chill, even bringing the festival to life right here wouldn't fix all of this. She'd still have to hide her real past from Preston. She'd always be holding something back. "It was a real pain in the ass," she finished thinly.

He must have noticed her shiver. "We'd better go, before it gets too dark."

She stumbled over the tree roots, and he steadied her. Bracing herself, palms to his chest, she murmured, "Too late."

"I'm starting to understand how you ended up in that swimming pool."

"Must really be great out here for stargazing."

But the moon was full and bright, and Preston's gaze was locked only on her. As if he could *see* her, through the mess she'd made and didn't know how to clear away. Like the moonlight reaching through the tracery of leaves and branches. No neon glow now, only pure silver playing over his dark hair, catching on his cheekbones, as he gave a helpless sort of sigh and leaned in and kissed her.

They were a furnace in the gathering night, Preston's strong, warm hands clutching her near, Harmony arching into him, feet tangled in the roots of a hundred-year-old tree, bathed in moonlight.

She wanted this, something alive, something lasting. It seemed all she was getting was more questions—and while she usually had a quick answer to throw at any that came her way, what she needed now was truth. And that seemed much harder to find.

Harmony knew she couldn't kiss her way to a solution, but, really, she should probably give it a go. Just in case. For science.

She backed Preston against the tree and tried.

CHAPTER TWENTY-FIVE
PRESTON

Preston sat in the chair at the desk in Harmony's hotel room and bent to tie his shoes. She'd left already, off to a meeting with Travis Weaver. She'd seemed nervous about it—maybe that was why she'd texted earlier, why she'd been delighted to hear that Lacey was at Mason's and Preston was free for a couple hours. Hopefully she was feeling a bit more relaxed now, after what they'd gotten up to in this very chair. And then the bed.

He was feeling better about his own upcoming meeting. Seeing Harmony stand up to the Weavers made him feel ready to tackle anything. The way she'd spoken up for Nina and Jordan made him more sure than ever of his love for her. She'd been fucking glorious. Harmony was such a force of nature, and behind all the brash business tactics and free ice cream cones, she was just as exuberantly kindhearted and used it for good. Preston would never ask her to give any of that up, even if he hated that her job would soon take her away. She never would, anyway. He was only glad to get to share it with her at least for a little while.

He was also glad to have the chance to leave something he'd gotten for Harmony in her room as a surprise. It was the only way he could tell her everything, without demanding what he didn't deserve. He slung his bag on, smiling despite himself, and headed out the door, into the slanting late-afternoon sun, making sure to pull the handle until it locked.

"Hey, man, this isn't Harmony's room?"

Preston turned to see a man about his age stopped at the top of the stairs to this floor, in jeans and a T-shirt, tattoos over his white skin. He didn't recognize him, and he wasn't about to point out anyone's hotel room to someone anyway, so he just shrugged. Harmony dealt with a lot of people for the festival.

"Nah, couldn't be the same room." The man shook his head, rubbing his neck with one palm. "Shit, I was really hoping to say hi before hitting the road again."

"Can't help you." Preston made for the stairs.

The guy sidestepped in front of him. His eyes narrowed. "You sure you don't know Harmony? Might be using a different name. They said in town she was going by Hale here, that's a new one. Big girl, but still hot."

Preston's lips pressed in a line. Who the fuck was this guy, and who the fuck did he think he was talking about Harmony that way?

The man's mouth curled up at one side. "You do know her. Aw, man, so what's her angle with you?"

"What?" Preston was lost. No script, not even a cast of characters to help him figure out what the hell was going on.

"You don't look that rich." The man tapped a fist on the metal stair railing. "Look, I did what I came here for, but I'd hoped to catch Harmony too. Give that bitch what she deserves." Now Preston's entire body clenched. The guy seemed totally at ease as he cast a glance down to the parking lot. "But I gotta get back to the city before my goddamn probation officer knows I've been gone. So. Warning a mark off is gonna have to do." He actually smiled at Preston. "I'm gonna do you a solid today. Hopefully you're worth more than you look—I'd love to cost her something big."

There was nothing confusing about the anger sparking all through Preston. "What the hell, man?"

"Oh." The guy laughed. "She's got you wrapped around her finger, right? Her specialty. Landed me in fucking jail with that shit."

"I think you must be looking for someone else—"

"No. I saw her in a picture online at the library in this town, tracked her down here. It's her. Get it through your skull, if you don't want her taking off with all your money." The guy angled his close-shaven head, leaning forward, setting the chain he wore swinging. "She's a con woman. A thief."

No. None of this made sense. Harmony worked promoting concerts. Preston didn't even have any money. This guy was mistaken, on drugs, on a prank show, something. "You're wrong. I'm not rich, I'm a librarian."

"Huh, yeah, she always did have that thing for books."

"This can't be the same Harmony." It couldn't. It couldn't.

"You're far gone, huh? Maybe I *should* stick around, see if she comes back."

Preston was still utterly at sea, but one thing clicked clearly into place for him. This guy intended to hurt Harmony somehow. And he had a probation officer in the city.

Having recently been punched by Raymond Vickes did not make what he did next any easier. Preston, who until this month had never in his life been in a physical fight, who was supposed to be a pacifist, *dammit*, knew how much this was going to hurt. Probably worse, judging by this guy's build. He was shorter than Preston, though giant biceps likely made up for that when it came to punching.

But nothing for it. He shoved hard at the guy.

All those muscles coiled with dangerous intention. *Oh fuck oh fuck oh fuck*— The other man immediately shoved back, knocking Preston into the hallway wall. He braced one arm across Preston's chest and lifted his other with a fist. "I'm telling you, man, she's not worth it. I lost six months for her. You wanna lose your fucking face?"

Ignoring his pulse lashing in his ears, Preston jerked his head at the security camera in the eaves over the stairs. "You want to go back to jail for her?" The guy stared at the camera. *Come on, put the pieces together, genius.* "What were you saying about probation? Probably not *great* to be recorded assaulting someone in a county where you're not supposed to be."

The man gave Preston another hard shove, before backing off.

Preston struggled down a breath. "Better hurry home."

"Fuck you. And fuck her." But he tromped down the stairs.

Preston's shoulders slumped down against the wall. What the fuck had just happened?

CHAPTER TWENTY-SIX

HARMONY

Walking into Travis's office the last hour before town hall closed for business, Harmony couldn't seem to quell the nerves zinging through her stomach. She wore her black jumpsuit and heels, and a confident, purposeful expression. Underneath it all, though, she was worried rather than enjoying the challenge of nailing a job. Maybe because of her confrontation with Travis the other night. Maybe because this time she had something to lose.

The mayor didn't ignore her today. Travis waited for her with a smile, hands folded on his desk. "Miss Hale." His white teeth flashed. "Good afternoon."

At least he didn't seem hung up on their little tiff at the café. She needed to pull this off to make the festival real for all of Brookville. For her and Preston. "I'm afraid it's not. We've run into a bit of a snag." Harmony sat. "Nothing that can't be solved. With money, as all things can."

"Oh?"

"Legend Watts, the headliner we've been in talks with, pulled out last minute. He's taking a loss defaulting on the initial agreement by walking away, but that leaves us without a headliner just as we need to move to promoting."

Travis pursed his lips. "That sounds like more than a little snag."

"True. If we don't start ticket sales as scheduled, that risks a depressed turnout, plus bookings for hotels, local recreation—and if we don't line up a replacement, that puts the entire festival, along with everyone's investments, in danger." Harmony rested her folio in her lap and sighed. "I'm going to be straight with you. We need an infusion of cash to save the festival."

Travis narrowed his eyes at her. "Miss Hale, you assured this town your company was experienced at putting on events like this." He didn't seem all that upset, considering how easily he always lost his cool.

"These things happen." Harmony raised a palm in an unconcerned shrug and shifted forward. "I know you don't like to put your money directly into ventures like this, but I think in the interest of so many of your neighbors, not to mention your business's investment, and that of your wife—"

Travis laughed.

Okay, he was taking this maybe too lightly. Harmony shifted in her seat. Her marks always scoffed at her first threats of ruin, but then she got them to come around. "To be honest, Mr. Mayor, I think this might be a good opportunity for you, not just with the potential profit as a major investor, but to restore your reputation after that unpleasant scene at the restaurant this week. It's a small town, and word gets around. Supporting the festival—saving so many of Brookville's businesses, creating opportunities for its children—that would go a long way for buying back goodwill."

"You think I'm going to have an image problem?" He laughed again.

This meeting was getting away from her. Travis was acting so strangely. She found herself moving too quickly to her biggest push. "I think the people will demand action, and if they know you could have saved them and chose not to?"

Travis flattened his hands on his desk and leaned forward. "And what if they know you've been lying to them, and me, the entire time?"

Harmony's grip on her folio slackened. "Excuse me?"

"Miss. Hale." A tight laugh wheezed from Travis, and he pinned her with his cold gaze. "Bullshit. You're Iggie's kid. Harmony Greene."

Ice water ran down her spine. This could not be happening.

"All grown up." Travis shook his head thoughtfully, his gaze on her assessing. Harmony's stomach churned. "It only came to me today, once I knew you were full of it. I started thinking you over more carefully after a visit I had from someone this afternoon. Zach Seeley?"

No, no, no. Harmony's hands, slick with sweat, slipped over the leather of her folder. She had to get out of here, she had to lie her way out of this.

"He said he'd heard you were in town and wanted to warn us. Told me all about how you like to spend your time." Travis pulled a frown. "What would my old friend Iggie think of what you've become?"

Fury seared away Harmony's panic. "Friend? You stole my father's work and tossed him aside like trash."

"He *was* trash, drunk or worse half the time." Travis scoffed. "I took his one good idea and made something of it."

Harmony's hands clenched. There was no point arguing with this monster. She could only try to leverage what power she had against him. "Brookville will still be on the hook, we still need to save the festival for everyone's sake—"

"*What* festival?" Harmony's chest constricted at Travis's scorn. "You've tanked my chances at franchising the arcade. I might have to scrap the entire endeavor." He shook a meaty finger at her. "You may have made a mess of my town, but the strongest will survive and eventually buy up the rest. You face a far bigger mess yourself, taking all those payments. Namely, unless you deliver a headliner by the date stated in our contract and move forward with the festival we both know you never intended to put on, you'll be inviting charges of fraud."

The threat rang in her ears, sending waves of desperation echoing through her—not only for herself but for everyone she couldn't pay back, after laying out the last of her money on the festival. And because, for once—for Preston—she didn't want to have to slip away in the night. Harmony fought to swallow, knowing she had no more cards left to play. No more tricks up her sleeve. Only more reason than ever not to lose. "Please," she said, and that word cost her everything, breaking her down, turning her into that same little girl waiting outside the room while her father pleaded with Travis. She was begging Travis now too. Her gut soured, but she mustered, "Please, help fund the headliner, and I'll make sure the festival is a success, and you can have all the credit."

"I don't think I need to worry about my image when the scandal of your fraud will be all anyone cares about once this comes to light. Now get out of my office."

She couldn't retreat without winning. She had the urge to run for her car and drive away fast, out of Brookville, before the truth of what had just happened could catch up and crash over her.

She hadn't even recorded Travis throwing his town under the bus, like she always did with her targets. Because she'd only wanted his help saving the festival for real. Which would never happen now. Just like her revenge for her dad.

Harmony rose from her chair automatically, like a goddamn puppet, and walked out of town hall in a daze. She'd driven halfway to Preston's house before she came back to herself and realized it. Yes, that was where she needed to go.

It was late afternoon, and people were walking their dogs, stopping to say hello, riding bikes, watching kids play on front lawns. This entire town was going to know she was a fraud and a liar. They would hate her, just as she'd wanted them to hate Travis. And she deserved it. Her scheme had put all their livelihoods at risk. Her manipulations had used their time and energy and passion. She didn't know how to fix this.

But she knew she needed to tell Preston the truth. She'd tried to turn all the golden lies on her tongue true, and failed, and all she had left was the ugly truth. All she had left was herself.

It took so long for him to come to the door, she thought maybe he wasn't home, though he said he'd be heading there from her hotel. Lacey would be back soon from Mason's. Then the door swung open, and she was so relieved to see him, in his scuffed glasses and shirt with the sleeves rolled up. "Harmony."

She dug her voice out from somewhere south of her toes. "Hi. Can I come in?" He stepped back, all the way into the living room, and she followed, the screen door creaking shut behind her, still struggling for what to say. She always had all the right words, but this was so hard now. She could not mess this up. She was afraid she already had. "So. Um. My meeting."

Preston looked her up and down, then stared at her face, forcefully, as if searching something out. He looked pale.

Harmony frowned. "Sorry, are you okay?"

His gaze drifted somewhere behind her. "Not really."

"What's wrong?"

He shook his head, but didn't say anything. He was spinning his ring at about a thousand miles an hour.

"Preston?" She stepped forward, reaching a hand out. "Did something happen? Is Lacey okay?"

He backed up and sat on the piano bench. "I need to ask you something."

She was at a loss, and she needed to *tell him*. But something clearly was bothering him, so she nodded. "Anything."

His voice was like gravel. "What's your real name?"

An entire sheet of ice water sliced through her this time, down to her fingertips, freezing her lungs. "What?"

"Someone told me today that you were only going by Hale. I think I should know the name of the person I'm—" His chest heaved, once, and he looked her dead on now, a terrible hope in his eyes. "Please, explain this to me."

She'd been with Preston only a couple hours ago. Now everything was falling apart. She almost whispered, "Who told you that?"

"Well, he didn't give me his name either. Too busy telling me how you're a con woman and threatening to knock my lights out."

"Shit." She was on one knee before him in a flash, trying to take his hands, but he threw them up between them. "Are you okay?"

"I already told you I'm not." His hands hovered over her shoulders. "I need you to explain. Who was that? Have you been lying to me this whole time?"

She rose from her crouch. Preston's gaze on her was too intense, too severe to withstand up close. She took a few steps back before she could make herself say, "Someone I used to work with." Harmony had shoved the threat of Zach into the back of her mind once she'd focused on actually pulling off the festival, on becoming everything she'd pretended to be. But that had been a fantasy—her biggest lie ever, told to herself. Preston raised a brow expectantly. Her shoulders dropped. "As a con woman."

He grabbed off his glasses and ran a palm over his face.

"I was coming to tell you. I wanted to tell you—"

"Did you?" He shoved his frames back on. "Why would you do that, if you're in the middle of a—" He waved a hand as if he could find the word he wanted and pull it out of the air. "A con?"

"Because I was trying to stop it. Change it. I didn't want to lie anymore." *Because of you*, she wanted to tell him, but she'd never in her life told someone she was in love with them, and the words wouldn't come in the face of Preston's glare.

"So you were lying." He shot to his feet and paced away until he ran out of space. "The festival is a scam. You were trying to steal from the town."

"Not the town—"

He spun back to face her. "You had me *helping* you."

"No, I told you, that was because I wanted to see you."

"Sure." There was an edge of bitterness to his words now. "How am I supposed to know what's real? You just say whatever you want." He raked both hands through his hair, the blue of his eyes like shattered glass. "Fake. It was all fake. Of course."

"*No.*" She started toward him, but he cut her off with his next words.

"So there is a festival?"

She wanted there to be. "The festival—" She'd *tried*. Her answer tangled in all her lies, all her history, all her hopes. "It's complicated."

"No, it's very simple," Preston said with deadly precision. "Real or fake. Truth or lies. Right or wrong."

It must have been so easy to see things clear-cut like that when you grew up with a home like this you knew you could always come back to, and two parents, even if one was a shithead. Preston had no idea what she'd had to do to survive, having zero safety net and telling herself she liked it that way. He'd never understand if she tried to explain how she felt about him, how everything had gotten into such a jumble because of the strength of that, the truth of it. Instead she did what she always did, and said the first thing that came into her head. "Yeah, you got me. I'm a dirty criminal, you sure are lucky you found out now before I stole your bike!"

She thought she'd seen the full force of Preston's scowl before, but the disbelief and scorn his face wore now blew that way, shriveling Harmony's impulse to argue. "Do you think this is a fucking joke?" His voice ground down to a growl. "I let you be around Lacey." He seemed to startle at his own words, and Harmony sank against the back of the couch. He didn't know her past because she'd lied to him about it. He was always so careful, and she'd made him trust her and then betrayed that trust. He was right to be horrified at inviting her into his life.

"Okay," Preston muttered, maybe to himself, drumming his hands on his thighs and pacing again. "It's fine. Fucked up, but fine. Same result. I always knew you were leaving."

"Right," Harmony croaked. "You're not losing anything you care about."

Now he looked truly furious. "Of course I fucking care about you. I'm not the one who's been faking everything."

"Not everything. I was trying—" But she hadn't been good enough. Her eyes were burning. "I wanted to make it for real, even though you never said you'd want me to stay. I *wanted*—" She choked on how much she wanted, on her fear of how she could never have it now. How she didn't deserve it.

Preston practically shouted, with shock or frustration, "I just didn't want to hold you back."

"*Why not*?" Her voice was between a rasp and a wail. "Why doesn't anyone think I'm worth hanging on to?" Travis's words back at his office had slithered deep inside her, that she'd already failed her father, let him wallow and waste away, and that was why she'd become something worse than trash trying to make up for it. "After he lost everything, my dad drank himself to death, because I wasn't enough." Maybe she was always going to turn out this way, loud and lying, but maybe that was why she was *so much*, trying to fill that hole. "Why am I not good enough? I'm never *enough*."

"Fucking *hell*, Harmony." Preston had gone very still and glowered. "You were a kid. It wasn't your job to fix everything."

That reassurance somehow both terrified her and gave her strength enough to say, "But I need to fix what I did here."

"No. You need to leave."

Harmony clutched at the sofa and summoned every scrap of her shredded bravery. "I want to stay."

"For what?" He was back to looking past her. "So they can arrest you for theft or fraud or whatever?"

For you. But that was impossible now. Preston didn't want her anywhere around him, his sister, his careful life he'd constructed for himself.

"How is anyone supposed to hang on to someone who's been lying about who they are? How are they going to hang on to you if *you're in jail?*"

His phone ringing made them both jump.

Preston snatched it from the entryway table and tapped the screen. "Sarah? Is Lacey all right?"

Sarah's voice was small over the line. "Oh, good, I texted, but you didn't answer. Lacey actually headed home a little while ago, but I was driving to the grocery store just now and saw her on her bike over here."

Preston's face was blank. "That's the wrong way."

"I know, I thought maybe she'd gotten lost, but I couldn't find her once I turned around."

"Okay." Preston ran a hand over his hair. "Okay, thanks, Sarah. I'll track her down."

"Just wanted to let you know. I'm sure she's fine."

Preston's hand holding the phone dropped to his side. "Why would she—" His gaze pulled toward the screen door. "She must have come home and heard us. Shit."

Harmony straightened and dug for her keys. "Do you want to go look for her? I could drive, or you could stay here in case she comes home?"

Preston slid his phone carefully into his pocket. "I want you to leave."

"Preston, please." She owed him far more but could at least do this.

"I can't deal with this right now." He pulled his keys from the hook by the door.

"Let me help, we can talk more later."

He looked only at the keys when he said, "Please, go."

"I still need to explain—"

"Tequila."

A painful bubble rose in Harmony's chest at the flat finality of his tone, the harsh line of his profile as he refused to look at her. She swallowed it down, fighting back those tears again. All she could manage was a nod.

And then she left.

CHAPTER TWENTY-SEVEN
PRESTON

Unexpected phone calls always set Preston off this way. Ever since his mom. His father had called him while Preston had been walking to class. He hadn't had a meltdown, not until that night, though Dani seethed later, unable to believe "that jackass" hadn't called someone at the school, to be there to tell him in person, to take him back to his apartment. Preston had dropped his phone. Watched it fall toward the pale concrete path across the humanities quad, time seeming to slow, to stretch into a clear line marking the before and after of learning what he'd lost. He'd made all the arrangements—the funeral and flowers and emailing his professors that he'd be finishing his degree online—on the shattered screen.

Now Preston's anxiety flooded through him as he raced toward downtown, looking for his sister and trying not to think about Harmony. Even before he'd jumped on his bike, his pulse had been speeding. He was worried for Lacey, no time to be upset for himself. He shouldn't even be that angry. Only at himself, for being foolish enough to believe any of this could actually have happened to him for real. For thinking anyone, let alone Harmony, could have felt enough for him to barge into his life like she had, forget sticking around.

Why would Harmony bother, though, once he'd signed that lease? He coasted a moment, a sick dread falling through him. He'd never seen Harmony look like that. Defeated. Small. He'd never heard her sound like that, her voice broken.

But it was an act, right? It had to be. Right? Because she'd seemed heartbroken, and he knew, he *knew*, no one could love him like that.

He swung around the corner toward the greenbelt path he always took with Lacey, away from traffic. No sign of her.

Even before he'd found out Harmony had been lying, he'd known they were only short-term. And even if she had been sincere in her feelings for him, she still had to go or risk being arrested. Of course she did. One way or another, everyone left.

He'd reached the center of downtown and scoured each bench, the gazebo, the patio of the ice cream shop, for Lacey. Where would she go? Her bike wasn't outside the library. It was going to get dark soon. He chose a street and kept going.

Was Harmony already driving out of town? If she was in danger of arrest, she *should* go. He'd meant it that he needed her to leave. That had been half his panic back there, that he wanted her to go and be safe as much as he wanted her to stay and be who she'd said.

The whole way home from the hotel, and after, he'd wanted so badly for Harmony to explain it all away. He'd even waited to call or text, not wanting to interrupt her important meeting if it all turned out to be a misunderstanding. Mind churning, he'd gone through chores on autopilot, sure that with enough time things would settle into some shape that made sense.

But they didn't, and she hadn't. There was no escaping the truth, that she had only been here as part of a con, and that he had monumentally fucked up by thinking he might have actually found someone, even for a short time, and having her around Lacey.

Who had heard something about Harmony's lies and run away and *what if something happened to her?* He'd only just started letting her ride around the neighborhood on her own, not because of her own lack of skills, but because sometimes people were shit and thought it was funny to take advantage of autistic kids and *fuck* maybe he'd better call Dani.

He pulled over to the sidewalk and dug out his phone. He was too hurried to text, but she didn't pick up. He left a message. "Hey, Lacey got upset and took off. Not sure where she went, but can you keep an eye out, maybe drive down your road in case she's headed out there?"

"Mr. Jones!"

He spun at his name. Across the street and halfway down the block, Jordan was standing and waving, next to a bench outside the smoothie shop, where Nina sat—beside Lacey.

A wave of relief hit him. "Never mind, found her. Call you later."

He swung off his bike, left it against a tree with his helmet swinging from its handlebar, and jaywalked over to the girls. "Hey," he said to Lacey, who was holding a small smoothie cup with a bright pink straw. "I wasn't sure where you were."

Nina looked from Lacey to him. "She was stopped here and seemed kind of upset, so we thought we'd better hang out with her. Bought her a smoothie."

"Thank you. That was very kind of you."

Nina knocked her own cup against Lacey's in a little toast. "No problem."

"Yeah," Jordan said, "we all have to watch out for each other, right? Like Ms. Hale did for us."

The relief of knowing Lacey was okay receded, leaving behind all the pain of the last few hours. He really wanted to go home. "Lace, you want to take that smoothie to go?"

She nodded, but her face screwed up with concern. "Am I in trouble?"

"No, Lace Face. I understand." He was the one who needed to apologize to her. At home.

Nina sighed and stood. "I have to get home too." She tossed her cup in a recycling bin. "My parents think I'm at prom committee. Which they already told me I can't go to with Jordan."

"Hang in there," Preston told her, trying not to sound too bleak, as Lacey got her bike. "I did the countdown to college thing too."

"Pfft, I won't survive senior year in that house. The second I turn eighteen in September I am out of there." She slipped her hand into Jordan's. "Mr. and Mrs. DaCosta say I can stay with them. If I do make it into Berkeley, I plan to major in crushing student loans. But sometimes you just have to make a break for it, right, Lacey?"

Lacey shot a finger gun at her, and both girls did them back. It was all Preston could do as they rode home to hold it together a little longer. Back at the house, the empty drive, with no ridiculous red car parked there, looked bereft. He must not have been hiding his distress as well as he'd hoped, because before he could even sit Lacey down to talk, as they came through the front door, she asked, "Are you sure I'm not in trouble?"

He set down her smoothie and dumped his keys and phone. "We need to talk about going places without telling anyone, if you're going to bike on your own. But you're not in trouble."

Lacey's hands twisted into the sleeves of her hoodie. "But everyone's mad."

Preston sat on the sofa, eye level with his sister. "Hey, remember when we talked about how people being upset around you doesn't always mean they're upset with you? This is one of those times. I'm sorry if you heard something that made you sad or scared. We can talk about that if you want?"

She sat at the other end of the couch. "Is Harmony in trouble?"

He took a deep breath before saying, "Maybe."

"Why?"

"She made some mistakes."

Lacey scrunched her mouth to one side, considering. "Is Harmony a liar?"

"Yes." He swallowed.

"So do you hate her now?"

"No." The word was out before he could think, but it felt true. "No, I don't hate her. You don't stop caring about people just because they make mistakes. I want to be sure you know that." Because Preston could shield Lacey from their father's parenting, but not from knowing he'd given up custody and refused visitation. "No matter what, I'm going to be here for you, okay? I love you."

Lacey was fiddling with the drawstring of her hoodie. "Do you love Harmony?"

A dark feeling spread through his chest, like sticky tar, making it hard to breathe. He shoved it down, down. Rubbed a palm along the arm of the couch, right near where Harmony had leaned this afternoon. All he could finally say, fully aware of what a hypocritical asshole it made him, was, "It's complicated."

He kept holding it together as best he could through dinner, and a quick text session with Dani reassuring her about his earlier voicemail, and Lacey's piano practice, because he thought sticking to their routine would be good for both of them. He would go back to that, his straightforward schedule of afternoons and evenings full of piano lessons, long days at the library as long as they let him, running Lacey to class and sessions, pretending being busy all the time meant he didn't ever feel empty. Telling himself trying for anything more was foolish for someone like him.

Lacey went up to bed, leaving him at the piano, alone, again. He dragged himself to his feet, too ready for this day to be over. As he switched off the lights, he noticed a pillow on the couch had tumbled over, from when he'd sat there with Lacey. The red stain of

Harmony's lipstick burned into his vision. He hadn't ever tried to wash it off.

Preston grabbed the pillow and threw it across the room.

He was a liar. Because like he always said, it wasn't complicated at all. He did nothing halfway. He still loved Harmony with his entire, broken heart.

CHAPTER TWENTY-EIGHT
HARMONY

Harmony flung her suitcase on the hotel bed and began shoving clothes inside. Thanks to their afternoon tryst yesterday, her sheets smelled of Preston's soap, and she'd lain awake half the night running their argument through her head, again and again. She had to get out of here, not because of Zach and Travis and fraud charges, but because she couldn't take another day trapped in this room with memories of her and Preston before her lies ruined everything.

Shoes, makeup bag, laptop. Not much, easy to be gone. No more bringing problems into Preston's life. She didn't need to stick around here to be made to feel like shit. Everywhere she went, all she had to do was flash her smile and people gave her whatever she wanted. Why had she ever thought of leaving that life?

She pulled open the nightstand to grab her last few things, but a book rested on top of her lip balm and earbuds.

Harmony lifted a green leather-bound copy of *Leaves of Grass* from the drawer and sat with a thump on the edge of the bed. Her fingers traced the gold embossing, then opened the book to Preston's careful, terrible handwriting on the endpaper.

Harmony—

"That music always round me, unceasing, unbeginning, yet long untaught I did not hear,

But now the chorus I hear and am elated."

—P

How dare he. Now she was trying not to cry *again*. Because she knew exactly what he meant. Only once she'd been with Preston had she realized how much she'd been wanting this, all of this, but couldn't admit it. Getting together with Zach had been part of that, looking for something that might last longer than the alias she wore that month. How she'd stopped finding hookups ever since. Only with Preston did she learn how much more there was to want, how it could feel to let herself be seen, as she was, all of her. Only with him had she hoped, maybe, someday, to be loved for it.

For such a long time she'd told herself she only wanted revenge—building up her chance to take down Travis for her dad, building up her accounts like those numbers would prove her worth, and his worth, that she could still have what he'd always dreamed of for them.

But she'd made her promise to him when she'd been that angry young Harmony, younger even than Jordan. And the truth was, if she focused on getting back at Travis, she never had to think about losing her dad.

He was gone, and nothing Harmony did to Travis would change that. What would her dad, for all his big dreams and big talk, really want for her? To destroy Travis? Or to find a life she loved and live it well? He'd named her Harmony, but she'd ended up so solitary for so long.

It didn't matter now. Forget getting whatever she wanted handed to her, she couldn't beg her way now into what she *needed*. Preston had sent her away. The music was over.

A knock at her door startled her. She tucked the book beside her on the bed and considered not answering. It could be Zach. Or the police.

It could be Preston.

She checked the peephole, and opened the door. "Dani. Thank god. If you're here for vengeance, I will happily walk into your kiln myself."

The woman barked a laugh. "No, honey. I wanted to check on you, because I wasn't sure you had anyone to do that." She shoved a small casserole dish into Harmony's hands. "Ziti. Heartbreak requires carbs."

More tears threatened to rain all over the ziti. Harmony drifted backward until she bumped into the bed and sat again. She set down the dish before she could drop it.

Dani followed inside and leaned on the desk. "That bad, huh?"

"Preston told you? How did you know—" Harmony swallowed down a knot of tears and probably disgusting mucus. *Ugh, feelings.* "How did you know it was heartbreak? He thinks I was lying, and even before that, we were just casual."

Dani let out a sympathetic sigh through her nose. "You may be a great big liar, but I've seen you around Preston. No one's *that* good an actress. And Preston's never been casual about a damn thing." She crossed her arms. "Now look, I meant what I said that time. You were good for him. Not my place, maybe, to tell you this, but I've known Preston his whole life, and that boy needed shaking up."

"Well, I think I managed that," Harmony said miserably. The memory of Preston's distraught face was going to stick with her no matter where she drove off to.

"The question is," Dani said, with a pointed look at the suitcase behind Harmony, "what are you going to do now? Sometimes you have to start over. Maybe run from things. Maybe take what you have and try again with it."

Harmony pressed a palm onto the leather cover of the book. "He wants me to go away."

"That's what he wants?" Dani's tone was a challenge. But of course he did. Sometime close to midnight Harmony had gotten up the nerve to text him, asking if Lacey was all right, and he'd replied at once with a curt *Yes* followed by *You should leave town*, and *Please* just after that. She couldn't bring herself to respond to that with any of the explanations she'd been hoping to share. Excuses. Just more talk. Preston had seen the real her and couldn't stand being in the same town with her anymore.

At her silence, Dani shrugged. "As much as he likes to think he can control everything if he just tries and worries hard enough, Preston is not actually in charge of the world. So what about you? What do you want, Harmony Whatever?"

She wanted to stop running—from her actions, from her own fears of not being enough. She wanted to do real good. But for that to happen, she was going to have to be real. Be herself. And that meant facing the harm she'd caused. With more than talk.

Jail wasn't exactly the more permanent home she'd been aiming for, but maybe it was where she needed to start, if she was serious about making amends and creating a different kind of life for herself.

Bracketed by book and pasta, Harmony made her choice.

It would be her greatest challenge yet. And she'd always loved a challenge.

CHAPTER TWENTY-NINE
PRESTON

Preston arrived early for the inquiry meeting.

He wasn't eager, only anxious. After everything that had happened, he didn't hold much hope for things turning out for the better today. Probably they would get worse, just as he had felt worse the past few days, still going about his routine like nothing at all had changed, except for how he felt like a hole had been blown straight through his chest.

But Harmony and her magic were gone, and the town only had him, so he'd assembled all his notes and come to the town hall chambers ready to speak up for the library.

Cheryl was there already, chatting with a couple of her friends and Travis, who leaned on one of the tables at the front of the room. She shot Preston a superior look. As he took a seat on the far aisle, he could hear her murmuring about "that exposed scammer" and Travis laughing. Preston stared only at his notes while listening to them debate his lack of judgment for dating her. Rumors about Harmony and the festival had been flying all over town.

People were worried. Cheryl clearly thought this would only benefit her today.

He was concentrating so hard on not looking at anyone and keeping a brewing stomachache at bay, he didn't notice at first how full the chambers were getting. But the shuffling and conversations grew too loud to ignore.

The seats were filled with people. Ellie Vickes and several other friends of Cheryl were near her in the audience now, but Libby and Bonnie and Sarah were sitting off together on the other side of the room. Sarah caught Preston's eye and waved. Libby gave him a thumbs-up. And all around them, other library patrons had come. He twisted in his seat to see the entire GSA was sitting behind him. Holy shit. He'd halfheartedly posted about the inquiry on those new social media accounts, but as Harmony had said, no one tended to show up except to complain.

The town had come out for their library.

Nina propped her crossed arms on the back of the seat next to him. "Why didn't Ms. Hale come?"

Before he could reply, Jordan asked, "What they're saying about her isn't actually true, is it?"

His mouth opened and closed once, and he looked down at his notes as if the answer to their questions might be found there.

"Because that's BS," Jordan said darkly. "She wouldn't do that. Like, she's the one that got everyone here."

Preston looked up, the room seeming to go quiet and empty again, except for Jordan's words. "What do you mean?"

"Emailed everyone, posted everywhere, made us all promise. Mr. Jones, she's not really gone, is she?"

Nina slumped back in her seat. "If there's no festival, then all our work was wasted."

"It's not wasted," Jordan huffed. "She said she'd teach me stuff and she did. I'm not stopping. Wait till your mom hears me during open comments, and that's just the start. I have a whole strategy for the next city development meeting." She jabbed an emphatic finger in the air, in a way Preston knew she'd picked up from Harmony. "They are gonna *listen* about the risk of soil erosion and wildfires and harming the burrowing owl habitat, before they clear-cut any more land." Her brow pinched. "You really think she didn't care at all?"

Surrounded by all the people she'd gathered here, Preston suddenly found he couldn't answer that.

They were interrupted anyway, as the rest of the council had arrived and Travis called the meeting to order. Cheryl spoke first, all her carefully couched concern for children, for parental rights. She called into question the judgment of the library staff and proposed a committee appointed by the council to oversee culling the collection, new acquisitions, programming, and staff. Preston studied the faces of the councilors. Travis was a given to act in his wife's favor. But he couldn't get a read on anyone else. Was this going poorly already? Was this one of those times people went through the motions but already had their minds made up?

And then it was his turn.

As he took the podium, with hands that were not shaking enough for anyone to tell, he hoped, Preston couldn't help remembering Harmony's advice—because why wouldn't he be thinking about her right now when everything depended on his keeping it together? *People want you to succeed.*

All these people she'd gotten to come. They were rooting for him. And they were counting on him.

He launched into his prepared statement. All the information about the library's mission, the statistics about patron usage, circulation and attendance numbers, plus the American Library Association's statements on the First Amendment. He used all his regular tricks, looking at the councilors' ears rather than eyes when he lifted his gaze, matching facial expressions. He couldn't tell if this was going well, but when he reached the end of his notes he found he wasn't done speaking.

He steered his gaze directly into Travis's eyes. "Ultimately, our library needs to exist for everyone in our town. It needs to serve every race and disabled and LGBTQ+ patrons." Preston went on, to the rest of the council, "It needs to include them in its materials and programming, because to not do so would mean actively erasing them. It would be telling the children who use the library that who they are, or who their siblings or friends or parents are, is not okay. That they should not exist. That's a statement to the people of this town, to its children, that this council could but should not make." He broke his pretend eye contact with the people at the head of the room to turn in Cheryl's direction. "We should accept everyone, even if they turn out to be different from what you thought. Even if their lives are different than yours or what you imagined."

He wasn't sure if he was trying to convince her to finally get her head out of her ass about Nina, or somehow trying to talk to his own father, a hundred miles or two decades away.

Or maybe himself, as he felt all over again what a shit he'd been to Harmony when she'd tried to explain about her past.

Cheryl adjusted the sleeve of her blouse and murmured something undoubtedly spiteful to her friend next to her, but Preston was too busy hoping Harmony was long gone, far beyond the reach of the Weavers and his own sorry treatment of her, to care much.

He gripped the edges of the podium and finished, "I think the library should be a place of more imagination rather than reflect only one kind of person or one kind of life. I trust the people of Brookville to each use their own judgment in how they and their families make use of our services and materials that we aim to enrich the lives of all patrons with, just as I trust this council to decide in the true best interest of everyone."

Preston pivoted and took his seat again and promptly sat on his hands because they were definitely shaking now.

Someone clapped him on the back. Jordan, leaning forward. "Kickass, Mr. Jones."

He blew out a breath. "Thanks."

The meeting opened to public comments, which took well over an hour. That was what Cheryl got for pushing for a special meeting—at monthly town hall sessions there was a cap, but today person after person streamed forward to take the podium. A few spoke for Cheryl's side, but far more supported the library. Sarah mentioned the tutoring club her eldest, Joey, had used in middle school. Libby mentioned the value of the library to the school district's families and praised the book club, noting specific titles they'd chosen for their first year, some of which were on the contested list. Nina beamed encouragement while Jordan spoke confidently about the GSA—her voice didn't even tremble, like back at the band auditions. And so many others.

Preston couldn't help feeling more than ever the absence of one person. Harmony had done this. The rumors were all saying she'd reneged on her promise to help the town, but she'd made these connections that were working today to save something important. And he'd accused her of simply trying to steal from them all. He fought to hold himself together. He had to see this through.

At the end of comments, Travis adjusted his mic, mouth halfway open already, but Vinitha Newell spoke first. "Thank you, Mrs. Weaver and Mr. Jones, for sharing with us here today." She addressed the crowd. "And thanks to all of you for being here and letting the council know your thoughts on this important issue. I have to take a moment to say, I have been concerned about the direction Brookville seemed to be taking, with regards to the library and free speech. The calls for censorship have both a chilling effect on freedom and, I believe, a part in provoking actual physical violence against public servants, which is something I would very much hate to see happen in our town." She paused a moment, looking at Cheryl and Ellie Vickes beside her. Then she tipped her head to Preston. "No matter how forgiving our wonderful public servants may tend to be, we have a duty to speak up against such things whenever we can."

Travis looked like he was struggling to hold a mouthful of marbles in. He pulled his mic closer and said, "Everyone on the council is eager to discuss the matter, but it's gotten rather late. Perhaps we ought to adjourn and move that to our next private session?"

Ms. Newell gave a pleasant shrug. "I think it won't take very much time for the council to come to a decision on this." One or two on the council were blank faced still, but all the others nodded. Some of the audience drifted out while a few councilors made their own comments or asked Preston to answer a question—thank god for his over-prepared notes—or Cheryl, who talked a lot without saying much. After what seemed like an age in this room under the whining fluorescent lights, but also far too soon, Ms. Newell made a motion to vote on a resolution affirming the work of the library and taking no action to direct a change in materials, programming, or oversight. The motion was seconded, the vote taken, and it passed.

A grim-faced Travis struck his gavel and it was over.

Preston was honestly still trying to catch up with what had happened when the GSA cheered with the volume only a group of teenagers could achieve, and he covered his ears. People came up to congratulate him or thank him. Sarah and the others too. When he thanked them for making their comments, Libby rolled her eyes and said, "Cheryl talked about trying the same stunt at the school board meeting, aiming for the school libraries, and I'm incredibly grateful she'll probably think twice about kicking that hornet's nest now. We *just* got everyone calmed down about the new state sex ed curriculum."

Most were filtering out of the chambers, and Preston made for the back door that would avoid any more small talk and take him straight to the parking lot and home to Lacey and Dani, who would be eager to hear how the day went and were probably wondering what had taken so long.

Dusk was falling, Venus already winking in the sky, and Harmony's friend Alice was leaning against the first row of bike racks.

"Hey," he said. "How's it going?" It wasn't small talk—Alice was fairly new in town, and he could imagine it felt pretty shitty to make a friend only to have them turn into the top story in that month's town gossip and disappear. "You doing okay with the whole . . . Harmony thing? Had you two gotten close?"

Alice stood, hopping off the base of the bike rack she'd been perched on. "Hmm, thing is, I've actually known Harmony kind of a long time."

"You—" He was a little fried from the meeting, but the implication hit. "You work together?"

She scrunched her nose. "Yeah, at least until she decided to go straight because she fell in love with you."

Preston inhaled sharply. "What?"

His whirlwind of thoughts about *that* were interrupted when Alice lifted a finger and screwed up her sharp little face. "Do not tell her I told you so, or else I'll call in my guy who knows how to make problems go away."

Preston's *what* didn't even make it out of his mouth this time.

"I'm kidding." Alice laughed at his expression. "We don't operate like that. No violence."

"You sure?" Zach had seemed pretty quick to resort to it.

Her eyes flicked up to one side as she considered. "One time Harmony got shoved into a swimming pool when she almost got caught, but the only casualty that night was a silk gown."

"That story was true?"

"Oh, yeah." Alice cackled. "She looked like Kim at the Met Gala."

Preston didn't know what that meant, but you'd think his brain could give him a break and not *immediately* subject him to an image of Harmony in dripping, clingy silk. Had Alice come just to rub everything he'd lost in his face?

"Neither of us could stop laughing the whole drive down from Beverly Hills. I love working with Harmony, because it's fun."

The ache he felt in his chest carried to his voice. "Yeah, that sounds like Harmony."

Alice shoved her hands into her jeans pockets. "Most people in our business will treat you like crap, but Harmony never let it turn her into someone like that. She got me away from that kind of thing. I'd follow her anywhere, even if she decided to try settling down in a random town in the middle of nowhere."

He wanted to believe it, that she'd been telling the truth about wanting to stay. Even if she was already gone. Even if it made that hurt a little more.

"Where I actually really like it, turns out." Alice shrugged. "Small-town girl at heart. Anyway, Harmony has always looked out for me, and she's kind of been acting like an absolute churro lately—love, what can you do?—so I thought there were some things you should know. Like, Harmony only chooses marks who deserve it. People picking on the little guy. Or girl." She scuffed the toe of one of her Chucks into the base of the bike rack. "Or seven girls over five years, until Harmony bankrupted his church and shared the proof she dug up."

"Shit." This didn't sound like what he'd imagined when Harmony had confessed to being a con woman.

"Yeah. Or like Travis, who stole her father's work."

"What work?" Preston frowned. He felt like everything was shifting under him. "He wasn't a music exec?" Harmony had said her father had lost everything, but he'd pictured a *Behind the Music* kind of downfall.

"He did I.T., when he could keep down a job, which doesn't sound like that often from the little Harmony's told me. But he created some code that Travis used to make his millions, and Travis cut him out completely."

So when Harmony had said that about her father—this cast everything she'd done here in a different light.

He was still trying to catch up, but Alice went on, "And she always pays back anyone else caught up in a scheme. The people here never would have lost a dime, only the promise of more, and she honestly thought she was helping them to learn not to fall for that kind of thing again."

Harmony had tried to tell him. That she'd been trying to steal only from Travis, not the whole town. In the moment he'd been so overwhelmed and upset—

"But then she met you, and she decided, instead, to make the festival real and deliver on all those promises."

"That's . . . that's ridiculous." He straightened his already straight glasses.

"Yup. I told her that. But like I said, love." Alice pulled her hands free and fluttered her fingers around her heart and batted her eyelashes.

"She'd never actually put on anything like that before?"

Alice shook her head. "That's how true her feelings were for you."

The evening was deepening toward night, suffocating the light out of the sky. Preston fought to swallow down a breath. There was so much to process, lies and truths, but at the bottom of it all, the only thing that mattered was it seemed maybe—his heart stuttered with the thought—maybe Harmony's feelings had been real, as real as his love for her. While Alice was throwing around that word pretty freely, he couldn't know for sure just what Harmony felt, couldn't even be certain this wasn't another ruse, but he could remember the crushed look on her face when he'd sent her away. That had felt true and terrible.

Shit, what had he done? He'd thought he'd been okay with things, his whole history with his dad, but clearly he'd still been cutting himself off, shutting himself up, trying to make it not hurt—to not get hurt again. Instead he'd ruined everything with someone who saw him and accepted him and deserved far better than being treated like that.

He deserved better than that too. Maybe he really did need to get back to therapy.

"Harmony's always taking care of me," Alice said. "Of everyone who's been shoved down or overlooked. She'd be pissed as Christian Siriano was when she returned that gown if she knew I'd come to talk to you, and I don't even know what I hope you could do, but I can't sit by while she's hurting herself."

Preston sank down to sit on the bike rack beside Alice. "I'm sorry I hurt her." He scrubbed a hand through his hair. He couldn't say how much. "But she's better off away from here." He didn't have much experience with love, but he knew, despite what the poets wrote about it conquering all, it wasn't going to stand in the way of a prison sentence.

"Yeah, she would be."

"Would be . . . if what?"

"If she *left*."

"She—" Fuck, it felt like his chest was cracking open. "*She didn't leave*?"

Alice threw up her hands. "She's still sitting in her goddamn hotel room."

Preston gripped the metal frame of the bike rack, resisting the sudden mad urge to grab his bike and get to the hotel as fast as he could. "Why?" The word almost snagged on all the emotion welling up inside him, confusion and fear and hope. If she'd stayed, then that meant it was all true.

Arching a brow, Alice wiggled her fingers around her heart again.

"But she—she *has* to go. Without a festival, it's fraud, and Travis or the others will have her arrested."

"What do you think I've been telling her? She won't listen. She insists she's going to that contract meeting with Travis next week as scheduled. She's going to admit everything. And listen, no one has *anything* on my girl. That's why Zach was so pissed—there's nothing to point anyone to, no trail leading back to her, not without implicating himself in crimes our marks didn't even report because then they would implicate *themselves* in worse stuff. But if Harmony marches in there and confesses?"

Preston stared at the town hall building, darkening into shadow. "What do we do? We have to talk her out of it."

"I've tried." Alice shook her head. "She keeps saying talk isn't enough, only actions. That's why she was working so hard trying to turn the con into a real festival."

"Well," Preston said, and he was definitely clutching at straws, "can we do that?"

Alice snorted. "No way. The whole point is how impossible it is to get a headliner at the last minute, without a huge fee. Everything hinges on that. We're out of money, and Travis isn't coughing any up. So unless you know any A-list music stars who owe you a huge favor. . ." Alice blew out a breath sounding like a cartoon explosion.

Like a lone note rising from a long silence, a fragile hope broke through Preston's desperation. He angled his head at Harmony's friend. "Funny story."

CHAPTER THIRTY
HARMONY

Harmony took care getting ready for her final meeting with Travis, putting on a light bit of makeup and her electric blue dress. She wouldn't put it past him to have the sheriff's office on speed dial and have her hauled into a holding cell before the day was over. It might be her last chance to look this good for a while.

Although, as she'd reassured Alice when she'd been begging her to leave town, she looked great in orange. And she'd always loved a jumpsuit.

Her hand didn't wobble at all as she traced on her eyeliner. She was going to be absolutely fine. She always was. No matter how alone or how far life shoved her down the stairs.

Besides, this had been her own doing. She'd hurt people—Preston was only the start. She'd used the town's enthusiasm for her own ends, and the little she'd done to help with the library didn't even begin to pay them back for all that.

Time to face the consequences of her actions.

As it turned out, Travis was an even bigger asshole than she'd believed her whole life and had a sheriff's deputy actually in his office with him, along with several men she recognized as members of the Brookville Business Association, all ranged around the conference table at one side of the room. Oh, yeah, very intimidating.

She left the door ajar (some instincts for quick escapes die hard) and took a seat at the far end from Travis. "Afternoon, gentlemen." They nodded hello.

"Harmony," Travis said with an obnoxious familiarity.

She grinned. "Travis." She was making amends, but she never said anything about showing this dipstick any undeserved respect.

He gestured to the others. "The heads of the business association wanted to be here, in light of the information that has arisen calling into doubt your ability to deliver on your end of the bargain." Harmony had been lying low but monitoring things online, and she'd seen him riling everyone up about the festival falling through.

"Rumors are such nasty things." She raised her brows. "Imagine, I heard one recently that you came by your success through no genius of your own but by coopting the work of others without proper compensation!" She sighed with a smile and shook her head. "Gossip!"

But Travis knew he was untouchable, and he had her dead to rights. "People are always jealous of success. Now, to the matter at hand." He glanced at the empty table before Harmony. No folio. No bag. "I am very concerned about seeing if, per your agreement with the town, you've brought the signed contract to register on file here today."

Harmony's throat stoppered up with a decade of sharply watching out for herself, a lifetime of scrabbling to survive. Her thoughts chased around inside her, her instincts shouting while she stared back at Travis and avoided looking at the deputy. *Lie. Run.*

The only way out of this—to the Harmony she wanted to be, to a Harmony who might be worthy of someone like Preston someday—was through. She swallowed hard. "I have not."

Shoulders deflated. A few of the business owners shot grim looks at each other. Travis tapped his pen with an admonishing clatter. "So—" he began darkly.

A knock came at the door, which was immediately swung fully open by Preston.

Harmony gaped, officially speechless. What was he doing here? She'd heard his library inquiry had gone in his favor; he should be off enjoying that, not showing up to witness her arrest. Maybe he wanted to yell at her some more. She deserved that. It would complete this whole amends thing she was trying. She didn't even really mind—it was so good to see him, tweed jacket and pressed shirt and stupid perfectly curling hair she was never going to run her hands through again.

"I have, though," Preston said. "Brought the contract." He set a packet of papers in the center of the table. "Sorry I'm late."

Travis stared at the papers like they were a dead fish Preston had dropped into the middle of the meeting. "This is the headliner contract?"

"Signed and ready to go." He wasn't looking at Harmony or the *what the fuck* look she was very subtly giving him.

The silver-haired owner of a small local chain of coffee shops leaned forward with interest. "Who's the headliner?"

Preston braced his hands on the back of an empty chair. "Legend Watts."

No, he couldn't be doing this. If he'd faked the paperwork or something, he'd be abetting fraud. What the hell was he thinking, he had Lacey to take care of—

"Forgive me," Travis said, spreading a hand toward the papers, "but what with the rumors going around about the festival, what assurance does the town have that these are legitimate?"

Preston nodded. "I thought you might have concerns. Luckily, while we could have taken care of all this with electronic signatures, my roommate from music school had been looking for an excuse to visit." He called into the hallway. "Will?"

With varying levels of confusion about what this had to do with anything, Harmony and the others all turned to look at the door, and some old friend of Preston's, apparently.

But it was Legend Watts who walked into the room.

Excitement crackled through the office as everyone realized. A large man, Legend Watts wore a white T-shirt, faded jeans, and a haircut that all screamed how expensive they were, and a shy smile on his pale face. And Alice of all people was standing behind him in the doorway, looking like a professional assistant in black slacks and a ponytail, tapping away on her phone. Legend Watts gave a casual wave. "Been far too long since I came back to Northern California. Glad to stop by on my way back from my Asia tour and check up on Preston."

What was *happening*? But if there was one thing Harmony was going to do, it was roll with the unexpected. She leaned forward on crossed arms. "I know he's a huge fan of yours. He has all your albums favorited on his playlist."

Legend Watts turned a gleeful look on Preston. "He does, does he? Aw, mate, and here I thought you were too much of a classical snob to care about my little career." He winked at Harmony and jerked his head at Preston. "Won't even use my stage name."

Preston's tweed-clad shoulders bristled. "I'm not calling you that."

Legend waved a hand between them. "You gave me this nickname."

"As a joke, because you were always talking until three A.M. about how you were going to be a star."

"And was I wrong?" He turned back to everyone around the table. "I ask you!"

Delighted smiles and laughs came from everyone but Travis, who only looked shocked.

"Anyway," Legend said, "I'm very excited about kicking off this festival. Been looking for something just like this back home, honestly, so this came at the perfect time." He nodded toward the papers in front of Preston. "I assume everything you need is there. Preston's always so particular about details, so if that takes care of business—"

"Oh," Preston said, with studious innocence. "Nice of you to offer. I'm sure everyone would love if we could take a few minutes for an autograph or photo or two."

Legend looked for a second like he was considering murdering his old friend, then scratched at one eyebrow. "Right. Let's do it."

After that, the meeting was clearly over. Harmony rose slowly from her seat, still not quite sure what had happened, as a real estate agent and the deputy posed smiling on either side of Legend.

But Preston finally turned to her. And suddenly she felt more scared than when she'd been about to go to jail. Which maybe she wasn't doing after all? Because of Preston.

"Hey," he said. "Sorry for interrupting, but you seemed to have gotten into a tiny bit of trouble."

"Always a possibility." She made a small, tense shrug. "That's working without a net for you."

His eyes searched over her face. "Hope you don't mind I caught you." It was a question. He pressed his lips together, watchful, waiting.

Harmony fiddled her ring up and down her knuckles. He'd done it, what she'd been trying to do to wash away the lies between them. He'd also told her to leave town. "Why did you?"

"Why'd you make sure half the town showed up to my inquiry?" He glanced at Legend. "Alice has got him. She'll help him escape in a minute. Can we go talk?"

Harmony looked down the table where she'd been about to confess to her crimes. Travis had grabbed the paperwork and was flipping through its pages. The café chain owner was giving him a stern look. "Thank god you didn't tank this for the town. Spreading those rumors could have cost a lot of people a huge opportunity."

"Speaking of that," Alice said, stepping forward, edging behind the radio station owner snapping pictures of the others.

"And who are you?" Travis asked Alice. "Lady Gaga?" Leave it to him not to recognize Melissa from Indiana now that she was back to being an assistant.

"Alice Burrows, assistant festival manager, Rhythmic Events," she answered in a clipped tone. "I'm afraid we've had to amend the vendor list. We're trimming your VR tent and your wife's business from the merch booths." She pulled out a folder she'd had tucked under one arm and showed him the updated paperwork.

Travis thumped a palm on the table, making the pages flutter. "You can't do that. If there really is a festival, then we deserve to benefit—"

"Sorry, we can."

"Then I'll be expecting our fees back. You can't have your cake and get a free lunch too."

Holy shit. Harmony squeezed past the photo op to tell Travis, "All agreements include strict co-promotional clauses." Her next words came with a rush of satisfaction, a memory flashing through her vision of Iggie Greene throwing his arms up and spinning in his chair after nailing a tricky bit of code. "Including nondefamation clauses."

Alice nodded, paging through printouts in the folder. "And we have on file you and your wife's statements in several public forums online defaming Rhythmic, Ms. Hale, and this specific event. All fees are forfeit in such a case."

Harmony tsked. "Gossip." It wasn't all his millions, or anything like what he owed her dad, but Travis's fee for that big tent was a serious chunk of change. Goodbye, franchise dreams. Maybe even the entire arcade, unless Travis liquidated other assets. The cash would be enough to fund a local grant program, it occurred to Harmony, her mind working as fast as her mouth ever did. She bet Jordan and Nina would have some great ideas for deserving recipients. And helping to run something like that would look great on college and scholarship applications.

Harmony leaned nearer Travis to murmur, "Really should have read the contract more carefully." The idea of making amends was nice, but *that* felt fucking fantastic. She straightened and told Preston, "Let's go."

They slipped down a hallway and out to the edge of the town square. The sun was still high, the sky a clear blue, and people were spread over the benches and blankets, enjoying the warm day. The statue was dressed in a party hat with a banner slung between its hands wishing someone a happy birthday. They walked along away from the town hall steps, gradually slowing, and finally facing each other.

"So." The triumph drained out of her. Harmony wanted to ask again why he'd done this for her. If it was only his noble impulse for taking care of everyone, even if her lies had ruined things between them for good. "That was . . . quite the show."

"Yeah, well, it's not on my résumé, but distracting business owners with pop stars is one of my secret talents." Preston's hands flexed at his sides. "Now it's up to you to put on the festival."

She let out a little helpless laugh. "I don't actually know how to do that."

The corners of Preston's lips curled up. "How many times do I have to say it? You're good at everything. You can do it. And you'll have help. Alice is all in. Plus Will, whose ego rivals yours."

She gave a mock gasp. "Impossible."

"It's true. Antarctica-sized, at *least*."

She shook her head, still taking it all in. "Your college roommate was Legend Watts."

Preston laughed, rubbing the back of his neck with one hand. "I honestly thought I'd told you. Sometimes I forget people don't know everything running through my head."

She looked down at her heels and his loafers, biting her lip. But she'd been as brave as she'd ever been coming here today, so why stop now? "Like what else?"

He lifted her chin with a gentle finger. His eyes were bluer than the sky, the feeling in them deeper. "Like how I really missed you." Her pulse sped, and she needed to know if that meant she hadn't ruined things, if he could forgive her someday, but she couldn't think of any words at all, not even to tell him how much she'd missed him too. His hand moved to her shoulder, running down her arm, holding on to her. "And how I'm sorry. For getting so upset and not listening."

Harmony swallowed, trying not to get too distracted by how his touch set longing chasing through her blood. She still had so much to tell him. "I know you need time to process stuff. And it's understandable. *I'm* sorry." She took a deep breath. "I lied to you."

"I know. Alice explained some things to me. Your cons. Your dad."

Harmony fought down the old panic skittering over her skin at the thought of someone knowing her whole deal. She could trust Preston with anything. His saving her ass proved that. "I suppose, because she clearly helped get you and Legend here today, I won't hold that against her." She definitely wouldn't go command Evan to ask Alice out just to get back at her, or thank her, one or the other.

She took Preston's big hand in hers and ran her thumb over his knuckles. "I came to Brookville for one reason, and that's where all the lies came from, but then I chose something different." *I chose you.* Why was it still so hard to say? She kept going, talking her way around to it. "I gave up the revenge for it. What I can give my dad is being better and being happy. I was trying to figure it out, how to undo all the lies so that nothing would be in the way of us—" Everything she felt made her breath hitch. She was going to murder her feelings later, but for now, there was no helping how they made her voice waver, caught up with hope and fear.

She had come here today to tell the truth. So that was what she did. "I love you."

Preston's own breath went a little uneven, his hand clenching hers. He murmured, "I love you too," and actually, Harmony decided for once and all, feelings were pretty spectacular, because those words sent fireworks of joy shooting through her. "I was so stupid not to tell you," Preston said. "And so scared, because you were leaving, and you make everything better, and brighter, and I was really an asshole to doubt you."

"No, you weren't." She reached up with her free hand and brushed back a lock of his dark hair that had fallen forward as he bent to meet her eyes. "I like how careful you are."

His hand skated back up her arm, pulling her just a little nearer, almost by accident. "I like how reckless you make me want to be."

Harmony looked up into Preston's intent gaze. "Oh, really? Like what? You spend the last week zip-lining or race driving or something?"

His lips pursed in a gentle scowl, but his eyes fell to her own mouth. "More like thinking about kissing a wanted criminal."

She gave his hand a playful shake. "Hey, I'm not wanted, I've always covered my tracks. And you took care of this last job for me very neatly."

"Oh," said Preston, voice dropping to that rumble that Harmony could feel in her chest, where her heart was kicking like a goddamn chorus girl, "I think I can say with some certainty that you are very much wanted."

His hand lifted to cradle her head, and he dipped his to brush a sweet kiss against her mouth.

"Please stay." His words were mere breath against her lips between light kisses but carried an iron conviction. "I want you to stay. Not only for the festival. For me."

She answered him wordlessly, falling into a kiss with Preston that felt like an overture to so much more than even Harmony could have dreamed up.

"Hey!"

Preston barely pulled away and didn't break his gaze from Harmony's.

"Let's go, lovebirds!" Harmony grudgingly looked to see where Alice, with international pop star Legend Watts in tow, was shaking her keys from the steps of town hall. "Before the Brookville paparazzi arrive. We're going to an undisclosed location to get drinks to celebrate."

Preston made a little growl into Harmony's hair.

Harmony leaned back and quirked a brow at him. "Such a bully. I can tell her off if you want. I need like eleventy more of those kisses to make up for the past week. Maybe at an undisclosed location rather than the town square."

A heady look cast through his eyes just at those words, but he shrugged and smiled with a dawning sort of delight. "We have plenty of time."

He kept Harmony's hand in his as they walked over. "Is the undisclosed location my house?"

"Maybe," Legend admitted. "You owe me at least a bottle of wine for using me as a distraction to get your girlfriend out of there without any more questions." He smirked. "Besides, it's easier than braving the public trying to hide this renowned face."

"It's a good face," Alice said with an appreciative nod, and she listened, rapt, as Legend began telling her about visiting Preston's house back in college when he couldn't go home over the holidays. Good thing Harmony wasn't going to jail, because Alice was never going to be done needing her help staying out of trouble.

Preston leaned in to kiss Harmony's temple and gave her hand a squeeze. "Let's go home, sweetheart."

EPILOGUE
HARMONY

Lanyard bouncing against her chest, Harmony hustled through the crowd from the beer garden where she'd been hosting some music execs who'd flown in for the festival. It was day two, and the festival hadn't fallen apart as a complete disaster (yet), but Harmony was still running on frequent giant coffees furnished by her excellent interns and a boatload of nerves.

She found Preston and Lacey at the tables around the Italian slushies stand where he'd just texted they were hanging out between sets at the youth stage. Dropping with a thump into a folding chair beside them, she accepted the bright green drink Preston shoved into her hands and clicked off her wireless headset and its constant stream of chatter from the control center backstage. "Thank you, I'm in dire need of hydration after wooing those guys."

"Hey," Preston said, kicking his foot against the side of her sneaker. "I'm the only guy you're supposed to woo."

"Schmoozing, then." She tore the lid and straw off her mint slushy and gulped some down. "We'll just have to see if it worked."

She made an anxious grimace at Lacey, who was eating gelato out of a cup. A gentle rumble of music from the main stage carried from over a slope.

"You're the best at schmoozing," Preston said. "No one can resist your charm. Someone once told me that, and she never lies." He picked up his own lemon slushy. "She also looks really cute today."

"Hmm. You're pretty good at wooing yourself." But a sharp pain in her head made her groan. "Ow, brain freeze."

Preston chuckled sympathetically and brushed his fingers over her temple. "Slow down. Five minutes."

"I just hope they were impressed with what we've managed. If they come on board as sponsors, we can get some more big names next year." She took a smaller, slower sip. "We can't rely on your old classmates to fill the lineup every year." With a hopeful look, she said, "Unless you took music theory sitting next to, like, Halsey?"

Preston tilted his head. "I think the girl I sat next to became a riding instructor out in the boonies?"

"Wait, *this* isn't the boonies?"

He laughed, but in truth the festival site was beautiful all set up, the walnut trees shading the food stalls and merch stands, the cleared fields and rolling hills providing perfect spaces for the main stage and smaller performance areas. Preston said he was glad to see it all put to good use, even under the feet of so many attendees (thank god, ticket sales were strong). A bunch of locals were taking a break here too—*other* locals. Harmony was one now as well. She'd gotten an apartment with Alice, who was holding things down backstage, though Harmony spent plenty of nights over at Preston's.

The other night, after an endless video call with some of the stage prep people, Preston had sat her down for her own private concert of a song he'd written for her. She recognized it from that day she'd taken him and his bloody nose home. He said he'd begun composing it the day he'd met her, and she definitely did not cry and wipe away any tears before he turned around at its end, but she definitely did kiss him silly before they went to bed. He claimed he was going to have to get the piano retuned from how she'd knocked them both against it.

Legend was going to have to work hard tonight at his show if he wanted to compete with that performance.

She asked Preston how the kids had been doing at the youth stage near the front gate, then got into a fencing bout with Lacey, her straw against Lacey's neon plastic spoon. Part of her wanted to take off her headset and lanyard and stay with them the rest of the day, but she had work to do.

"We'll walk you back to the main stage," Preston offered, gathering up their trash and taking it to the recycling bin.

As they cut through the tables, people waved hello, to both Harmony and Preston.

"Hey!" Sarah, sitting at a table with some friends, raised a slushy that Harmony had to assume was the version on the menu spiked with actual limoncello. "There's our girl!"

Libby waved too. "Festival seems like a huge success!"

Cheers of "First annual!" rose from the surrounding crowd. It had become a rallying cry in town and at planning meetings. Harmony was hopeful about that. She didn't want to let them all down. Festivals were a shit ton of work. But it felt good. Not just as a different way of making amends but as a way of making something that really was good for a community—that she was a part of.

And it was pretty fun to raise her arms to the cheers, to run through a clump of teen performers collecting high fives.

She was looking forward to collapsing face-first in bed for about two weeks after this weekend, though. Hopefully Preston's bed. He still refused to allow breakfast in bed, because crumbs, but she'd bought a coffee maker to keep at his place, and he did plenty of other nice things in that bed that made staying there sound like the perfect way to celebrate surviving the *first annual!* festival.

As she made her way back toward where Preston, Lacey's hand in his, was shaking his head and rolling his eyes at her, people began streaming back toward the front stage for the next performance. Walking with Libby and Bonnie, Sarah stopped and gave Harmony a pat on the shoulder. "Hope you get a good break after this."

"Never too early to start work on the *second annual* fest." She made a little cheer as she said that.

"It won't take all year!" Sarah laughed. "What else are you going to do?"

"Ooh," Bonnie said, drink in hand. "You should join our book club!"

She could do that. She'd also been thinking about finding something steady, in town or online. Social media management? Teaching drama classes? But she liked when she had time, mostly before things ramped up for the festival these last couple weeks, to drag Preston along for a bit of fun out with friends and to help out with Lacey. And most of all to spend quiet evenings with Preston, entertaining him while he cooked with stories of how she'd talked her way into a better deal on lighting equipment or what she and Lacey had gotten up to that afternoon while he ran to therapy. Or squeezing onto the couch together with a couple of books. She loved listening to him get carried away ranting over some bit of poetry or romance plot; he pretended he didn't like her dramatic readings of wonderful or terrible lines, or jokes about showing her his Balzac, but he'd eventually laugh so hard, jostling her head where it rested in his lap, that she couldn't even read anymore. And while this weekend's financials would take several weeks to wrap up, when Harmony had asked Alice for an initial report on how they were faring, the woman had practically gotten dollar signs in her eyes. She had some breathing room to figure everything out.

Libby mused, "Ever think about going into local politics? Travis Weaver's up for reelection in two years, and I think the shine is off there with most of the town. With a couple successful festivals under your belt, you'd be a contender."

Harmony laughed. "Why don't *you* run against him?"

"No!" Libby said grimly. "I don't have time for something like that."

"We'll see." Harmony waved as they went off, and finally reached Preston's side. She took his free hand, meeting his growing smile with her own, sure she'd find something good to keep her out of trouble.

Right here in Brookville.

ACKNOWLEDGMENTS

The two most magical places I know in the world are the theater and the library. Both are buildings like any other you might pass on the street but open up into so much more, entire secret worlds of transportive stories conjured on their stage or playing out in the pages of their books. And when their powers combine? As the master Meredith Willson knew, we go from magical to miraculous.

Both this book and I owe so much to these worlds of performance and books and the people who champion them, and now that our show's over, before we raise the house lights, allow me to throw a round of applause to everyone who helped bring Harmony and Preston's story to life.

This book simply would not exist without the inspiration of my sister, Melissa Watson, and the day we were ranting together about (what else?) musical theater, when the idea of a bookish hero and a slick con woman marched into my brain. But my gratitude goes further back, to all the years we spent performing in community theater together, or watching, awestruck, the PBS airing of *Into the Woods*, or listening to showtunes on endless repeat, all of which inform my storytelling now. Thanks for reporting back on all the Broadway productions you see before anyone, so I can imagine the stories while playing the OBCs.

Melissa and I performed in the chorus of *The Music Man* together as children, and later in different productions she played Ethel Toffelmier and I played Mrs. Paroo—along with so many other sidekicks, villains, and mothers in so many other shows. While I loved my time in the theater, that casting sent a message to me about who was allowed to be the star, who was fitting to be the ingénue, who was worthy of having her story told. This book is for all the fat girls always cast as the joke or the mom but never the heroine, my chance to give the fat woman the starring role in her own romance, where she is desirable and pursued and fully humanized. Justice for Ethel Toffelmier!

I also have to thank our parents for introducing us to the world and stories of theater, for putting classic movie musicals on the television, for driving us to all those rehearsals, for saving up and taking us to touring productions (yes, even Webber). Thanks to my mother, Leslie Kuss, who house managed and sewed costumes and continues to read every draft I write—even when I suggested perhaps not this one (my first adult romance). And thanks to my father, Cameron Kuss, for running stage lights and joining us in so many of those community theater productions, and who made a delightfully sleazy Charlie the anvil salesman. You always showed me I could be anyone I wanted. I love you both.

Thanks also to all the theatrical and musical directors, choreographers, drama teachers, and castmates who made growing up in the theater the best and most fun upbringing a kid could have. There's truly no people like show people, no community like the theater community, and if you've been a part of it anywhere, all the Easter eggs are my flowers to you.

The other sanctuary of my childhood was the local library (thanks, Mom and Pop, for taking me there all the time too), and I hold heartfelt gratitude to all the librarians who made every branch I've visited through my life such a magical, welcoming place, as well as the librarians I've met online who have taught me so much about their field. They're currently facing some of the greatest challenges to books and the community built by libraries in a long time. As I revised *My Kind of Trouble* I watched, horrified, as bigots disrupted more and more storytimes, threatened library workers, and a miniscule number attempted to ban important books for all readers. Librarians shouldn't have to be heroes, but they are absolutely heroes to me, for fighting to keep books on shelves and events on schedules, and for the infinite small everyday things they do that benefit us all. This book is my love letter to libraries and librarians. You can shush me any time you like.

Thanks also to those other champions of books, my local(ish) independent bookstores, including the owners and staff of Mysterious Galaxy Bookstore, Meet Cute Bookshop, Casita Bookstore, and The Ripped Bodice, for welcoming and supporting me.

And thanks to Davis, California, small town of my heart and home to the Yolo County Library, Avid Reader Bookstore, and so many bicycles. Brookville may not look exactly like you, but it owes the best parts of its spirit to you.

Of course I owe the greatest of thanks to my brilliant editor Jess Verdi, the absolute best person/former theater kid to shepherd this book to publication. Your tireless, insightful work has my endless appreciation; this book is so much better than before thanks to you. I'm grateful to the team at Alcove and Crooked Lane, particularly Thaisheemarie Fantauzzi Perez, Mikaela Bender, Dulce Botello, Rebecca Nelson, Stephanie Manova, and Megan Matti. Sincere thanks to cover artist Stephanie Singleton for creating such beautiful artwork for my first official cover with both protagonists front and center, showing an autistic man so sweetly smitten and a fat woman so deliciously confident. And enthusiastic thanks to Emil Lundmark for continuing to make seriously swoony promotional character art that celebrates all bodies.

Deepest gratitude to my agent, Lee O'Brien, always there with calm support when I'm anxiety-spiraling worse than Preston and who didn't even blink when, on our first call discussing my young adult fantasies, he asked what I was working on next and I sheepishly replied, "Well, do you like musical theater?" Your excitement for this story meant the world to me, and your guidance in revising brought out aspects that made it so much stronger, some of my favorite parts now that I couldn't imagine the book without. Sorry for sending you black licorice to celebrate selling it.

So many friends helped as I engaged in Iowa levels of stubbornness through all the writing rejections and decided to try my hand at romance. Cate Baumer and Heidi Christopher, I could never do any of this without you. Thanks for keeping Preston company in music class and calling out from work so he and Harmony could find a little time together in the stacks.

Jenny Howe, you continue to always lift my spirits with both your work and your friendship. Preston is a huge fan as well and can't shut up about your books. Courtney Kae, you are a treasure just like your books, and I'm so grateful to call you my friend (and for Lacey to as well). And I'm so grateful to all the others who welcomed me as I forayed into Romancelandia, including Kyla Zhao and Charlotte Stein.

Thank you also to my Inklings, the funniest and most loving circle of support. I'm so glad I get to hang out every day with all you brilliant writers.

Piles of gratitude to everyone who read this book in early drafts, including Sheena Boekweg, Alechia Dow, Sabina Nordqvist, Samantha Elden, Jules Arbeaux, Chloe Maron, Birdie Schae, Haley Kral, Kara Allen, Michelle Bui, and Amanda Weaver (sorry I'd already named the villain before I met you!). Thanks for loving

Preston and Harmony and all their friends and yelling at me to send them to my agent already.

Hugs and finger guns to my brilliant and brave children, Sophia and Nate, who inspire me and impress me and will hopefully never read this book. Thanks to Cindy and Larry Schwartz for all the love and support, and the tax information. And, as always, every last scrap of my gratitude to my husband, David. I was always a hopeless romantic, but the emphasis was on hopeless till there was you. Your love is the great beating heart of my life, filling my days with music and flowers just for me, and your pride in my career as an author is what's allowed me to reach as far as I have. And yeah, fine, I admit it, you're a pretty great kisser.

Finally, I want to thank you, readers. My greatest hope for this book is for it to find those who see themselves in Harmony and Preston, or to help others understand what it's like for those who do—including the possible loneliness and exhaustion but also undeniable joy of being autistic. Whether you bought this book or borrowed it from a wonderful library, thank you for spending time with me in Brookville.